I0623790

ALEMANA

A Story of Love and Life

M. Carolina Bento

House of Riverenza

Copyright © 2018 by M. Carolina Bento

First edition published in the United States of America on May 28, 2018.

Revised edition published in the United States of America by House of Riverenza on November 11, 2022.

All rights reserved. No part of this book may be reproduced in any form without written permission from House of Riverenza.

ISBN: 979-8-9854689-6-0

For my beloved daughters,
the light of my life!

ACKNOWLEDGMENTS

Thanks to Stephanie for her continuous support and gracious contribution of the cover picture, which fits the theme of this story so well.

In tribute of one of the luminaries of German literature, hereby mentioned are a few of the countless meaningful quotes by Johann Wolfgang von Goethe (1749-1832), the most relevant for this context being:

'Nothing is worth more than this day.'

CHAPTER ONE

A TRIP TO THE PAST

*M*y son Gabriel has become a resounding presence in the music world, he is one of the most talented violinists that Europe has seen in the past decade!

He is a wonderful son and includes me in his life, very busy life, as often as possible, setting aside time for us which he calls 'Mama and Son Vacation,' occasionally inviting me to accompany him on his European tours.

We are ready to start his spring tour, beginning in London, continuing to Madrid, Rome, Milan, Paris, and ending in Zurich. But the days preceding the trip with Gabriel have been very tense and anxious.

I have been back to London, where I lived for years, many times since I moved to Germany. I loved it, it is always a delightful experience to visit the regal city where my son came into this world, healthy and perfect, despite the most daring circumstances, protected by the love of my dearest friend and the most kind-hearted man, George. He was tender with Gabriel and proud of showing off 'his baby boy!'

Together with George's mother, who couldn't contain her joy in holding 'her only grandchild,' we became a family!

An unusual and happy little family for a while…

But I have purposely avoided returning to Spain, my country, and now that I agreed to go on this tour I am overwhelmed with memories of my earlier experiences in Madrid.

The prospect of going to my hometown brings up many emotions, some sad, others unsettling. I believe that returning there now is my opportunity, once and for all, of letting go or resolving unfinished feelings resulting from the events that culminated in my sudden decision to move to England thirty-two years ago.

It is fair to say that I never regretted leaving Madrid, life has proven that I made the right choice. Our lives, my son's and mine, have turned out to be surprisingly better than I could ever foresee.

Anyway, right now I'll leave these memories where they belong… in the past.

I have other issues here at home to be dealt with.

Lately my husband has been cold and withdrawn with me. I know it is his way of not asserting issues that are bothering him.

After our quiet dinner I followed him to his study.

"Karl, are you upset because I'm going on the tour with Gabriel? Please tell me if you want me to stay home!"

"No, Clara, I think you should go. I understand that you love to spend time with him."

"Since I came back from New York, from being with our girls, you have been very cold with me, let's talk about it, Karl. Lately I feel like you don't care if I'm around or not, I wish you would tell me what is on your mind."

"I really expected you to bring Katie back home, you continue enabling her in prolonging her stay there. That was not the deal, she should have returned as soon as she finished her MBA."

"Karl, when things don't go your way, you blame me. She is a daddy's girl. Why don't you demand that she return? She is enjoying her internship on Wall Street, she does not need my consent or approval to remain there.

And I truly believe that there is something else going on here with you. Please tell me!"

"There is nothing to talk about now, Clara. When are you leaving?"

"Early in the morning. I'm flying to London, Gabriel is already there rehearsing. I'm leaving our itinerary on your desk with the information about our flights and hotels.

It would be nice if you could join us for a concert. Gabriel would love to see you, and I would too."

Karl had a very sad expression. During our twenty-six years of marriage we had a few dark spots like this one, but we always turned them around.

I love my husband, but I can't stand his coldness. *'Doesn't he love me anymore? Have I become a burden to him?'* I have so many doubts and unanswered questions! I am frustrated.

He is a towering, powerful, strong willed man, but also a workaholic, stubborn and domineering. On the other hand, he is a great father and friend, he puts family above everything.

I am tired of fighting my way through. I am afraid we are drifting apart, he hasn't shown any affection towards me lately. In consequence I have withdrawn too and moved to another bedroom when I came back from New York this last time.

It is enough for now!
I will deal with all of this on my return...
I am ready to enjoy my amazing son's company!

The tour begins...

On our first evening in London, Gabriel and I had dinner together and we discussed everything that was going on in the family. He talked about Elise, his love and long term girlfriend. I love her too, she is a wonderful girl.

3

I told him about the girls. Katherine, our Katie, is very excited about her internship on Wall Street and taking her time to return home. Amanda, Amie, our younger daughter, is a doctor completing an internship in pediatric hematology.

Gabriel is a caring brother, he sees his sisters as often as he can.

"How are things with Dad? Was he OK with you leaving him to come with me, Mama?"

"I think he doesn't care, lately he has been indifferent. Anyway I asked him to join us if he wants."

"I'm sorry, Mama, I know he loves you, my sisters and I grew up in a loving home, maybe it is part of him getting older, this shall pass! I just want you to be happy, you deserve it, and you are not old at all, you look beautiful and youthful, I'm proud of showing you off."

"Thank you for lifting me up, son. I'm happy being here with you. For the next weeks I'll enjoy your company and your divine music."

The next two evenings Gabriel was extremely busy with his concerts at the Royal Albert Hall. For being British born, he is highly recognized and has an enormous fan base in England.

The concerts were very successful.

During the day I visited our old neighborhood, like I always do when I come to London.

Walking by Kensington Gardens I had vivid memories of Gabe as a toddler, fetching his first ball with George's help, and then many years later, after a long period of solitude, walking down that same path with my German man.

Good memories!

We proceeded to Madrid, our flight was booked on the Spanish airline. Again, that brought me many flashbacks of the time in my distant youth when I worked for that company.

I was almost reluctant to board the plane.

"Mama, I am sure you are feeling anxious about going back to Madrid."

"Yes, son, I am emotional, but I'm looking forward to walk through the streets of Madrid and visit some familiar places. It is about time, I'm ready for it!"

The stewardess offered us some magazines, among them there was an airline publication. I curiously flipped through the pages and saw pictures of the board of directors, among them, Miguel Fuentes-Terrades, Vice President of Operations. My heart skipped a beat!

'This is not possible!'

I felt a chill running through my body and thought I was going to pass out!

'*He is back at the airline!*'

I controlled my breathing, trying not to reveal any emotion that would disturb Gabriel's rest, he was napping right there beside me. I refrained from the impulse to tell him.

I looked at the picture again.

'*Miguel came back to Madrid! Thirty-two years have gone by, he has aged of course, we all have, but is he the same man?*'

I discreetly folded the magazine and put it in my bag. I reclined, closed my eyes, pretending I was asleep, and like in a movie our past flashed back as if it just happened yesterday...

***

The year was 1978, I was twenty-four years old and in a relationship with Miguel Fuentes-Terrades for more than three years. I was in love for the first time!

I was very lonely when I met him. My mother had died years before, she had serious health issues, the reason why we moved from our hometown of Caceres to Madrid for treatment a decade prior. I didn't have a father, my mother was the only family I had, we were very attached, she was the kindest and the bravest person I had ever known. She taught me acceptance and resilience in the face of adversity and hardship.

During the last year of her life my mother couldn't work anymore, she was bedridden, she was desperate that she couldn't support me financially, and I couldn't afford to continue in school. That was devastating, I wanted to learn English, I thought it would advance me professionally.

But my mother told me over and over not to give up and to nurture my dreams.

'Maria Clara, believe you are strong and capable of building a good life for yourself. Go on, my daughter, go on.'

We were poor, very poor, and we were living in a small room with my mother's aunt. I was still a teenager when Tia Carmelia helped me find a job in the same department store where she had worked for many years.

After Mother died, Tia Carmelia told me that my mother had concealed from me that my father was not dead, as I grew up believing. He had abandoned us right after I was born and moved to Andalusia with a woman who owned some land and offered him a better life. My mother didn't tell me to protect me, she was afraid that I would grow up feeling rejected.

When I turned eighteen, Tia Carmelia suggested that I try to get a job in another place that would offer me more possibilities of professional growth, she suggested the airport.

"You have a good presence, you are outspoken and skilled with customers, and besides they will provide a uniform and you won't have to spend money on work clothes anymore!"

On that day she also told me she was planning to retire and move back to Caceres to join some of her old relatives. She kindly urged me to find another place to live.

I was devastated to leave the humble house in the outskirts of Madrid, one of those places that tourists never see, but for me, it was the home that I had shared with my loving mother and dear Tia Carmelia for a long time.

Within days Margarita, a friend from work, offered to share a room with me in her mother's house, for a price, close to the department store downtown where we both worked.

I took my aunt's advice and found a job as a ticket counter agent for The Royal International Airline. Along with the new job, I had the opportunity to train in customer service and basic English. I was thrilled!

I completed all courses offered by the company, got promoted, and by age twenty I was able to share an apartment with Pilar, a flight attendant, very close to the company's headquarters, which offered direct transportation to the airport and made my commute much easier and faster.

That was the first time in my young life when I was able to afford a room of my own!

Soon I heard that the company was sponsoring English language courses at the city college. I immediately signed up, that was as close as I would get to obtaining a college education.

The teacher, George Bentlenn, was a young Englishman, very pleasant and dedicated to all his students. He was contracted for two years, at the same time he was advancing his studies in Spanish literature. He loved Spain, and he told us that upon returning to the U.K. he would become a professor.

George became friends with some of the students, including me. I loved his witty sense of humor, his kindness and patience with us.

Many times he organized exploratory outings with our participation, I always attended them. That's when I had the opportunity to visit many sites and landmarks of my own beautiful city, and shared the experience of discovering new places, new foods.

Outside of the classroom George told us how close he was with his mother. He was very proud of mentioning his father who was a missionary doctor and died in a senseless battle while he was on one of his missions years before.

During his stay in Madrid, George took time off to visit his mother in London. I thought he was a caring son!

I met Mrs. Livia Bentlenn once when she came to Madrid to spend time with her son. She invited me to visit London and stay with them.

"George told me you are his friend and one of his favorite students, I'd like you to come, Clara, stay with us!"

His friendship meant much to me. I started believing that one day I would fly on my airline's wings to visit my friend in the royal city of London!

Days after his mother left, George felt he needed to clear things up. On a winter evening after class, while sipping hot chocolate, he had a conversation with me:

"Clara, you are a very attractive and pretty girl, and I like you very much, so did Mother, as a matter of fact she is always looking for a girl for me, if you know what I mean! I do appreciate our friendship, our conversations and your company. What I want to say is that I like you, but as a friend, I have no other interest. The truth is I am a gay man, do you understand?"

"George, of course I understand. I never had a friend like you before, and that subject is taboo here. I don't care about this gay thing! I love you as a friend, but I'm not in love with you. Not that you are not attractive, you are!"

"Thank you, Clara, I expect this to stay just between the two of us, there is much stigma about this issue and I want people to continue respecting me for my work and for who I am."

"I understand, George, people sometimes are cruel, they make demeaning comments. Don't worry, the other students never said anything about you, they all like you and respect you. Thank you for trusting me."

"I treasure our friendship, Clara, I live an isolated life, and it is good to be able to talk openly with someone who is non-judgmental. And as my mother said, if someday you want to come to London you'll be very welcomed in our house."

"Thank you, George. Let me tell you a secret too, I met someone recently in the company bus coming back from the airport. I have seen him twice so far and I can't stop thinking of him… I never felt this way before."

"That's good news, if he is smart he would not let you go, you are a jewel, Clara. Does he work for the airline too?"

"Yes, downtown at the headquarters, and he is very kind to me, and a good person. Miguel is also close to his family, he travels quite often to Barcelona where they live."

I was twenty-one years old and I had no idea how those two men were about to impact my life: one as my best friend, the other as my first love.

I started nurturing dreams of a life with Miguel, he was caring and attentive to me. He was the one who told me of a position in the Customer Service Department at the headquarters and suggested that I apply for it. As a benefit we would work closer and would have more time together.

"But it requires fluency in English," he added.

"I can handle it, Miguel, I'm doing very well with the English course, I'm really good at it, and with my years of experience at the airport I believe I would qualify!"

I applied and got the job.

Over the next years our romance flourished, Miguel and I spent much more time together in my apartment alone when Pilar was away on her flights.

We were happy! He was passionate and promised to love me forever!

Miguel came from a very traditional family. His father was a banker in Barcelona. Miguel had come to Madrid years before for grad school, found a job at the airline and stayed there a couple years longer, but his family expected him to return and join their business.

He assured me he would never give up his independent life in Madrid, he loved the city and his job. 'Aviation is in my blood!' he would often say.

George extended his contract for another year and eventually he returned to England. I was sad to see him go, but we remained friends and in contact.

On one of our calls he sounded very sad and he asked me when I was going to come to visit him. He was lonely, living alone, he had lost a dear friend, and his mother had decided to move to a cottage she owned in Henley-on-Thames.

In that same period things were not going well with me and Miguel. He was under pressure from his family to return home, but always promising me that he was not going to leave me.

To appease his parents he went to Barcelona for a week, and I took that opportunity to visit George in London.

That was my first international trip!

George took me around and told me much about life in the city, and he also told me he was desperately concerned about his own health. He confided in me that his friend had died of a serious disease that was plaguing the gay community.

I did not know anything about it, and that was the first time that he told me about an autoimmune disease and that he was at risk. He asked me for secrecy, he would never tell his mother, he couldn't bring that worry upon her.

"George, you are healthy, you'll be alright. Take good care of yourself, and if you need me I will help you any way I can! At least talk to me, don't keep it all bottled up."

Before returning to Madrid I spoke to him about my concerns regarding the demands of Miguel's family, I was scared that he would succumb to their pressure. He had been going to Barcelona quite often.

"I'm afraid of losing him, George."

"If you ever need anything or if you want to change your life, come here, Clara, I'll help you, true friendship works both ways!"

I appreciated George's sincerity and friendship, his words stayed with me.

I didn't have a hint that a couple of months later I would be the one calling him, begging for his help.

Back in Madrid, Miguel was annoyed that I went to see George, he did not approve of our friendship.

I reassured him, "George and I are good friends, that's all! I haven't told you but I guess you should know he has absolutely no interest in girls, we are like brother and sister, we are kindred souls!"

"Kindred souls? Maria Clara, how can you be friends with someone like that?"

"He is a wonderful human being, you are being prejudicial, Miguel. Please open your mind."

"I don't want to discuss this, I'm just very conflicted about disagreeing with my parents, and in the end they might be right!"

"Miguel, did you ever tell them about me, about us?"

"I never told them about us, with no offense, you are not the kind of girl that they expect for a daughter-in-law. You are smart, beautiful, but they have plans of me marrying someone of our same social class."

"You don't think I'm good enough, do you? Are you embarrassed by me? That's why you didn't introduce me to your mother when she was here in Madrid visiting you!"

"I didn't think she would understand why I am in love with you. We come from very different backgrounds, Maria Clara, *very different...*"

"I'm worried about us, Miguel, you keep repeating that you love me, that we are going to be married someday, and now you are telling me this? What is going to happen to us? I love you like I never loved anyone before."

"Maria Clara, I promise we will be together. No matter what!"

He hugged and kissed me with passion like he always did, and I believed him like I always did.

We stopped discussing his family.

Weeks later he surprised me with a weekend getaway to an exciting place I had never been to before.

"We are going to Mallorca, it is off season, the best time to be there!"

I couldn't believe it. A trip for the two of us! I had never been on a trip with him before.

On the flight over, he told me, "I have a surprise for you, Maria Clara, this is our honeymoon!"

I was astonished. "What do you mean?"

"There is an Orthodox chapel in a small village in the northern side of the island where they perform weddings on the spot, we don't need to make any arrangements! I am taking you there and we are getting married!"

I was in disbelief.

"Is that why you invited me to come? We are getting married! Is this for real?"

We got married in a short and simple ceremony and we enjoyed a few days of our honeymoon. It was like a dream, we made a commitment to be together as husband and wife.

I asked Miguel when he was going to tell his parents and if I was going to move into his apartment in Madrid with him.

"Not yet, I can't tell this to my parents now, but in time I will. We are together forever, Maria Clara."

That didn't sit right with me, but I was willing to wait until the day when he would bring me to his family to introduce me as his wife.

Oh, how naïve I was!

Weeks later I had a troubling revelation... I was pregnant!

I told Miguel, and unexpectedly, he reacted with anger.

"You can't have a baby. You need to get rid of it!"

I was devastated.

"Miguel, please, I need you to understand, it is our responsibility, it is our child, we love each other, we are married!"

"Maria Clara, I can't have this kind of commitment with you. That was all a make-believe ceremony, it was not a real wedding, you knew quite well!"

I felt faint, his words were cutting me deeply. Before he left he threw some money at me.

"Get rid of it! I'm going away, and when I come back I don't want to hear anything else about it."

I couldn't do anything and waited for his return, hoping that he had come to his senses.

When he came back and asked me if I had done it, I told him no, there was a new life to be considered. He became very angry, like I never saw him before, and shouted:

"I can't have a bastard child! I have agreed with my family and

I'm on the verge of committing to a girl from our social circle.

Be reasonable, if you insist with this, you are going to lose everything, including your job! What do you think they'll do when you show up unmarried and pregnant?"

I couldn't believe it, he was the same man that for almost four years told me he loved me and would never leave me. My heart hurt so much, all I could say was, "Go away, Miguel, and don't come back."

"Why not? We can be together after you get rid of it, I'll give you some time, but if you don't do it there'll be consequences. You will regret it!"

I had no strength to respond.

He left.

That was the last time I saw him...

I spent the next days sick, I couldn't even move. It just happened, I lost Miguel, I was about to lose my job and the respect of my superiors and co-workers. I was on my own! All I had was a new life growing inside of me. How would I be able to protect the life of my baby?

I made a sudden decision and called George.

"I need your help, I need to start a new life, I am pregnant. Can I come?"

"Come, Clara. We will help one another."

Without further consideration I quit my job, packed my possessions into two suitcases, took my savings and closed my bank account. I gave Pilar the money that Miguel had thrown at me for the rent until she would find another roommate. I lied to everyone when they asked me where I was going, saying that I had located my father in Andalusia and I was going to join him.

As soon as I arrived in London, George opened his home and his heart to me.

"Clara, I also need to confide in you, I was diagnosed with a virus, the same that killed my friend. I am under treatment, experimental drugs, which might prevent me from developing full blown AIDS. I have to keep it a secret, I could lose my career, it is a very scary time, people are paranoid about this new disease."

"I will help you, George, tell me what I need to learn and do."

"Please, don't tell my mother, she would die if she knew, I can't bring this hardship upon her. I'm thinking of bringing you to her cottage in Henley-on-Thames this weekend. My mother has a kind heart, I'm sure she will help you with the pregnancy and plan for the baby."

We went to Henley, Livia was very welcoming.

"A baby is a blessing, you and your baby will be alright here with us."

She invited me to stay with her for the week while George went back to work in London.

I had the loveliest time with Livia, I felt calmer walking through the charming historic town and along the riverside. I was impressed with the most beautiful scenery and gardens.

She kept repeating, "Don't worry, Clara, don't worry. Marius and I will take care of you!"

"Marius?"

"That's my son's middle name, it was also my father's name. That's my term of endearment when I think of him. All my side of the family have Latin names. I named him after his father, but in my heart he is my little Marius."

"You say it so sweetly. I also like Latin names and already decided that my baby will have my Mom's name, Gabriela, and if it is a boy, Gabriel!"

"That's a beautiful name, Clara. But let me ask you, are you planning to raise your child in England? Or are you returning to Spain after the baby is born?"

"It makes me so nervous thinking about going back to Spain. No, I'll never return, I am afraid Miguel would find me, and I don't know what he would do. I am also certain that I will never find a job like the one I had.

I want to stay here, and after my baby is born I will find work to raise him or her by myself, like my Mom did.

Livia, I want to tell you that I am very grateful for you and George's support, but I won't be a burden, I promise. I brought all my savings and I'll take care of myself until I start working."

"It is not that simple, Clara, medical costs out of your pocket can be very high, and to get a job, you need the proper documentation. But don't worry now, there is a solution for everything!"

Alone in Livia's guest room, many nights I cried, and no matter what she said I was worried. And incredible as it seemed I missed Miguel, I loved him, all I wanted was to rip him out of my heart and forget about him.

I would get angry at myself sometimes. How could I have been so gullible?

Once Livia told me that I was too naïve and he was too deceiving. It was a bad combination!

I was more relaxed when George arrived on the weekend. Livia sat both of us down for a talk and made the most astonishing proposition.

"I have been thinking and I came to the conclusion that this is the opportunity for you, George, to protect your reputation and your career. You know, son, I love you and accept you the way you are, but the world is cruel and judgmental, and you will suffer if the truth comes out.

And you, Clara, need to protect yourself too, you need a permanent home and assistance, therefore I suggest that you both get married. You love each other as good friends, both of you don't expect anything but an honest mutual friendship, and you can help each other!

I would be happy knowing that you are not alone, George! Please do it for me and for Clara."

I was flabbergasted!

George, on the contrary, thought his mother's suggestion was not bad at all!

Later on, he took me for a walk alongside the river.

"I can't accept this idea, George, I know your mother means well, but us getting married is flatly outlandish!"

He smiled and told me, "Mother has a point, it could be very positive for both of us. Let's support one another, it doesn't have to be forever, if someday you want to start a new life, you will be free to go on, in the meantime I will stand with you, I will be your baby's father figure. I like the idea of being responsible for a new life, I love children, it fills me with hope and purpose!"

"George, this is not reasonable, we can't make a decision like that, led by emotions or convenience."

He went back to London to his job, and Livia insisted that I stay with her a little longer. She started introducing me to her friends as her son's Spanish girlfriend.

A couple of weeks went by, and as I started realizing that I needed medical attention during the pregnancy, I warmed up to her idea. George would come every weekend to see us, and just like that, we both said yes to her proposition.

Livia arranged our wedding in Henley.

We made her happy that day!

I moved in with George into his house in South Kensington, London, not far from the college where he was an assistant professor. We lived separate lives, like brother and sister. He supported me and continued helping me to perfect my English. I took care of him and kept his secret.

As impossible as it seemed, I had a healthy and happy pregnancy, forcing myself not to think about Miguel, even if I felt then that I would never stop loving him, I was wrong! Eventually, after my son was born, all my attention and love was bestowed on him, and Miguel became nothing but a sour and distant memory.

***

The airplane started descending to land at the Madrid airport. I felt that my heart was going to jump out of my chest.

Gabriel held my hand, "Mama, you are trembling. I know you are emotional, we are about to land, I'm here with you!"

I was able to smile at him.

16

"You were with me when I left, you are with me now, it is just you and me, my baby, my son!"

I did not tell him that I had a plan. I was determined to contact Miguel, and this time he would listen to what I had to say.

On our first day in Madrid, while Gabriel was at rehearsal, I called the airline's office to confirm if Miguel was in town. I identified myself as an old colleague who worked with him decades ago.

I hired a driver at the hotel reception who took me around the city, revisiting landmarks and sites.

For most of the tour it looked like time had stood still, Madrid was regal, beautiful as always, rich in tradition and history. I made a few stops at internationally famous art galleries, at the Palacio Royal, I strolled through the Parque Del Retiro, an ideal place to relax between visits to the great art galleries and museums of Bourbon Madrid.

At the Plaza Mayor I visited the Arcades at the base of the buildings, filled with cafés and craft shops. Then I went to the Centro de Arte Reina Sofía, an outstanding museum of 20th century art, a new building that I hadn't seen before, it is entered by highly original exterior glass lifts. Impressive!

It was daunting returning to Madrid, but that feeling dissipated as I experienced the familiarity of the places, the people.

'Home at last!'

On the way back to the hotel, I saw the building occupied by the airline company.

'I'll be there tomorrow!'

I got ready for Gabriel's concert at the Auditorio Nacional de Música, home to Spain's National Orchestra, where most high profile performances are held. I took my place backstage and enjoyed another magnificent concert.

Gabriel always adapts his repertoire according to the crowd's local preferences.

It was a huge success! He was pleased, and I was proud!

Back at the Ritz we had a late supper together, but I still did not tell him about my findings regarding Miguel, I couldn't divert his attention, he was very focused on his next performance.

CHAPTER TWO

THE REUNION

In the morning I told Gabriel I was going to walk around and would meet him later at the Concert Hall.

I didn't know what to expect, how Miguel was going to react, but I felt very calm and confident! I was anticipating some satisfaction in surprising him. He would be caught off guard, and I would be ready to face him.

Purposely I dressed up very elegantly, showing my best, to make a good appearance to get Miguel's attention. I sure know how appearances are important to him, at least they were.

When I arrived at his office I introduced myself to the receptionist as Mrs. Weisenwert, an old colleague. She opened his office door, "Mr. Terrades is waiting to see you, Madame."

Miguel was sitting at his desk, I walked in his direction confidently and slowly.

He paused, stared at me, got very pale like he was seeing a ghost. When I approached his desk, he stood up.

"Maria Clara! You are here!"

"How are you, Miguel?"

He came around to shake my hand. He was visibly trembling. I was cool and collected, enjoying the moment of taking him by surprise. He was silent for a little while, then he pointed to two sofas at the other side of his large office. He sat right across from me.

"You look amazing, Maria Clara, as I remember..."

"Thank you. So, when did you come back to Madrid? Didn't you move to Barcelona in 1978?"

"I did, but I returned fifteen years ago, aviation was in my blood. How did you find me here?"

"Flying from London two days ago, I saw your picture in the company's magazine. I was very surprised!"

Awkward silence.

Then he continued, "Since I came back to Madrid I hoped that one day I would see you around the city, I didn't know if you had left for good."

"I did leave for good, this is the first time I returned here since... I am with my son on a business trip."

"A son! Do you have a son?"

"I have a big family, a husband, a son, two daughters, an older stepson, a daughter-in-law, two grandchildren."

"Two daughters? Now I'm absolutely sure I saw you in New York at JFK Airport, summer 1996. You were walking fast with two girls, I was coming in the opposite direction, I stopped and followed you with my eyes. I was not sure it was really you, and off you went into a Lufthansa gate."

"Yes, Miguel, it was me, I took that flight and I still do, very often, to go back home. I have lived in Germany, Dusseldorf, for the past twenty-six years."

"Dusseldorf! I thought you were living in London! That day at Kennedy Airport I really wanted to approach you, but I didn't know how you would react."

"I would have talked to you. That summer I was returning home with my girls after leaving my son in New York City, in school. That's why I came here today, to talk to you about him."

And with no hesitation, I dropped the bomb!

"My son Gabriel was born in London on October 6, 1978, and you are his biological father."

Miguel suddenly got up, he became very nervous, took a few deep breaths.

He sat down again, changed his tone:

"I have wondered, Maria Clara, and knowing you I thought there was a possibility that you had raised the baby by yourself, and for the longest time I felt guilty. My son Fabio José was born in 1980, and when I held him for the first time I realized there could be another baby out there that would never know his father, that I would never call my child. I'm so sorry for what I did."

"Miguel, I did not come here today for apologies, I came to ask you if you would like to meet Gabriel. He knows everything, when he was younger he asked many questions about you. A couple of years ago he was in Barcelona, looked for your name, but did not find it in the phone book. He said he could easily do further research, but he was going to leave it to destiny to maybe find you someday...

Gabriel does not need anything from you, maybe just a little time to get to know you.

My son was always loved, he got the best of everything, he loves and respects his father, my husband Karl, but sometimes he is curious, which is very natural in children that are adopted, they want to know their biological parents."

"He might hate me! I'm so ashamed. I'm not the same man, I have grown mature, life proved me wrong. Does he hate me?"

"Gabriel is a good hearted and sensitive man, he doesn't hate anyone. My son is an outstanding human being."

"Maria Clara, this is so surprising! Could you stay longer? I want to know more about him. Does he know you found me?"

"No, he doesn't, and I can't stay, but I can call you tomorrow morning to see if you want to meet him."

"I don't need to think until tomorrow, yes, I want to meet him, anytime, anywhere he wants. Please call me to confirm. Where are you staying?"

"At the Ritz by the Prado. I'll call you in the morning, Miguel."

Talking to him was easier than I had thought. But there were also mixed emotions. I left his office relieved and conflicted, feeling a little sorry for Miguel, he had lost his attitude of pride, he was humble and obviously shocked to see me, and more so with the news.

All of a sudden it hit me that seeing him intensified sad memories of my undeniable past, for a moment I almost regretted contacting him. I should have let go... I thought.

'Oh, no! Gabriel needed and deserved closure, I owed that to my son.'

At the same time I was feeling liberated! Conflicting as it was, I had nothing to fear, no memories, no old feelings could ever defeat me or keep me away. I reconnected with my young self and my beautiful city!

Arriving at the hotel I felt exhausted, emotions are tiring!

Later, I got ready and went to the Hall to meet Gabriel. He was prepared for his performance, and I was excited about the news I was about to give him.

And again, it was another majestic concert!

At supper, back at the hotel, Gabriel was relaxed.

"I'm glad everything went well, I'll sleep late tomorrow, then to Rome we will fly, Mama. Did you enjoy your time here in Madrid?"

"I did and I had a surprising encounter today. Gabe, I met Miguel Terrades, he is back at the airline and I talked to him about you!"

"What? How unexpected! I don't know what to say! How did he react?"

"Better than I thought, he was humble, apologetic, and he wants to meet you. I didn't disclose anything about you. I wanted to discuss it with you first before I offered him more information. Would you like to meet him?"

"This is so surprising, I always wanted to meet my biological father, but now I feel strange. Do you think this is the right time, Mama?"

"It's entirely up to you, son, I was clear telling him that you don't need or want anything from him, just a little time. I think you have the right to know him."

"Was it hard for you to see him after all this time, Mama?"

"No, I was prepared, I even took some satisfaction out of surprising him. He was distraught and emotional, he has regrets."

"What if I don't like him and want nothing to do with him? What do I do?"

"Well, just say, 'Thank you for coming, it was nice meeting you.' You don't owe him anything, Gabe."

"I am really curious now, I want to meet him. I'm not coming back to Madrid anytime soon. I think we have some time tomorrow before we leave for Rome."

"Perfect, I'll invite him to come here by lunchtime. I'll call him in the morning to confirm. Should I tell him more about you? He has no idea that you are the greatest violinist of our time."

Gabriel laughed.

"Of course, my name and picture are all over the papers, just tell him not to divulge this meeting. The world knows that my father is, and always will be, Karl Weisenwert!"

"Dad would love to hear that. Oh, I miss Karl! I'll talk to him in the morning, it's too late now. Sleep good, son."

I called Miguel's office around 9:30 a.m.

"I thought I'd give you some time to prepare. Would you like to come and see Gabriel by lunchtime? He wants to meet you, Miguel!"

"Absolutely, I was anxious for your call, I hardly slept, there is so much I want to know about him."

"You'll have time to talk to him, we'll be leaving the hotel around four o'clock. Is twelve thirty good for you?"

"Yes, it is, should I meet him at the hotel restaurant?"

"No, it is better if you come to his suite, I'll leave your name at the front desk, ask for Gabriel Bentlenn! Have you heard of him? My son is one of the greatest violinists that Europe has known!"

"What? I almost fell off my chair right now, Gabriel Bentlenn? The violinist? I saw an article on him in the paper just yesterday. How amazing is that! I'll spend the rest of the morning researching him."

"He asked you not to make any comments about this meeting. Please keep it private."

"Absolutely, I imagine he is pursued by the media. I'll be there on time, thank you, Maria Clara."

I called Karl right after, he was working from home again.

"Are you taking a day off? How are you feeling, Karl?"

"I'm fine, Clara. How are you and Gabriel?"

"Everything is going very well here, the concerts have been magnificent, he is very pleased. Last night we were talking about you, and he said he misses you, Karl, he'll come to visit after this tour is over, and I realized I miss you too."

"The house is sad and empty without you, Clara, I'll be happy when you come home. But for now have a good time."

"If you need me, let me know, I'll come home, Karl. Take good care of yourself."

Maybe the wall is coming down, he sounded a little mellow. *'Oh, Karl!'*

I spent a quiet morning resting and packing for our trip in the afternoon. I knocked at Gabriel's room at noon.

"I'm awake, Mama, come in."

"Son, Miguel is going to be here in half an hour, I already ordered brunch for us, I thought it is more private here."

"I'm excited and curious to meet him and I'm starving."

Room service was delivered, looked fabulous, Gabriel couldn't resist and started eating.

The front desk announced: 'Mr. Fuentes-Terrades is coming up.'

He knocked at the door. I opened it.

Gabriel got up and went to greet him. They both looked nervous.

They shook hands.

Miguel could only smile at him, he was lost for words.

I observed both of them side by side, *'They are physically alike. My son is taller, has fuller hair, but there is a resemblance.'*

Gabriel told him, "Come and have something to eat, this is brunch for me."

"Thank you, I don't know if I can eat anything right now, this is a very special moment for me."

I poured some fruit juice and offered him a glass.

"Relax, Miguel, drink something."

Gabriel started a conversation about the city.

"It's not my first time here, this is a great city. How do you like living in Madrid, Miguel?"

"I like it very much, I have been back here for fifteen years and I'll stay for always. Do you live in Dusseldorf too?"

"I live in Vienna, the land of the waltz, it is idyllic, it is where I recharge after all this travelling, but I visit my family in Dusseldorf quite often, I grew up there."

I commented, "Gabriel has a magnificent property in Vienna, but most of all he has the most beautiful and talented Austrian girlfriend."

Miguel seemed more relaxed. "By the way, I just learned about your musical talent today, and I am amazed. I'll never miss a chance of attending one of your concerts."

"The tour is continuing, maybe you'll catch up somewhere else."

I ate a little bit and excused myself, I felt they needed to talk alone. "I have to finish our luggage, you both continue your conversation."

Hours later I returned to tell Gabriel that the limousine was waiting to take us to the airport. He had given Miguel the tour itinerary and our phone numbers. They said goodbye.

Their first meeting went very well, Miguel left with a smile on his face, and I had a lighter heart. Mission accomplished! My son met his biological father and hopefully now he will have the answers to all of his questions.

On our way to Rome, Gabe related to me, word by word, how their meeting went. He was the one that initiated the conversation with Miguel:

"I always wanted to meet you, Miguel, I really wanted to know you, thank you for coming."

"Since the moment I knew about you, I wanted to meet you, Gabriel.

Over the years I had haunting thoughts that I could have a child that I would never know. I need to tell you that I'm entirely responsible for how things happened and I think your mother could have done nothing different to protect you.

I want to confess how much I regret my actions, I was immature and succumbed to my family's pressures, I was not strong enough to resist them. I loved Maria Clara, she was an inspiring young woman, she made a noble life for herself, she became a great professional, respected and envied by many at a very young age. I loved her and I wanted to spend the rest of my life with her.

I didn't realize then that in breaking your mother's heart, I also broke my own, and it became impossible to mend it.

If I only could go back in time, I would have changed everything. I'm sorry for my actions, I'm not that weak young man anymore, and I have learned my lesson. I regret not being the father you deserved. Please forgive me, because I can't forgive myself!"

"I appreciate your sincerity, Miguel, and understand we do things in life that later we might regret, but the past is the past, we can only move forward into the future.

My mother told me the truth, but you telling me now, it looks more painful. She is strong, she has an incredible resilience and a heart full of love. She gave me a good life, I never missed having a father, my sisters and I were raised in a beautiful home with much love and everything we ever needed or wanted.

She moved on, look at her now, I don't know any other woman more wonderful than my mother, I'm proud of being her son!"

"You are right, Gabriel, I'm happy to see how she transformed her life, the talented man she raised. She rose above everything, poverty and hardships, she is an incredible woman. I loved her, to be honest with you I never stopped loving her, I wanted to find her in every woman that crossed my path, and I never found it, she deserved so much more than who I was."

"Thank you for being so candid with me, Miguel."

"I sincerely want us to be friends, and there is nothing like truth and honesty to connect us, is there? I'm so glad we had this heart to heart conversation, you heard of who I was, now you know who I became."

"I'm not going to judge you, Miguel, and I appreciate your sincerity. We might become friends."

"How is your relationship with your father? Are you close? Did you ever miss having your real father?"

"No, I never missed having a father. First George, I don't remember him, I was too young when he died, but I know he gave us a good start in London. Then Mom and Karl met, and pretty soon they were married and we moved to Dusseldorf to a castle!

I was mesmerized by Dad since the moment I met him, for me he was the image of a superhero, invincible, powerful! He was loving too, he treated me like he treated my older stepbrother Erik. I was proud of being his son, I still am.

There was just one time that we disagreed, when I decided to go to Julliard for my musical training, but in the end he let me go and told me, *'I'll support you in New York for whatever you need, but you have to be the best you can be in the music world and you have to come back and develop your career in Germany. Always remember you belong with your family!'*

Father had a hard time letting me go. All I wanted was to make him proud."

"I'm glad you have such a strong fatherly presence in your life, Gabriel, you didn't miss out on anything! Why don't you use his name professionally?"

"Because he is well known and powerful in Germany, I did not want to start my career in the shadow of his name, he understood, I use Mother's name before she married him. But everyone knows that I'm Karl Weisenwert's son!"

"I understand, I'm surprised that Maria Clara married George! They were friends, I knew that she had fled to London, and I assumed she was with him, but I didn't have his address or even his last name. I couldn't locate her."

"George and Mother married to legalize her permanence in the U.K. Now you know everything about my family, Miguel, what about yours?"

"I moved back to Barcelona, and a few months later I married the daughter of one of my father's friends. A year later my son

Fabio was born, and two years after, my daughter Marina.

We tried to be a happy family, but we never were. I couldn't get along with Silvia, my wife, not her fault, I just didn't adapt to her lifestyle... But I loved my children, I stayed until they were old enough to understand. We divorced, and I came back to Madrid, I was lucky enough to get the job that I longed for.

Later, Fabio came to live with me, we are very close, he is a pilot now, and he looks and sounds like you, Gabriel, he is a wonderful son and I'm very proud of him. Marina is a good girl, but turned out to be like her mother, the socialite type, she is happy with her life in Barcelona. I do visit her occasionally, she knows her father loves her.

When Fabio is not flying he spends time with me, we have a good father and son companionship. Would you mind if I tell him about you?"

"I don't mind, I just don't want my personal life being publicized."

"Absolutely, maybe someday you and Fabio will meet, I believe you'll have a lot in common. And I also would like to come to a concert of yours soon, before the tour is over."

"Mama, that's why I gave him the itinerary, I feel good about this first encounter, he seemed sincere, we might become friends someday. However I made sure he knows my father is and always will be Karl. I miss him, I'm going to see him after the tour is over."

"I did call Dad earlier and I was going to ask you to come and see him anyway, I also called the girls, they are always following your steps online, they are very proud of their famous big brother. We should have a family reunion soon, I miss having all of our family together."

Gabriel continued talking during the flight to Rome.

"Mama, you never denied that you loved Miguel in the past. How did you feel meeting him again? Did it bring up any old feelings?"

"No, not even resentment. My feelings died long ago... I do love my husband, even when he is grumpy and moody!"

"Miguel talked a lot about you. He said he loved you and still does. He tried to find someone like you and he never did, that's the biggest regret of his life."

"Well, maybe he can make peace with himself now."

On our following day in Rome I got an unexpected call from Miguel.

"I tried to get a ticket online for the concert tomorrow night, but they are sold out. I really want to see Gabriel playing."

"I can't help you, Miguel, I don't have any tickets available here, but if you take the trip to Milano, I might have a ticket for you there. It is going to be a black-tie gala at La Scala."

"Yes, definitely, I'll come to Milano. Where are you staying?"

"At the Pierre Milano, Via de Amicis, the gala is on Tuesday. I'll leave a ticket for you at the front desk."

"That's perfect, I'm looking forward to it. Thank you, Maria Clara!"

During the second concert in Rome, Gabriel played a special Rachmaninoff piece for all the mothers in the audience celebrating Mother's Day. It's one of my favorites!

At the end he called me to the stage, "Ladies and gentlemen, I have the privilege to introduce to you my beautiful mother Clara!"

He hugged and kissed me in front of all.

I was emotional and grateful for my son's acknowledgement. The next day the local papers had our picture all over, 'Mother and Son – Happy Mother's Day!'

At the hotel the next morning, before leaving for Milano, my daughters and Karl called me, wishing me a Happy Mother's Day! He told me:

"You couldn't be in better company than Gabriel's today."

"He is the best company, Karl, but I wish I had all my family around."

"So do I, Clara."

"Karl, you sound lonely, do you want me to come home?"

"No, I'm fine, enjoy the rest of your tour."

We arrived in Milano on Sunday evening.

On Monday morning Gabriel went straight to La Scala to get

acquainted with the symphony and to practice.

I was alone in the hotel all day, walked around a very nice area for a little while, feeling upset. The anticipation of seeing Miguel again didn't sit right with me.

I also felt uneasy about hiding this from Karl, I will tell him face to face, I don't know what reaction to expect from him, something is going on with him, and this reminds me of a very difficult time we had fourteen years ago when I supported Gabriel's decision to go to New York City.

Oh, that time was so painful! But we got over it, we lived happily until these recent months when his demeanor changed again.

'What is going on with Karl?'

I was worried and emotionally exhausted!

Gabriel and I had a quiet dinner, and he noticed that I was a little upset. I told him I was just tired and went to bed early.

In the morning Gabriel left for the theater to return in the afternoon to rest and get ready for the concert.

"This is an opulent one, I have to be in my best form, Mama."

"You are always at your best, son! Remember, Miguel will be at the theater tonight."

"I'm pleased he is coming all the way to Milano to see me. He may join us after for supper, if he wants."

As soon as Gabriel left, I got a call from Miguel.

"I'm here at the hotel, I arrived late last night and did not want to disturb you. We have a whole day ahead. Would you like to have lunch with me, Maria Clara?"

I thought for a while.

"Maybe we can go to the café next door."

We met in the majestic hotel lobby.

"I had no idea you were going to stay here, Miguel!"

"I just wanted to have the chance to talk to you and Gabriel. I assume he is at rehearsal now."

"Yes, he is, he will come back in the afternoon to rest and

prepare. He will see you after the concert, he invited you for a late supper."

"Absolutely, I won't miss any opportunity of talking to him."

We went to the café and sat down.

"Maria Clara, I don't mean to intrude on your life, but Gabriel told me that you married George when you moved to London, I knew you were friends, but I was puzzled... I believed he was gay. What happened to him?"

"First let me ask you not to call me Maria Clara anymore, just Clara, please! George was my best friend, we had a strong friendship and I respected his lifestyle. By marrying him I was able to provide my baby with a loving and kind father figure. In return, I helped George, taking care of his health and also keeping up appearances.

Remember, he lived in a time when being a gay man was taboo, there was much misinformation, discrimination and fear. He was a college professor and was afraid he would lose his job if they knew he was carrying a virus. I didn't know anything about AIDS then, he taught me all.

For three years he was doing very well, he was extremely mindful of me and Gabriel. But after his mother's sudden death, he was devastated, we both were, his immune system was compromised...

Months later George contracted pneumonia, had to go to the hospital, where he died unexpectedly. His heart gave out in an adverse drug interaction. It was tragic!

George was a wonderful man! He was like a loving and protective brother to me, I missed him terribly."

"I'm sorry, Clara. It still amazes me how unbiased you are, you appreciate people for who they are, and that is the way it should always be! What did you do after he died? Were you working? Where did you live?"

"I was working in a five star hotel by Hyde Park since Gabriel was six weeks old. I continued living in George's house in South Kensington, which I inherited. I had help with my son right there, the lady that lived next door took care of him while I worked. Agatha was a wonderful caretaker, she loved him and was a good friend to me."

"I imagine those early years in London were not easy, you had the courage and determination to go on raising your son alone. Did you meet Karl there?"

"Yes, at my job in the hotel's customer service office. He was a guest, he came to discuss an issue, and from then on we didn't stop talking...

By that time Gabriel was five years old, I had been alone for too long... Karl and I connected instantly. He returned to London to see me often. To make the story short, we got married, I moved to Dusseldorf, he adopted Gabriel, we had two daughters and together with his son Erik we built a beautiful family..."

"You smile when you talk about Karl and your family. Is your marriage a fairy tale? Is he a good husband? I know he is a good father, Gabriel raves about him."

"He is an outstanding man, husband and father. You are asking me too many questions, Miguel!"

"I feel compelled to know how Gabriel's life was growing up, imagining him running to his father's arms, being a happy little boy."

"He was well loved and cared for, he adored his father. It was mutual, Karl loved him like his own."

I gave Miguel the ticket and told him to be at La Scala by eight o'clock, I would go with Gabriel earlier.

"Are you sitting with me in the audience, Clara?"

"No, the conductor's wife and I are invited to the Mayor's Box."

We walked back to the hotel in silence. I didn't feel I had to continue the conversation. I was feeling uneasy in his presence.

At La Scala I took my seat with the other guests and looked straight at the audience, I knew exactly where Miguel was. He was also looking around, he saw me and nodded his head.

The lights dimmed, the symphony started playing an introduction, then Gabriel walked onto the stage, the audience effusively applauded. He had a commanding presence, standing tall and handsome he brought his violin to his chest and started...

In a world of his own, where all his feelings and emotions connected to the musical notes, rich melodies invaded the theater, in silence and in awe the audience listened.

My heart was filled with pride. I can't help it! Sometimes I feel like shouting, 'This is my talented, beautiful son!'

At intermission, I went downstairs and saw Miguel.

"It was such a magical experience, Clara, I could never imagine being part of something so beautiful, more than ever I feel a rush of joy and appreciation for music!"

"I know what you mean, Miguel, but go to the lobby, have a drink, compliments of the house!"

"Good idea, I need one! By the way, Clara, you look fantastic, regal, it is hard to believe you are Gabriel's mother, you look like his sister."

"Thank you."

In the second part, Gabriel looked straight at me and started playing one of my favorites, the Rachmaninoff Concerto.

Oh, sound divine! I was taken by emotion. That was our song, Karl's and mine, how many times we were immersed in those notes, together, loving one another, enveloped by that beautiful, passionate melody...

When the concert was over, Gabriel was exhausted: "I gave it my all, Mama!"

"It was superb, son, I couldn't be any prouder! Absolutely wonderful."

When we arrived at the hotel Miguel was waiting for us in the lobby. As we were going up to the suite Miguel told Gabriel, "I am in awe of you, I just had the most unforgettable experience of my life. I don't even have the words to describe it, I felt all deep emotions, in this moment I feel like I am coming back from a trip to Heaven!"

I had ordered room service earlier, and they promptly delivered it to the suite on our arrival.

"I'm always famished after a performance, let's eat, Miguel!

I'm not in a hurry, I can sleep late tomorrow."

I served them some wine. They start chatting, this time Gabriel was asking more questions to Miguel. They were both relaxed and engaged in conversation. I excused myself.

"I have things to prepare for our trip to Paris tomorrow."

Miguel got up in an attempt to hug me, I stepped back and shook his hand.

"It was nice of you to come, Miguel. Have a nice trip back to Madrid."

"I'll always be there, Clara, call me if you want to talk or need anything."

I kissed my son goodnight.

I woke Gabriel up by noon to get ready to proceed to Paris. During the trip he told me he had a good time last night.

"Miguel has a wicked sense of humor, we laughed a lot, the things he said and how he said them were familiar, it reminded me of myself sometimes! Maybe that's the only aspect of our personalities that matches.

We also had a very interesting discussion about nature versus nurture! Like you, Mama, I tend to think that we are the result of both, but I wonder sometimes... Genetically I am a hundred percent Spanish, but I was raised German. What really determines who I am?"

"Gabe, you are very scientific today! You are unique, you are your own self, I never met anyone as talented as you, son."

"I always wondered where I got the musical gene from. Miguel told me that his Grandfather Antonio, a banker, was a cellist! He adored his cello and played at every family reunion. He said that after his grandfather died he felt sorry that he was too young to appreciate classical music and his cello playing. And he also said that the adults in the family always said, 'Grandfather was a musical genius.' Miguel is going to explore it and eventually he will give me more information."

"You wonder if that is where your musical gene came from, son? Was not from my side, that I can tell... And I see that he found a way of keeping the conversation between the two of you going."

"That's true, Mama, I almost feel sorry for him, he is making an effort to connect with me. He also talked a lot about Fabio, he is proud of him. I think he is trying to show me that he is a good father and friend. As I see it I have my father, Miguel can only be a friend!"

"I'm glad that things are working out this way, you have closure now and answers to all of your questions."

"It seems like you were uncomfortable around him, Mama."

"I had nothing to talk to him about, I was just trying to be polite."

There was only one concert scheduled in Paris, but it required more preparations, Gabriel modified the program and rehearsed with the symphony for two days. The President of France would be attending.

The day after our arrival in Paris I received another unexpected call from Miguel.

"Gabriel is not here, he is at rehearsal."

"I thought so, I want to thank you again, Clara, and tell you that I admire what you did with your life! You gave your children the best life, married a powerful and rich man. You did it all!"

"I didn't marry Karl because he is rich, I married him because I loved him. And for the first time in my life a man made me feel valued and truly loved…"

"I know your values and your character, Clara, what I want to say is that I'm glad you got the happiness you deserve."

"Thank you, I'll let Gabriel know that you called."

In the meantime, I did some sightseeing around the area, reminiscing about old trips that we had taken, sometimes with the children. Paris was one of the places the family enjoyed coming to, especially the girls! I miss them!

I called them in New York, Amanda told me she spoke to Karl, and he seemed sad and lonely.

"Daddy asked me and Katie to come home this summer, he can't wait until the end of the year to see us."

"I know, Amie, as soon as the tour is over I'm going to Dusseldorf, and this time I'll stay longer with him. I miss you girls, but I won't come to New York anytime soon."

In the afternoon before the concert, Karl called me!

"It has been a long time, Karl, since I heard from you. Are you alright?"

"Yes, I am spending a lot of time in the house, it is quiet here. But how is Gabriel and how are the concerts coming along?"

"Wonderful, a success, he is getting ready for a special one tonight at L'Opera, the President of France will attend!"

"That's good news! When are you coming home, Clara?"

"As soon as the tour is over, Karl, tomorrow we will leave for Zurich. Can you come and join us there for the last concert?"

"Sorry, not this time. I wish you were here, I miss you, Clara!"

"Karl, I haven't heard that from you for the longest time! I miss you too, and I think that instead of going to Zurich I'll come home tomorrow."

"Is Gabriel going to be alright with that? Are you coming by train or plane?"

"He will understand, I'll tell him later. I'll call you in the morning to confirm."

"Thank you, Clara, I'll send Franz to pick you up."

I felt right about that sudden decision. I sensed that Karl was lonesome and he missed me… I had the urge to rush to him.

At L'Opera I accompanied Gabriel to the dressing room.

"It's going to be especially French tonight, Mama. I have a special introduction for the President."

"It's going to be fantastic, son, as always. You are in your best form!"

The concert started, Gabriel walked onto the stage under applause, he bowed his head to the President and played La Marseillaise. The audience stood up and sang along. In the end the President applauded effusively. It was a great start!

The symphony joined in and they played a repertoire very pleasing to the French audience. Spectacular sounds of joy and triumph!

During the intermission, champagne was served in the atrium for the public. I went backstage and crossed paths with a government official with a message:

"The President wants to meet Gabriel Bentlenn after the concert is finished. Please ask him to come to the Presidential Box, Madame."

"He will be honored!" I responded.

Gabriel was changing his shirt for the second part, and I gave him the message.

"You'll come with me, Mama."

The concert ended with a fun and vibrant can-can, with the whole audience clapping and participating, including Mr. President.

I met Gabriel backstage and we walked together to the balcony. The President and his entourage offered the best compliments:

"You need to come to Paris more often, we truly enjoyed your music, it is superb."

"Thanks, Mr. President, I love Paris and won't miss any chance to come back. Let me introduce you to my mother, Clara Weisenwert."

"Madame, thank you for sharing your gifted son with us."

There were photographers around and many pictures were taken, and after a toast of champagne we said goodbye and the entourage left.

Back at the hotel I told Gabriel:

"Tomorrow you are going to be all over the papers with the President!"

"And you too, Mama, I'm always proud to show you off."

"Gabe, I didn't want to distract you before the concert, Dad called this afternoon and he sounded down, he asked me to come back, and instead of going to Zurich tomorrow I'll return home. Do you mind? You know how much I appreciate being with you, son, but I believe he needs me now."

"Absolutely, Mama, you should go. It is just one more concert, I'll be fine. From there I'll go to Vienna, to Elise and to rest, then I'll come to see Dad and you in Dusseldorf. Give him my best, and tell him I love him."

Early in the morning I made arrangements for the flight change and called Karl to confirm that I would be arriving late afternoon.

He sighed!

"I'm glad you'll be home today, *meine liebe*! Franz will be waiting for you at the airport."

Gabriel and I left the hotel together.

He proceeded to Zurich, I went back to Dusseldorf.

CHAPTER THREE

IN SICKNESS AND IN HEALTH

*F*ranz, our loyal driver, was waiting for me at the airport.

"Thank you for coming. How is everything at home?"

"All is quiet, Frau Clara. We'll be there soon."

When we arrived at home, Karl was waiting in the library, reclining in his favorite chair.

I was anxious to see how things between us would unfold.

"Karl, I'm home! How are you?"

He smiled.

"I'm fine, Clara. How was the tour?"

"Exhausting but wonderful. I brought clips from newspapers, including the last ones from Paris."

"I know Gabriel is a great success, I'm proud of him."

I sat close to him.

"How are you really feeling? You look pale, Karl. What's wrong?"

"Just a little under the weather, don't worry."

I put my arms around him and kissed his face. My sixty-eight year old towering man looked a little down, but he is still an impressive figure.

"I'm glad you asked me to come home, I was thinking you didn't miss me anymore."

"I missed you, Clara, more than you know, you light up our house."

Hilda came in. "Welcome home, Frau Clara."

"I'm glad to be home, Hilda. How are you?"

"I'm quite alright. Franz brought your luggage upstairs and dinner is ready. Would you like it to be served now?"

"In a little bit, Hilda, I'm going to freshen up. I'll be right back."

Franz and Hilda are a married couple who work and live on our estate. They contribute to running the house and other staff. I have true affection for the couple, they have been part of our family for more than twenty years.

Hilda is our trusted governess.

Karl was waiting for me in the dining room. During dinner, he told me that he has been delegating more responsibilities to Erik and working from home often.

"I am preparing Erik to assume my position in our company."

It was obvious that Karl was not enthusiastic about letting go of his responsibilities, he is very attached to his work and his power.

After we finished dinner, we went to the den.

Karl looked at me with tenderness…

"What happened to us, Clara? We were so close. I admit that I have been stubborn, but you used to overlook that. Now you spend so much time away with the children. Are you tired of me? Is it because I'm getting old and you are still young and vibrant?"

"Karl, I was never silent about the way I was feeling, many times I felt like I was one of your possessions decorating the house, you had very little time for me and my feelings. You provided me with everything, but you were not validating me. I needed to keep afloat, it was exhausting fighting you, and I was hurting because throughout everything, even when you withheld affection, I loved you. No, I don't see you as an old man, you are strong and powerful."

"Until very recently I didn't understand what you were talking about. I provided well for the family, I thought I was doing my best, but lately I have had time to reflect and recognized how demanding I was, sometimes a bit unreasonable, I am afraid to say."

"And cold, Karl, very cold with me. I felt you didn't love me anymore. Old memories of our past trouble surfaced, I thought you had some other interest out there. I needed to protect my heart, and spending time with our children filled my life with joy and purpose."

"Clara, I never stopped loving you, the apparent coldness was my way of not dealing with issues. I'm sorry for being insensitive to you."

"You say you didn't stop loving me, but indifference is the absence of love, that's how you have been treating me, and that hurts."

"Did your feelings for me die? Are you resentful of me?"

I came closer and caressed his face.

"Karl, I married you because I loved you, you are my husband, my children's father, I always admired you as a man and a father. When I made that vow to love you 'till death do us part' I meant it with all my heart."

He was teary, which was totally unlike him, and he hugged me.

"I love you, Clara, and I need you, of course you can always spend time with the children, they adore you, but I need you here as well."

"Is there anything you need to tell me, Karl? I feel like you are holding something back. Is the business in trouble?"

"Not at all. I don't want to spoil our time together tonight."

"Karl, after we were married, you would tell me you loved me mostly in our intimate times… Yes, my place is here with you in our house, maybe we will visit our children together from now on."

"My wife, my sweet and beautiful wife, I hope there is still time for us."

"What do you mean? Of course we are going to grow old together!"

I rested in his arms for a little while, listening to his heartbeat, the strong heartbeat of a good man, and I started getting sleepy.

"Sorry, Karl, I'm falling asleep, I'm so tired."

"We'll talk more tomorrow, *meine liebe.*"

He held my hand and we went upstairs, walking slowly. We stopped by our suite where I haven't slept in a few months, he didn't say anything. I asked him:

"Do you want to be alone, Karl?"

"Of course not, I was afraid to ask you."

I came in the suite with him, got ready for bed.

"I just need to sleep, Karl."

He held me close and we kissed softly.

"Sleep well, *meine liebe.*"

It was almost noon when I woke up.

'Oh my, I slept for ten hours! Where is Karl?'

I put myself together and went downstairs to the kitchen, grabbed a cup of coffee and asked Hilda if Karl had gone to work.

"No, he is in the study. Lunch will be ready in half an hour, Frau Clara."

"Karl, I never slept so long in my life, I'm well rested. How are you feeling today?"

"I'm fine, I feel happy that you are here."

"Would you like to go for a walk in the garden, Karl? I almost forgot how beautiful it is in the spring. I used to enjoy gardening, I'll do it again!"

"Yes, it is beautiful. Every time I look out this window I remember you walking around, pushing my father's wheelchair and talking to him, even if he could not understand you. His dream came true, he lived with his family in a house full of children, song and laughter. I'll always be grateful to you, Clara!"

Lately Karl has reminisced quite often about his father Johann Gustav, the one who gave him everything, the automotive industrial park, the mansion.

Johann lost his wife when Karl was twelve years old. Katarina died in a boating accident in the South of France, where she was celebrating her fortieth birthday with some of her girlfriends. He was working in Dusseldorf when that happened.

For many years, Johann dedicated himself almost exclusively to his work and his son, but he had a dream of owning an estate in the Old Town, on the east bank of the Rhine River.

When Karl went to university, Johann finally found the property of his dreams in a beautiful location with a magnificent view of the Rhine. It was much larger than he had dreamed of for many years, but he bought it anyway, planning that in the future the whole family would live there.

He counted on Karl getting married and moving into the mansion with his family.

By then Johann was in a relationship with a widow who already had grown children away from Dusseldorf. The two of them moved into the estate while he started a complete overhaul.

Karl got married at age twenty-eight, but he continued living in the west side, closer to the commercial center and their city office. His first wife Elsa did not want to move away from the life she was used to.

Elsa enjoyed the nightlife, bars, nightclubs, she was out frequently. She stepped out of the marriage, and when Erik was in kindergarten she had an affair with a count from Bavaria.

Karl divorced her and got full custody of Erik. Elsa moved to Bavaria with her count and would visit her son only a couple of times a year.

Johann's dreams of having his entire family living with him were crushed again. But Karl and Erik visited him often on weekends or holidays, and Erik would spend vacations at the mansion with his grandfather, enjoying the pool, tennis court and boating.

For Karl and Erik that was their retreat, only twenty minutes away from downtown.

Years later Johann was diagnosed with Alzheimer's, and as his health declined his companion left him. Karl closed the mansion and brought his father to live with him and Erik in the city, to better assist him.

Johann's condition was progressing, needing constant medical supervision. Karl had to place his father in a specialized nursing home.

When Karl and I met, his father was living in the nursing home. Only after I agreed in marrying him and moved to Dusseldorf, Karl brought me to the mansion.

In this same garden, he told me this was his father's property and he would like to live here with me, Erik, Gabriel and hopefully have a baby of our own. I spontaneously told him:

"This is a mansion, it is immense just for us, it was your father's dream to have his family here. Why don't you bring him home? You can hire a nurse to take care of him properly, I'll keep him company too. This is his house and his dream, and you can make it happen, Karl!"

Karl had a new suite set up on the ground floor for his father and his nurse. A month later when we moved into the house he brought his father home. Grandpa Johann was already having difficulty talking and remembering even his own son's name. He never called me by my name, for him I was Katarina, and Gabriel was Karl. His mind had stopped in a time when he was happy with his wife and his little boy…

Contradicting the medical prognosis Grandpa Johann lived for four beautiful years, surrounded by love in his house full of children, Erik, Gabriel, Katherine and Amanda, as he always dreamed of!

Walking together in the garden, hand in hand, Karl made a comment:

"Your bed of tulips is in full bloom, Clara, and pretty soon your summer roses. You make everything beautiful!"

"It is nice to know you appreciate that, Karl. I love this place, but sorry to tell you sometimes I don't feel this is my home. You fight me on everything I want to do, replacing old furniture, even changing old drapes."

"That was silly of me, you are the lady of the house and you can make any changes you like, no budget approval is necessary." He laughed, and that was the first time I saw him laughing in a long time.

It was a warm, sunny day. Hilda served lunch outside on the patio.

"Karl, you look tired and you are acting different, you can't hide it from me. It is time to tell me what is going on. Have you seen a doctor recently? Is it Alzheimer's? You were always concerned, whatever it is, please tell me."

"I have seen some doctors and I'll go straight to the point, Clara, nothing is wrong with my brain, but I have cancer, I'm fighting it for a while. Initially I thought it was something simple to take care of, but while you were in New York, I started having other symptoms, it has spread, I need to go into very aggressive treatment soon."

I was in total shock!

"Cancer! What kind of cancer? Where did it spread to? Are the doctors sure?"

"It is a tumor in the liver and a little spot on the left side of the lung. Unfortunately the doctors in Frankfurt confirmed all the test results and diagnosis from the ones done here."

"Oh, Karl, you went to Frankfurt and I didn't know. All this time that you have been cold and distant was to hide this issue! I can see it now. You should have told me. Why didn't you tell me yesterday when I came home? I came for you!"

"Initially I was in denial and believed I was going to be alright, there was no point in worrying you, and yesterday I didn't want your pity, I didn't want you to come only because I'm sick."

"I'm here because I love you, I want to help you. Do you want me to take you to the cancer hospital in New York City, the best in the world?"

"No, Clara, we have all the treatment available right here. The doctors said it is going to be a rough process, I might need to hire a nurse for that period."

"You don't need a nurse, I'll take care of you, Karl. We will deal with this together. You are strong, you can overcome this!"

"I don't want you to be upset, Clara, but I accept your support to fight through it, we are stronger together."

I was crying, brought my chair closer, put my arms around him and leaned close.

"I'm here with you for always, Karl, in good and bad times, in sickness and in health… My husband, my love."

He held on to me, and for the first time he let tears roll down, my big and strong man was crying.

"I didn't mean for this to happen, I wanted to be here with my family for a long time."

"I understand now why you are sharing more responsibilities with Erik and why you want Katie to return home. Does Erik know?"

"Yes, and he is very concerned, I told him I trust him with the company, but it is too much for him to handle alone."

"I'll talk to Erik, he does have an enormous responsibility, and I'll tell him that I'm with you all the way. He will know you are being taken care of. I want to go with you to all your treatments and doctor's appointments. When is the next one?"

"On Thursday, they are going to schedule chemo and radiation."

"I'll be with you and I also want to ask your doctor what I can do to help."

"You being here with me makes all the difference, Clara. I have realized that in the end all that matters is to be surrounded by the ones we love. Family and love take us through everything. I want my family around, I want joy, laughter and music in our house like we had when the children were younger."

"You'll have it all, Karl, I promise."

We stayed in silence for a while.

"Clara, I want to have the biggest Christmas celebration this year, with many lights and an enormous tree in the family room and our children, all of them around, with Gabriel playing his magical violin and the girls accompanying him on the piano and caroling. I want memories, beautiful memories like the ones you created for my father. I hope now, somewhere in the corner of his mind, he knew he was loved. I want everything to be the best, like if it were the last…"

"It will be wonderful, Karl, and we will have many others to celebrate, but before that, we are going to have a family reunion in the summer.

Amie and Katie are coming, so is Gabriel. As a matter of fact he is coming as soon as he takes a break after the tour, he misses you."

I served him some lemonade.

"I'm going upstairs to get something to show you, I'll be right back, Karl."

Alone upstairs, I couldn't contain the tears, I was overwhelmed and devastated. I dried my eyes and went back to the patio.

"Look at this, Karl, I brought clips of newspapers with reports about Gabriel's performances. This one was in Rome, he celebrated Mother's Day and called me on stage. I was flattered!

On the way out of the theater a reporter asked him why he didn't use his father's name and he responded:

'*My father is a very powerful man, his name is well known in Germany. May you all know that I respect and love my father, for that reason I didn't want to use the prestige of his name to launch my career. He supports me, he always did.*'"

"Gabriel said that? In public?"

"Yes, Karl, look, it is in writing!"

"I'm proud of him, Clara, I was hard on him sometimes, but I love him, he is my son just like Erik!"

"I know, Karl, you never made any distinction between him, Erik and our daughters. I have more to tell you, but you might be tired, maybe take a nap."

"I'll rest in my study for a while, but leave me the papers, I want to see them all."

"Rest, Karl, I'm going to talk to Hilda. I'll check on you later."

I met Hilda in her small office outside the kitchen.

"When did you and Franz know about Herr Weisenwert's health issue?"

"A couple of months ago, when you were in New York. He forbade Franz to tell you anything, he didn't want to worry you. Franz has driven him a few times to the oncologist and we knew something was wrong with our Master."

"Did Karl ask you for special foods or medications? Anything?"

"Yes, he said his doctor recommended that he would eat less meat and more vegetables, basically like you always ate. He also asked to keep the maid out of his room, he didn't want her to mess up the bottles of medication he is keeping on the side table. Since then I'm the only one cleaning the suite."

"Hilda, thank you very much for taking good care of Karl, from now on I'm here, I already told the girls that I'm not going to visit them anytime soon. And you and I are working as a team, we can do this together."

"Count on me, Frau Clara, Franz and I want to help any way we can. This news has been very sad, you are like family to us."

"And you and Franz are part of our family, Hilda, I thank you very much."

I went to the study to check on Karl and he was asleep. I went upstairs to our suite, on his nightstand he had new picture frames of us and the children. *'They were not here before, maybe he looks at them every night.'*

The bottles of pills were in the drawer, I took them out.

I looked around the room, there was no reason not to share it with him. I have missed my husband and I'll be with him until he is whole again!

I decided to freshen up our room, the comforter and drapes have been there for ages, time to renovate, especially now that he is going to spend more time there during his recovery.

I was compelled to start making changes and brought my American comforter and pillows from the other room. *'Much better, I never liked anything stuffed with feathers.'*

I came back to the study, Karl was awake, looking at the newspaper clips. "Did you rest well, Karl? You had a long nap!"

"I feel rested and I was enjoying this news about Gabriel's concert, he is such a celebrity and he did it all by himself with his talent alone, what a boy!"

"He is very sincere, he plays with his heart and soul, and people feel it. Karl, tomorrow I'm going to call the children and tell them what is going on here."

"Please, Clara, don't tell them now, let's wait until they come in the summer."

"If you prefer, Karl, they are all adults, they should know. Anyway Gabriel is coming soon and we will tell him when he is here, alright?"

"I do not want them worrying, Clara. You mentioned before you had something else to tell me. What was it?"

"Nothing important, we had a very emotional day, let's relax."

"I spoke to Erik in the morning, he is coming over after work, I told him you were home, Clara."

Erik and I were always good friends, he has a special place in my life and my heart. He was thirteen years old when I married his father, he was raised by a governess and had not experienced the care of a loving mother. As a teenager he was a little reluctant to accept me as a stepmother, but we did bond, more like a big sister and little brother.

He confided in me, listened to my advice and became my partner and my critic when I was learning German, even getting a kick out of my funny accent. He helped me, he had the brilliant idea of sharing his school books with me and gave me some homework.

Erik was a great big brother to my son, he was the one who introduced him to the violin. He had a small violin from his elementary school years that he gave to Gabriel to play with, and taught him the first notes... He is, literally, the one responsible for Gabriel's musical interest!

Erik is pretty much like his father in terms of appearance and personality traits, maybe that's why I loved him right away.

He came around 6:00 p.m., and I gave him a big hug.

"You were missed around here, Clara."

"And I missed you all, Erik. How are Louisa and the children?"

"They are alright, Louisa is complaining because I have been working late hours recently."

"I know, Erik, family time is very important, but you have some extra responsibilities now, I understand. How are you feeling?"

"I'm worried, Clara, very worried about Dad."

"I'm here and I'm with him all the way, don't worry, you have too much to deal with. Your father will be fine, he is a fighter, we'll fight this together!"

"I'm counting on that, Clara! I'm glad our old man mellowed and begged you to come home."

"He didn't have to beg, I love him, my place is at his side. The best you can do is to keep the business going and take care of yourself and your family. We would like to see them soon."

"I'll bring them on Sunday, it might be warm enough for Lili and Will to enjoy the pool!"

I accompanied Erik to the study to see Karl.
"Erik just told me he will bring the family on Sunday!"
Karl added, "Sunday is good, we are going to see my doctor on Thursday, and I'll probably have some updates for you, come and see these papers all about your famous brother."

I left them alone. Erik did not stay for dinner, his wife and children were waiting for him. I walked with him to his car when he was leaving.
"Clara, I'm really worried about Dad, it sounds serious, and I'm so glad you are supporting and motivating him, he needs your optimism. When you called him yesterday morning to say you were coming home, he told me, 'The light of my life is back.'"
"Erik, I'm still in shock, I am so sorry I was not here when he was diagnosed, he only told me about his health issue today. I reassure you, I'll do whatever it takes to see Karl well again."
"I never doubt you, Clara. See you on Sunday."

Karl was waiting for me in the dining room. After dinner we stayed downstairs for a little while.
"What's your doctor's name? I'm looking forward to talk to him on Thursday."
"Dr. Jung. Are you sure you want to come with me?"
"Of course, *liebe*, I'll be with you every day until you get tired of seeing me around."
"Never, *meine liebe*! I think I want to go upstairs now."
I went right to his nightstand in the suite.
"Which pills are you taking at night?"
"These two, the others are to be taken in the morning with breakfast."
I pointed out the picture frames. "I see you are keeping our family close."
"I like to look at my beautiful family, my beautiful wife. Clara, are you making some changes already? Where did this come from?"
"From my other room, I never liked the feather comforters, you

50

are going to like this one, it is fluffy, light, but warm. And there will be more changes to come."

"Changes are good!"

"I still have my luggage in the other room, Karl, tomorrow I'll transfer it to our dressing room, I'm going to get something new to wear."

When I came back, he was reclining on the bed and he noticed my new silk nightgown and robe.

"You look beautiful, Clara, like I always remember my young wife."

"It's new, I bought it in Italy."

I got into my side of the bed, he pulled me close, and I rested my head on his chest.

"I'm sorry I'm sick and old, I wish I could love you like when I was younger and healthier."

"Karl, I'm pretty happy in your arms, this is just how I want to be, close to you again. We are together and we will not get any younger, but we will be healthier and stronger, I promise you, *liebe*."

In the morning he gently caressed my face, waking me up.

"Good morning, Karl. Did you sleep well?"

"Wonderful, I feel good this morning and I like the comforter, it is soft and warm, just like you."

He was in good spirits this morning.

I got up and served Karl's juice to take his pills.

"It all might change with the new treatment, maybe I won't need these anymore. We will find out at my appointment with Dr. Jung tomorrow."

"I have many questions to ask him, I'll be your partner in the treatment."

"You make me feel hopeful, *meine liebe*."

"Do you have anything to do today, Karl?"

"I have to read some reports that Erik brought me, and we can go for another walk in the garden like yesterday. You also mentioned that you had something to tell me, Clara. Is it about Gabriel?"

"Yes. I thought we could go down to the riverbank and talk

later, if you feel like it. In the meantime I'll do something upstairs."

I organized my clothes and talked to Hilda.

"I'll be making some changes upstairs in our suite and maybe some other rooms too."

"That's good, Frau Clara, I like changes and I would like to help."

I joined Karl around 11:00 a.m.

"I'm a little tired to walk now, let's just sit outside on the patio and you can tell me now what you want to say about Gabriel."

"Alright, Karl, it happened in Madrid, and I wanted to tell you in person, but when I came home our most important conversation was about your health and us. This was not as relevant, that's why I didn't tell you yesterday.

Do you remember when we first met, I told you that George was not Gabriel's father, that his *biological* was someone I left in Madrid?"

"I remember, you told me you were deceived by that man and left to give your son a life away from all of that, and your friend George helped you with a new beginning in England."

"I also told you that I was raising Gabriel with the truth. As a young man he became curious about his biological father, he had many questions and showed interest in meeting him someday..."

"I heard that is very natural in adopted children, they want to know their origins. No matter how good their adopted parents are, they can become anxious and even depressed about it."

"Exactly, Karl. I did promise to Gabe that I would introduce him to Miguel, if I would ever find him. It just so happened that during our flight from London to Madrid I found a picture of him in the airline's magazine. I couldn't believe it!

Miguel had left the company and Madrid in 1978, and he is back there at the same place. I spent a day in Madrid preparing myself and surprised him in his office when I told him about Gabriel. I didn't know what to expect, and in the end I was pleased to see that he was very apologetic and wanted to meet him right away."

"Did Gabriel meet him?"

"Yes, he met Miguel the day we were leaving for Rome. They talked. Now thirty-two years later, he was humble. Miguel showed interest in knowing more about Gabriel's career, and he went to his concert in Milano."

"Did Gabriel like him? Are they going to maintain contact?"

"Gabe was pretty clear, he told Miguel that he has a father that he loves and admires. Maybe someday they'll become friends, like many others that Gabe has all over Europe."

"Do you want to see him again, Clara?"

"Not at all, I have nothing to say to or listen from him. I was innocent and gullible when I first met him, I didn't know men could be that deceiving... No matter how remorseful he seems to be, he is in the remote past, that is where he is going to stay."

"In my opinion he should burn. Did he hit on you?"

"He had interest in knowing about my life. I told him I'm happily married to the best man I ever met, and I love and respect my husband."

"Did you tell him that before I called you and asked you to come home?"

"Of course, Karl, I spoke to him in Milano. I didn't know what was happening to you, but I always knew my feelings for you. I told him the truth."

Karl held my hand, "I love you, Clara. I'm so sorry there was a time I hurt you, I'm sorry I'm sick now and I can't be the best husband."

"Karl, I love you too. That wound in my heart healed, and you are the only man that I trust. Best of all, I was very pleased with Gabriel's reaction, immediately after meeting Miguel he told me you are and will always be his real father."

Karl's eyes welled up, "He is a good boy, I am proud of him!"

"He is fair, he has learned from you, Karl, you taught him how to be a good man, he remembers you treating him no differently than you treated Erik. Gabriel is your son, he is too good to be another man's child."

"When is he coming, Clara? I miss him."

"I'll call him to confirm on Friday, he should be back in Vienna."

"I'm sorry I didn't make it to his concerts, I couldn't this time, but as soon as I get better I'll come with you."

"I like the way you are talking, Karl! Yes, as soon as you get better we will do many nice things together."

We held hands and stayed quiet. All was right!

Karl is just like that, he only discusses personal matters once, I'm sure he won't be dwelling on this subject again.

I accompanied Karl to the study for a nap.

"I'll come back to see you later, *liebe*."

I took the time to search for mattress stores and found exactly what I wanted and asked Franz to drive me downtown. I purchased an adjustable, comfortable bed, very sleek and classy, to be delivered on Friday!

I also went to the home store. One thing led to another and I ordered new drapery too.

I returned home very excited with the car stuffed with new things for our suite. Mission accomplished!

Karl was already awake.

"Did you go shopping? What is all of that?"

"For our new room. I got the most comfortable bed, you can adjust it with a remote control, higher, lower, you are going to love it! It will be here right on time."

"If it makes you this happy shopping for bedding, keep going, *meine liebe*."

"Karl, I want to make you comfortable, and I also feel like it is a new beginning for us."

"Indeed, it is, we are going to spend much more time in our room!"

That evening we retired early, we needed to be at the Hospital early in the morning.

"Clara, it is going to be a long day."

"It's alright, Karl, all my time is available to you."

We met Dr. Jung at the Hospital.

"I'm here to learn everything about my husband's condition and the best way to help him heal, Doctor."

"I think you are helping already. You look very well this

morning, Karl!"

"Thank you. The light came back home!"

"I have everything decided and laid out for you. Dr. Linder, the oncology radiologist, Dr. Gutmann, the chemo specialist and I have discussed and agreed that you'll benefit from an aggressive treatment.

Due to your overall good physical health status, heart and otherwise, we expect very positive results."

"In this case you see that Karl is strong enough to endure all of this treatment! I'm glad, please tell me how it will work."

"Radiation and chemotherapy will be done simultaneously. Dr. Linder and Dr. Gutmann are in charge of those procedures, and they will give all the feedback.

During the treatment I'll be following up and available to both of you, if you have any questions or concerns.

It is going to be difficult for you, Karl, that's when your wife will be of great help to you.

Dr. Linder is going to see you next. She will discuss the radiology protocol. I wish you both the best of luck! Keep positive!"

We went to the radiology department.

Dr. Linder has vast experience in her field. She calmly and kindly described the treatment. Karl was scheduled for eight weeks of applications, starting on Monday. On the days he also has chemo he will stay in the Treatment Center all day.

She suggested we eat at the cafeteria before seeing Dr. Gutmann at one o'clock.

Karl was overwhelmed.

"I feel tired already, I wish this would be over."

"Don't get discouraged, it is much to deal with, but you are not alone, we will see this through together."

"I'm anxious about this treatment, it is more than I thought."

"I agree, Karl, but I have faith in you and the team of doctors, they are invested in you."

We met Dr. Gutmann.

He informed Karl they are placing the port in his chest. Karl was frustrated.

"Do you have to do it now?"

"Yes, it is a quick procedure, has to be done before the first day of chemo. We can start the treatment next Tuesday or Friday. What do you prefer, Karl?"

"Tuesday. I'll have time to recover and hopefully have a better weekend."

"Well then, for the next ten weeks you will be here every Tuesday, all day. Now please follow me.

Mrs. Weisenwert, you may wait in my office."

I kissed my husband, "I'll be here waiting for you."

I felt like crying when he walked away with his doctor. Karl looked defeated, I never saw him that way.

About forty-five minutes later, Dr. Gutmann came back.

"Karl is resting for another hour, in the meantime I'll give you a prescription for the nausea and painkillers in case he is uncomfortable with the incision. You can get them at the pharmacy on the ground floor."

When I returned, a nurse gave me some additional informational brochures and took me to Karl's recovery room.

I sat by his bed, "How are you feeling, Karl, does it hurt?"

"No, it's all numb, but I don't like this, it is right over my heart."

"I know, Dr. Gutmann prescribed some pills in case you feel pain. Franz will be here in one hour, you'll feel better once we get home."

The nurse came in a few times to check on him.

"You can start taking your pain killers as prescribed, at home. They will make you drowsy and sleepy."

I helped him put his shirt and jacket on. We walked downstairs. Franz was waiting for us, it was almost 5:00 p.m. What a long day…

Karl was silent all the way home. I felt emotionally exhausted, it was difficult to see him suffering.

At home I asked Hilda to bring dinner upstairs.

"I don't feel like eating."

"You need to eat, Karl. I know it has been a very long day. I'm sorry you are in pain."

He ate a little.

"Good, Karl, now you come to bed, I'll be here all the time, and if you wake up in pain in the middle of the night, please tell me."

He was sitting on the edge of the bed, I was standing right in front, he leaned his head against my chest, I held and caressed him and he let his tears and emotions flow, he cried, cried profusely, like I never saw before. He was so vulnerable. I let my tears roll down my face... relieving the anguish.

After a while he told me, "I'm so sorry I'm giving you all this grief, Clara, I never thought I would end my life like this, sick and dependent...."

"Your life is not ending, Karl, this is an enormous challenge, but you will overcome it. I'm with you every minute of every day in this ordeal."

"Clara, I didn't want to give you a hard time, I'm so embarrassed, I'm such a wimp!"

"You are not, it's right to let go of your anguish, you have reasons to feel this way. Rest now, *liebe*."

I stayed until he fell asleep, then I talked to Hilda and Franz.

"This is the worst part, we have to go to the Treatment Center every morning at eight for two hours, except on Tuesdays we will stay until five.

Hilda, tomorrow we'll discuss menus and other arrangements."

"Alright, Frau Clara. The store confirmed the bed delivery early in the morning, I will assist them. Is there anything else you need?"

"Yes, you and Franz, please check if we have an extra lounge garden chair, I want to make the suite's balcony more comfortable. Karl might like to sit out there in the afternoons. It would be nice to have some planters with flowers up too. Thank you, both, I couldn't provide all the care and attention to him without your help!"

Hilda and Franz serve us with pride! This is one of those times that I am glad I can count on them! But it was not always like this...

***

When Karl and I got married and moved into the mansion, he brought along his governess Greta. She was with them since Erik was born, and took over all the responsibilities of his house after his divorce, and continued doing the same at the mansion.

She didn't speak English and hardly communicated with me. She thought of herself as 'the lady of the house.'

I immediately started taking German classes with a tutor, Bertha, and in four years I was fluent, I had two babies and helped care for Grandfather Johann. I was a hands-on mother for Gabe, Katie and Amie, never needing much help from Greta, who just had eyes for 'her boy' Erik.

When Erik went to university, Greta finally retired and left us.

I was totally ingrained in the German lifestyle, but dealing with the mansion, maids, a cook, gardeners and still driving the children... It was too much!

Karl had Franz, one of his factory drivers, to take him back and forth to the Industrial Park and from his office downtown.

On one of those occasions Franz told him that he was having many problems, his wife Hilda couldn't recover from the loss of their only daughter Helga one year earlier.

Their little girl was born with muscular dystrophy and died at age four. Hilda was so distressed that she stopped working, and their bills were mounting.

They needed a new start.

Karl discussed with me that we could hire Hilda as a house manager and Franz as the driver and coordinator of the landscaping services.

I agreed and met them. Hilda was knowledgeable and very kind with the children. We offered them the job.

Soon they moved into a guest apartment over the garage.

Franz started driving the children to school. Hilda loved them, she said the children helped her mend her broken heart.

The girls adored her and the special cookies that she would bake for them on holidays and other occasions.

After Gabriel left, and then years later the girls went to college, we still needed Franz and Hilda's help.

I could take time visiting my son and daughters in New York, knowing that the house and Karl were in good hands.

***

I returned to the suite, Karl was still asleep.

He woke up later, complaining of pain. I elevated his back on the pillows, gave him another pill.

"Try to rest, Karl. Tomorrow you are going to sleep much better in your new bed."

He stayed awake for a while.

"You are treating me like a baby, I am a burden."

"You are not a burden, and I love being a Mom. Close your eyes, Karl, rest, rest now."

I remained awake, thinking of all that I had heard from the doctors, I was so scared...

In the dim nightlight I looked at his face, resting peacefully. I thought of our whirlwind romance when we first met, how strong and powerful he was, how protected I felt in his arms, how intensely we loved each other. Now he was frail, needing me...

'I want my husband back. Oh, Karl, I love you, I can't lose you, please get better.'

I woke up very early, and he was sitting up.

"I'm uncomfortable, my whole body hurts, I want to move."

"Karl, I can get you breakfast. Do you want to stay in the study? They are delivering the bed this morning."

"I'll go to the study."

I left him in his office and went to the kitchen to prepare breakfast.

I served him oatmeal with honey, and coffee.

The house was silent. Nobody was up.

"It feels good, just the two of us, doesn't it?"

"It does, Karl, reminds me of our old times in that chalet by the South Alps. We had many wonderful times there, surrounded by the picturesque ravines, the view of the mountain peaks, clear water of the lakes, wildflowers. It was like being in a dream!"

"I miss those times, Clara, when I get better we will go back there."

I met Hilda in the kitchen.

"Good morning, Hilda. Karl is in the study, he is probably going to sleep all morning, I gave him oatmeal, you don't need to serve breakfast. I'm going up to make a few calls."

"And I'll wait for the delivery. By the way, Franz and I found a nice lounge chair, we'll bring it up to the balcony."

My first call was to Erik.

I updated him on what I had learned from the doctors at the Hospital, and I told him that Karl was devastated and needed the emotional support of our family, now more than ever.

"Erik, at least for the next ten weeks your father is not going to be able to go to the office, but he is very confident that you have everything under control. He knows you have a challenging task and doesn't want to worry you. I'm here giving him hope, making him feel stronger."

"Clara, I'll be there as much as I can, and I think Father is very lucky for having you. Please keep me updated, I believe he is not going to tell me everything, you know how proud he is!"

"I know, Erik, and I also know that you have an enormous responsibility on your shoulders. Take care of yourself and your family."

"I'll be there on Sunday with Louisa and the children, we will cheer him up. What about you, Clara, do you need anything? You can come to me if you need a friend."

"Thank you, Erik, I'm holding up, I'll be strong for Karl and our family."

I called my son in Vienna.

"Gabe, I miss you, when are you coming to visit us?"

"What is going on, Mama? Did you and Dad make up? What was wrong with him?"

"He was hiding something very serious from me. Dad is sick, he has cancer and he is going to start an aggressive treatment on Monday."

"I'm so sorry, Mama, how devastating! I can't imagine how he feels. What is the prognosis?"

"We don't know yet, the doctors believe they are taking the best approach, but we will only know by the end of this treatment phase in ten weeks."

"Is there a better day to come next week?"

"He has chemo on Tuesday and they predicted that he will feel sick the following two days, you should come after Thursday. Bring Elise, we'd love to see her too."

"Yes, I'll come next Friday and I'll do whatever I can to help you both."

Karl was awake, still reclined on his chair.

"I spoke to Erik, he is coming on Sunday with Louisa and the children, we will have a fun day with the family. And Gabriel is coming next Friday."

"I'm looking forward to see my family, my sons! Did you talk to the girls?"

"Not yet. I'll call them later."

"What about you, Clara? I know this is very hard on you too, you don't have to put on a brave face."

"It breaks my heart to see you this way, Karl, but at least I have the comfort to make it a little easier on you, to remind you that you are loved and that you are not alone. You have me and all of our family…"

Hilda came in. "Franz is taking the delivery men upstairs."

I rushed to our room. They placed the tall, sleek headboard against the wall, assembled the platform and mattress, and gave instructions for operating the remote control.

Franz showed me the balcony.

"You did a great job, Franz, I love it. Karl will enjoy it, he can relax, have some fresh air out here on the days that he doesn't feel like walking in the garden."

I told Karl the new bed was ready.

"I'll go up after lunch, I also want to take a shower and rest before Peter Scheid, my lawyer, comes later."

"Why are you meeting your lawyer? You shouldn't be working today."

"It is not work, it's personal, there are a few things to be discussed. It won't take long."

We went upstairs and he was very impressed with the new adjustable bed. He practiced with the remote control and approved it!

I opened the French doors to the balcony, "Look, Franz arranged it for you!"

"It is fantastic, it is pleasant and breezy out here."

"You'll be spending time here when you don't feel like going downstairs, Karl."

"I will, thank you, *meine liebe*. I'm going to rest now."

I went to the next room to call my daughters.

Katie was not home, I spoke to Amie. She told me that she was preparing everything to be able to come home in June. Her internship at the hospital is demanding, but she will be able to take a week off.

Our younger daughter is very dedicated to her career as a pediatric oncologist. I know her understanding of the disease and above all her compassionate heart. I disclosed to her what is happening to Dad.

Amanda cried. "No, Mommy, I didn't know Daddy is seriously ill, I want to be at his side and yours as soon as possible."

"Don't do anything rushed, *liebling*. You have your commitments there, but we would love to see you, and I'm sure it will do some good for Daddy to see his little girl. Please, talk to Katie, she has to come along."

"Mommy, I'll do everything I can to stay longer, I want Daddy to be OK, and I miss you, Mommy, it is hard not to have you around here, but I understand, he needs you more now. Please tell Daddy I love him, he is going to be alright, I'll help him."

By the end of the day Karl was waiting for Peter Scheid, his lawyer and old friend. I greeted him at the door.

"It's nice to see you, Clara, it has been a long time."

"Yes, a long time, I was in New York with the girls, then went on a tour with Gabriel, but now I'm here to stay... Peter, I don't know what Karl wants to discuss with you, but please don't let him exert himself. Karl needs to rest."

"What is going on, Clara? He hasn't been in the office much lately."

"I believe he wants to tell you himself. Please come, he is in the study."

Their conversation took more than one hour. When Scheid left, he told me he would come back on Monday afternoon for Karl to sign some papers.

"I wish him the best results with his treatment. You are both my friends, please call me if I can help with anything, Clara."

"Thank you, Peter, it is good to count on our friends at this difficult time."

Karl was standing by the open window in his study.

"It's beautiful outside, I'll be admiring this view many times from now on, I am not going anywhere for a while."

He felt better on Saturday morning.

Our daughters called him, and he sounded very animated. Katie told him she is planning to come at the end of June for one week. Amie will come along, she intends to stay for a month, she is taking a leave of absence.

On Sunday we had a wonderful time with Erik, Louisa and the children. Liliane, 'Lili,' ten years old, and Wilhelm, 'Will,' eight, were planning a pool party, but the water was not warm enough yet, anyway they had a good time biking around the garden.

Louisa and I had a long talk about the upcoming summer.

"We should have a family reunion in July and celebrate Erik's fortieth birthday right here. That will keep Grandpa Karl's spirit up!"

"I agree, Clara, that will be fun!"

"You can also plan some weekends away with Erik and leave the children here with us, Louisa. They bring joy into the house, Karl loves when they are around."

"I'm glad you said that, Clara. Erik has been stressed out with work, that is creating a distance between us."

Erik and Karl spent a long time in the study, they came out laughing.

"We are going upstairs for a hair cut," Karl said. "I want to free myself and shave it before it starts falling out."

When they returned, Karl was wearing a hat.

"Let me see, what did you do, Karl?"

"Get ready, tonight you are going to sleep with another man, a bald one!"

I appreciated his sense of humor, at least for that day he was in good spirits.

Later in the evening, in our room, he opened the doors to the balcony.

We embraced.

"Look, there is a moon tonight!"

"We will be looking at the moon many times together, Karl. I really enjoyed today, you were upbeat, it is a great way to start this new phase, being positive about it…"

"I have decided to live every day to the fullest, every day with you is a good day."

"In sickness and in health, I'll always be with you, *liebe*, my husband."

CHAPTER FOUR

CHALLENGES

*W*e arrived at the Hospital for Karl's first treatment. It was not as difficult as we anticipated, but he felt weak and dizzy returning home. Tomorrow we'll spend the entire day at the Hospital.

I stayed at his side all day. The two following days were very difficult. This is going to be our new life routine for the next ten weeks, if we are not at the Hospital we will be at home recovering.

I comforted him and he rested his head on my chest, I touched his face.
"I wish I could do more to relieve your pain, Karl. Believe, this shall pass!"

On Thursday afternoon he said he wanted to go for a walk in the garden. I brought him a hat and a cane.
"A cane, why? This makes me feel really old."
"Makes you distinguished, and it's good to maintain your

balance."

We spent a long time out there and we went down the property, sat on a bench, looking down into the riverbank.

"Let's sit here, Clara, it has been a while...

Remember the day that I asked you to marry me? I brought you here, we sat down in this same place and I told you I wanted us to come and live in this house! You immediately suggested that I bring my father along.

Lately I have been thinking much about him, and you as the young woman, caring for my old man, now again here you are caring for this old man."

"You are forgetting one thing, Karl, two as a matter of fact. First you never asked me to marry you, you told me we were getting married! The other is I'm not that young woman anymore, I'm also getting older, and all I want now is to grow old with you."

"Sorry, I was not romantic, I just went straight to the point, and here we are twenty-seven years later in the same spot, contemplating the same river view. I wanted you then to be in my life, and I want you more so now. Clara, you are giving me the courage and reason to face all of this and go on."

We went back up to the house. Hilda told us that Gabriel had called to confirm his flight tomorrow.

"I already told Franz to pick him up."

I was anxious to see my son.

He arrived on Friday.

Gabriel immediately noticed that Karl didn't look as strong as before. He hugged him tenderly.

"I have missed you, Dad, it has been too long. How are you feeling?"

Karl got emotional. "I feel glad you are here, Gabriel."

I hugged my son.

"I am so happy to see you, you look rested."

"I have been only resting since I returned from the tour, next week I'll resume my activities at the recording studio."

He asked Karl, "How is the treatment going, Dad? Is it

difficult?"

"It is hard, I'm tired, but I have the weekend off, now I just want to have a nice time with you here. Erik is coming tomorrow to see you too, let's all have a good time!"

Gabriel's presence in the house filled us with contentment. Karl directed the conversation around his interests.

"You are successful, I'm very proud of you and I'm sorry I didn't always support your vocation. I was afraid that being an artist wouldn't give you a good quality of life, I was wrong, son!"

"Dad, you don't need to apologize, I always understood your concerns. And you did support me, I never forgot that you gave me the tools to become who I am, and I'm grateful for that. I only wish that you had more time to attend my concerts, I feel proud when you come."

"As soon as I am better I'll come to see you play, I'll be there with Mom. I also want to tell you that I know you met 'the biological' in Madrid. There is no need to keep secrets. Did you like him? Are you going to maintain contact with him?"

"I felt sorry for him, Dad, he looked remorseful and ashamed, he knows that it is too late to try to develop a bond between us. For now I think of him as an acquaintance that lives in Madrid, and maybe I'll see him again, if he is willing to come to my concerts. We'll see! I made it clear to Miguel that you are my father, and I love and respect you!"

"Thank you, Gabriel, you are my son, and I love you too."

There could not be a better feeling than this to heal Karl's heart. He retired early.

Gabriel and I continued talking.

"He looks weak, Mama, I'm worried."

"So am I. I'm anguished seeing him this way."

"Mama, you need to take care of yourself to be able to help him, I'm concerned about you."

"I know, Gabe, I am doing my best. It is grueling."

"All of this is making him softer, I would say more open, he even said he loves me."

"Yes, I think it is natural, when confronting mortality our values change, we pay more attention to the matters of the heart. He is very vulnerable now."

"Is Dad afraid? Are you afraid, Mama? You can tell me, I know you, I can see you are worried but showing optimism in front of him."

"I am devastated, Gabe, and I'm so sorry for his suffering, I'm suffering right along with Karl. I don't want to lose him…"

Gabriel embraced me. Oh, I needed my son's support.

"Dad wants to have the whole family here for Christmas, he wants a very special celebration this year. I know it is seven months from now, but you and Elise have so many commitments, please try to have Christmas off, it is very important to Dad and to me, he thinks it could be his last…

I keep praying that this treatment will work and hopefully he will be in better health by then."

"Mama, I won't accept any commitments at least for Christmas Day, and I'll ask Elise. She really wanted to come now, but it is opera season."

"I understand, the girls are coming in the summer and I thought of having a family reunion the first week of July, we will celebrate Erik's fortieth.

Do you think you can come? That will be midway into the treatment, I think Karl will be energized having the family around."

"Summer is fine, Elise and I will take some time off."

"This is not all about Karl, I also need you, son. You do understand me and I feel happier when you are around."

"We are bonded, Mama. By the way, Miguel called just to touch base and asked about you. I told him you were home with Father."

On Saturday Erik came with his family, and the two brothers engaged in conversation. Erik always treated Gabriel as his little brother and somehow he still does.

Gabriel, on the other hand, was interested in knowing how Erik was coping with his work responsibilities now that Karl is absent.

"It is overwhelming, I'm finding it very hard to have a balance between work and family life. I admire Father even more, I feel like he was always present when it was just the two of us, and then with all of us, I don't know how he did it."

"I understand, Erik, I also admire him for that."

Karl joined the conversation.

"No, boys, I was not the perfect father, I wish I could have been there more for both of you. I was always so busy, but when you get to be my age and look back, all you think is, 'I wish I had spent more time with my family.' In the end, family is all that matters!"

"But, Dad, if you hadn't worked so hard you wouldn't have given us the best of everything, a great life!"

"Yes, Dad, Erik is right, and I remember you always being present," Gabriel told him.

On Sunday Gabriel left for Frankfurt to work on recordings at the studio he owns in partnership with Gunther, his events manager and one of his best friends, who is also a mogul in the recording industry.

In the evening Karl and I shared a moment together outside on our bedroom's balcony.

"The air is fresh, fills my lungs up, I feel good!" he said.

"Breathe, *liebe*, breathe! We have another week ahead, but we will make it day by day, together!"

On Tuesday again he had a very bad reaction to chemo, however by the end of the week he felt better.

The girls called from New York to confirm they will come by the end of June, together. Katie will stay for one week, but Amie will stay for the entire month of July.

I was looking forward to have my daughters home, I missed them dearly.

Week after week went by, with each passing day Karl looked more frail. Dr. Jung and the others saw him often at the Treatment Center, they motivated him, reassuring him that he would improve.

Karl didn't waver, didn't miss any treatment, always accompanied by me. At home he spent most of his time in our room or balcony overlooking our gardens, now in full bloom.

"Lately I have been thinking about my life as a boy, I remember my father always working, investing his time and energy making the company grow. He built a colossal company, but he had very little time for me.

As I grew up we did spend most of the time working together, our connection was mostly about business.

My mother was very kind, but she would not give up her time for me. She was out frequently with her friends, complaining that my father didn't have time for her.

Then I got caught up in that failed marriage... I married someone just like my mother, she hardly had time for me or Erik.

Clara, I didn't know what love was until I met you. I told you that many times, didn't I?"

"Yes, Karl, you did! And I like to hear it."

"Still at times I failed you, with my pride and coldness, this whole ordeal is changing me, I hope life gives me time to make it up to you."

"I always felt loved by you, we will have more time together, now it is time to heal, you are winning this battle, Karl!"

In my heart, sometimes I doubted my own words, he seemed frail, but I wanted to believe that we would have more time ahead.

In the dark of the night, many times I left our bed and cried. It has been a very lonely time for me, I couldn't show him my pain and my concerns.

Hilda cheerfully prepared Katie and Amie's rooms for their arrival. She has much affection for our girls, and they for her, who they still lovingly call 'Hildie.'

My heart sang when they arrived!

Katie was so vibrant and full of energy, and Amie, loving and caring, they brought life into our home that has been under a cloud...

Karl was very emotional when he saw our daughters.

"Every time I see you girls you are prettier! How can you spend so much time away from your old Dad? I miss you!"

Katie told him, "Daddy, I miss you too, I'll stay with you all week long."

Amie was fast to say, "And I'll be going to the Hospital with you for the next four weeks, that's what I'm here for, Daddy. I am going to talk to your doctors and check on everything."

"I know, my *little doctor*, it is wonderful to have you here."

That evening we had dinner together like old times.

Later, as Karl excused himself, Amie held his hand, "I'll walk up with you, Daddy."

Katie told me, "Daddy is looking frail, it's scary, Mommy, and we came for you too, you look tired and sad."

"I'm not sad right now, my girls are here! But I am physically and emotionally exhausted, I need to put myself together for our family reunion, we will celebrate Erik's birthday on Sunday."

"That will cheer Dad up. Is Gabe coming too?"

"Yes, he is coming with Elise."

Amie was back downstairs.

"It is so sad to see Daddy this way. I'm going to help you too, Mommy, it is depleting to take care of him all the time by yourself."

"Thank you, Amie, I can use your help. I was just telling Katie that Gabe is coming tomorrow, and there is something I was waiting to tell both of you. When in Madrid during the tour, we met his biological father."

"Wow! Did Gabe like him?"

"I think so. Miguel was very apologetic and humble, he demonstrated interest in Gabe's musical career and went to his concert in Milano. They will be in touch, eventually."

"Does Daddy know?"

"Of course, we have no secrets. Everything is alright."

Katie asked me, "Miguel was a man that you loved, how did you feel when you saw him again?"

"I felt nothing! I had gotten over any feelings I had for him long before I met your Dad. And that is all!"

Changing subjects, Katie, Dad is going to ask you to spend time with Erik at the office. He thinks, and I agree, that your return to the original plan is overdue. You went to the U.S. almost three years ago to get prepared for an executive position at your father's company. It is time to come back home and start working with him."

"Mommy, I know I promised, but I need to stay in New York for now. Anyway, while I'm here I'll do what Dad wants."

"What is going on, Katie? Why do you need to stay there? You know quite well where you belong, you grew up in Dad's factories knowing and wanting to be part of it. Besides, if you like New York so much, you can always go back, we have the apartment there, you can go anytime you want to visit and enjoy it!"

"Tell the truth, Kat, Mommy needs to know," Amie told her.

"I know, Mommy, I have other interests there, I mean I have a new boyfriend."

"Why didn't you tell me before? Who is he?"

Katie got agitated. "I don't want to talk much about him right now. His name is John, he works on Wall Street. Please don't mention it to Dad, I think he'll get upset."

"I'm upset, you are hiding something from us. Are you afraid of leaving this John and ending the relationship? I can tell you, if that is true love and meant to be, nothing will separate you. Nothing!"

Amanda was looking at her sister apprehensively.

"Don't you see, Kat? Mom and Dad are going through so much anguish right now, this is not a good time to discuss your boyfriend drama."

Our youngest daughter is so sensible!

Gabriel and Elise arrived on Saturday! Sweet Elise, she is very welcomed in our family. They make the perfect couple.

"When are you going to marry her, Gabe? We could plan a beautiful wedding here, like the one we had for Erik and Louisa. Remember?"

"Yes, Mama, one of these days… We are both very busy now!"

Karl made an effort to participate, they had a relaxed afternoon by the pool.

After dinner, the girls asked Gabe to play with them. Karl told them to leave the music room doors open.

"I want to listen, I'll be with Mom in the den."

Sitting together, holding hands, we listened to Gabriel's divine violin sound, Katie and Amie accompanying on the piano and Elise's angelic voice echoing through the halls.

Life, music and laughter was back in our house!

On Sunday Erik, Louisa and the children joined us for a day of celebration.

Hilda had done a superb job catering for the occasion, and she and Franz were invited to participate.

On Monday morning Karl and I went to the Hospital for his radiation. When we returned, Amanda told me:

"I'll stay with Dad all day, Mommy, take a break, and tomorrow I'm going with you and spending the entire day at the Hospital."

"Let's go out, Mommy, I bet you haven't been out of the house for a while," Katie suggested.

"Good idea, Katie, I really want to do some shopping at the home store. I started making some changes in the guest bedrooms and never finished."

To downtown we went.

We shopped, had lunch together and for a few hours I forgot about the challenging times.

"I want our lives to be normal again!"

On Tuesday, while Karl was in Radiology I proudly introduced Amie to the doctors and nurses.

"Our daughter Amanda has an internship in New York, specializing in pediatric oncology."

Dr. Jung told her:

"I can introduce you to Dr. Altmann in the Children's Infirmary to get acquainted with our services."

"Thank you, Doctor, I'll be coming every Tuesday with my Dad and I'd love to visit the children."

While Karl was being prepared for chemo, Amanda went to the Infirmary.

She came back later, Karl was receiving the treatment, I was sitting by his side.

"Dad is napping, you can go back, Amie, I bet the children enjoyed your visit."

"I met some doctors and nurses, they are so very kind with their little patients. I'd like to spend more time there, but I'll come to check on you and Daddy."

During the afternoon she came several times, she sent me out for lunch and some fresh air, and stayed with Karl.

Later, on the way home, she held his hand, saying words of encouragement.

"I know it is hard, Daddy, but you are strong, you are doing well, you'll be fine!"

I felt happy having our daughter, at least for a while, to share Dad's care.

At home after dinner, I prepared Karl for bed, Amie stayed with him.

"You are just like your Mom, compassionate and caring, I'm a lucky man for having the two of you!" he told her.

Katie talked to me about her day at the office.

"The day with Erik was eye opening, it is serious work and an enormous responsibility. I realized that Erik and I have a lot in common the way we see business. Tomorrow he has a meeting at the factory and he is bringing me along. I haven't been there in years."

"I'm glad you are having this experience with your brother, now more than ever he needs to share his workload. You have to start getting ready to return home soon, Katie."

"But, Mom, I told you, I want to stay in New York!"

"Katie, life is not a playground, there are fun moments but also hard work to be faced.

Start preparing your boyfriend for the reality of your life. You have responsibilities with your family, and if he truly loves you the relationship will work out!"

"It is nothing like that, he has his plans to get rich on Wall

Street, he loves the thrills of ups and downs of the stock market."

"Well, some people get rich, some others lose everything. Who is he? A gambler?"

"Mom, you don't understand."

"I don't like your attitude, Katie, and I don't like what's happening."

Amie joined us downstairs.

"Daddy is sleeping, it is so sad to see him this way, I always thought of my Dad as invincible, and now he looks weak, sick, my heart breaks for him."

"I know, Amie, that's how I feel. What do you think of the Treatment Center? Is it comparable to what you see in New York?"

"Absolutely, they are very well equipped, all modern and updated. The doctors are very invested in the patients. You should see the Children's Infirmary, they are so caring with their little patients."

"We get so wrapped up in our problems that we forget to look at others, it is sad to see children going through this misery."

"It is, Mommy, but they are extraordinarily resilient, and it is a blessing that most of them do not know the gravity of their disease. Their hope and optimism helps them heal."

"The world would be marvelous if we could see it through the eyes of a child."

The next morning Amie came with us to the Hospital, and Katie went to meet Erik downtown. Karl was feeling horrible from the effects of yesterday's chemo.

When we returned home, Amie spent most of the day with her father.

"My *little doctor*, I'll never forget how you are nursing me back to health."

The following week, before Katie returned to New York, Karl reminded her:

"Christmas is here with the family, but I would much rather see you coming home before that, for good."

Every Tuesday Amie came to the Hospital with us, spending part of the day in the children's wing where she made new friends, among them a young doctor.

"I met Dr. Alfred Bautzer, he is so kind with his patients, I could learn a lot from him."

She returned to the Hospital also on Thursdays, and asked Hilda to prepare cookies for the children.

On her last week she came home in the evening all excited. "Mommy, some people from the Hospital invited me to a party tomorrow, I'd like to go. Do you think Dad will mind? After all I came here to spend all my time with him!"

"Of course not, Amie, you are young, you should see your new friends. Who are those people? Or, *one person* invited you?"

"Fred invited me, he will come to pick me up."

On Friday evening, a tall, skinny young man arrived at our front door, driving a beaten up car.

He told Amie:

"I know this is an upper class neighborhood, but you didn't tell me you live like a princess in a castle!"

I was close by, "Nice meeting you, Alfred. Would you like to come in?"

"Thank you, Mrs. Weisenwert, maybe on the way back if my car lasts that long. Amanda has told me about her father, how is he feeling today?"

"He is well today, thank you."

The next day Amie got up later and came to see her father, he was on the balcony.

"Would you like to go for a walk, Daddy? Or come down to the pool later, Louisa is bringing the children, we are going to swim this afternoon."

"I'll come out after lunch, Amie. Mom told me you went out last night with a new friend. Did you have fun?"

"Yes, Daddy, I met some nice people, all physicians and nurses from the Hospital, it was a dance party, they were good company."

"I'm glad you made new friends, there are a lot of nice people at the Hospital, I can tell."

Later she told me, "When we returned, Fred and I stayed in the den until about one in the morning. He is so interesting and he wanted to know more about my life in New York, he never has been to the States, he might apply there for a fellowship."

"I had a good impression of him. Is he just a friend, Amie?"

"I like him, but I told him I still have to complete my internship, and he also has plans to continue his training, we can only be friends for now."

"You have a good head on your shoulders, Amie, everything will come in time."

Karl's radiation treatment was over, and the days of July were coming to an end.

Sadly, it was time for Amie to return to New York. Her presence in the house had been uplifting, to say the least.

We were sad seeing her go.

Although all of those weeks of treatment had taken a toll on Karl, he was not anguished anymore, he was looking forward to recovery.

"I admire you, Karl, you are winning this battle."

"We are winning together, *meine liebe*. I have been thinking that I'm blessed for having all the support and love of my family, and fortunate to have financial stability. Not everyone has, and I want to contribute to patients and their families, to give them at least a little comfort. Mostly to the children, I can't imagine the little ones going through this, it is so unfair.

You can help, Clara, you can start thinking of how to make their lives better, I have contributed with money donations, but I think we can give more, maybe establish a foundation."

"Karl, you are compassionate. I'd love to help, I'll talk to Amie about it, she knows the Children's Infirmary well, I'm sure she has suggestions on how to improve the quality of their lives. I'm going to work on it, it is my new project!"

"Your eyes are shining with excitement, I know that look, Clara! The same you had one day, after Hilda and Franz came to help us, you had more time on your hands and you started the 'Day

Care Project at the Industrial Park,' which I initially dismissed. You didn't give up and finally convinced me to do it. And that was one of the best things we did for our employees!"

"Karl, I had experienced how hard it was for parents to care for their children while they are at work. In the end you became the 'businessman of the year' for that endeavor! And I rejoiced!"

Gabriel called us often to follow up with Karl's progress. He told him he had scheduled a few concerts in the fall in Germany. Between those concerts he will come to visit again.

He also said that Miguel called him twice lately, showing interest in meeting him again during one of his concerts.

"Are you looking forward to see him?"

"Yes, Mama, my questions about my heritage are being answered, I feel a sense of closure. He did turn out better than we thought, but you need to know that he spends half of his time asking questions and talking about you."

"What does he want to know?"

"I have mentioned that Father is ill, he wants to know if you are alright, when you are going back to New York, and he said he would love to see you again."

"Gabe, I have no interest in giving him any information about my life or seeing him. Your conversations should be only about the two of you.

Changing subjects, Dad wants to help the Treatment Center, and we might start a foundation. I'm going to invest time in that project after Dad is recovered, for now I was thinking you could participate in a fundraising concert."

"Absolutely, count on me, I'll make time for it. Maybe I could fit in a concert before next year's tour to the Scandinavian countries."

A week after the last chemo Dr. Jung gave Karl the results of the recent tests. Some were very positive, the small tumor in his lung had disappeared, the liver tumor was reduced to a very small size, and he recommended surgery to remove it.

We were disappointed. "Surgery? When?"

"I know it is disappointing, Karl, but this is actually a very good result and the prognosis is excellent. You need a few weeks to get stronger, and we'll discuss with the surgeon, Dr. Goetz. He will schedule it, better sooner than later."

Dr. Goetz explained that although small it was still a delicate surgery requiring a stay in the Hospital for a few days.

It was scheduled for September.

I had a knot in my stomach. I thought that the intensive treatments were enough, but there was one more bump in the road to recovery, it was not over yet!

"You will be free of this soon, Karl, your total recovery is happening!"

I called our daughters and told them of the upcoming surgery. Amie said she would come at least for a long weekend to assist her father. Katie couldn't come, she was overwhelmed with her job. She asked me to come to see her in New York.

"I'm very tired, Mommy, things are not easy for me lately."

"Katie, you are tired? Really? You know I can't possibly go, I need to be here with Dad."

Amie commented that Katie has been sad or sometimes angry and she doesn't talk about what is happening.

"But I know that is boyfriend drama. Don't worry about her, Mommy!"

"Have you met Katie's boyfriend? I sense that something is not right…"

"I never met him, and I feel the same way."

Everything went well with Karl's surgery, he spent five days in the Hospital.

Dr. Jung told us that it would be necessary to follow up with a four week round of chemo to eliminate any cells.

Karl was devastated, so was I, we believed the surgery was the end of it…

Amie came and spent three days attending to her father and convinced him that another round of chemo was necessary.

She took the opportunity to visit the Children's Infirmary and her friends.

The day after Karl was released and back at home, Amie returned to New York.

Erik came to see his father almost every day, keeping him updated on the business performance.

The family's support motivated Karl to continue fighting the disease, hoping for the best results.

Gabriel also called often.

"Mama, I'm on my way to a concert in Frankfurt, then another in Munich. I'll come to see you and Dad next week."

"Dad and I will love to see you!"

Days later, while Karl was taking an afternoon nap, I received a call from Miguel. I was unpleasantly surprised.

"I came to Frankfurt for Gabriel's concert, I thought you would be here, Clara. I haven't seen you since Milano."

"I'm very busy, Miguel. Did you enjoy the concert?"

"Yes, very much, it was brilliant, and I had a great time with Gabriel again. He told me that your husband is ill and you are attending to him. Are you alright, Clara?"

"I'm fine. Karl is recovering, that's all that matters."

"I'm so close to Dusseldorf, I thought I could come and talk to you, Clara. Would it be inconvenient for you?"

"Yes, it would be very inconvenient, Miguel. What is it that you want to talk about? Is it about Gabriel?"

"No, about us. I didn't mean to bother you, Clara, maybe we will meet some other time."

"I don't think so, Miguel. I don't mean to be rude, but there is no 'us' and I have nothing to talk about with you. Goodbye."

I was distressed by that call, I tiptoed in the bedroom and Karl was deeply asleep.

I went downstairs and asked Hilda not to serve him dinner, I was letting Karl rest until... "If he wakes up later, I'll bring something upstairs for him."

Gabriel came to visit after his concert in Munich.

"Dad, hopefully this will be the end of it, I see that you look much better now. In no time you'll be back to your own self!"

"I hope, son, I'm starting to feel useless. I want to go back to work, not like old times anymore, but I want to be back there!"

I told my son about Miguel's phone call. He was annoyed.

"Mama, I'm sorry I told him you were having a challenging time. He is out of place inviting himself to come to Dusseldorf to see you! He makes no sense!"

"I think he is confused, Gabe, he should free himself from feelings of the past and start a new chapter in his life. Remorse is doing a number on him!"

"Do you want me to say something to him, Mama?"

"That's not necessary. I think he understood I don't want to hear from him."

The next four weeks were extremely hard on Karl, he was depleted of energy and became depressed.

After all, Dr. Jung was satisfied with the latest test results. "Everything looks good, Karl, there is no evidence of the disease, but we will wait a little longer for further confirmation."

"How long, Doctor? Can you remove this port now? What can I do in the meantime?"

"The port will be removed when remission is confirmed! For now I'll keep you on oral medication, and you may resume your life as normally as possible. In three months we will run new tests. In the meantime, if you have any concerns or symptoms, please call me, I'll see you right away."

That sounded like music to our ears!

Karl was cautious, he knew the symptoms could show up again, but for now he was free of the grueling treatment.

"*Liebe*, from now on, everything is about recovering, gaining strength and enjoying life. The nightmare is over!"

"I want to enjoy life as much as possible, Clara, I have gained a new perspective after this experience, life can end in a moment… I'll live every day like if it were the last, I want to work, not only for the company but for others, I want our project to help the children in the Hospital to go forward.

I want to give you my love every single day, thank you, Clara, for standing with me."

"We are a team, Karl! First you need to get stronger physically, that will take food for energy, long walks, I love to nurture you back to health. And I already have a few ideas about our project. I have discussed it with Amie and Gabe, we will work on it, in time."

Karl's recovery was slow but steady, the bad days became far between.

In November I told him that I was working on the special holiday celebration we are going to have at home and also the Christmas party that Amie wants to be part of with her friends at the children's wing.

I did not tell him, but on Katie's last call she implored me to come to New York!

"Karl, if you don't mind I would like to go to New York to see the girls and do some special Christmas shopping, only for a few days."

"I wish I could go with you, Clara, but I still need a little more time. Go, you deserve a break, the girls miss you too."

"I feel sad for leaving you, Karl, I'll miss you!"

In New York City the first thing Amie told me was that Katie has been crying and she doesn't talk about what is going on.

"I didn't tell you before, Mommy, because you had more important things to do, but her behavior is concerning me, I'm glad you are here to help resolve whatever Katie's problem is."

I immediately talked to her.

"Katie, it is time to tell me what the problem is and how I can help!"

"Oh, Mommy, I'm glad you are here, I didn't want to worry you, but I'm in trouble, in a lot of conflict and I'm scared!"

"Katie, you are scaring me. Are you pregnant?"

"No, Mommy, that's not it. It is worse! John, as I told you before, is a very ambitious guy, months ago he shared with me his plan to make a fortune and convinced me to do an experiment, a game, selling out a great volume of stock. In consequence the market value starts going down, then you buy all back at a lower price to make a profit.

This is an illegal practice, a stock market sell out, some people might even end up in jail for doing it."

"So what, Katie, did you go along with that illegal trading? Go right to the point."

"John convinced me to negotiate my own stock, and everything went wrong, now the price is much higher and I can't buy my lot back, I'm desperate, Mommy, I lost part of the stock Daddy has given to me!"

I became irate.

"Katherine, I can't even begin to comprehend why you would do it, knowing that it is fraudulent! To please a dishonest gambler? You know better than that. Why? Just tell me why! And what are you going to do now?"

"I was in love, Mommy, I believed John, and I trusted I would buy my stock back and everything would be alright."

"Love? What kind of sick love was that? What happened to your intelligence and self worth? Oh, God, if Daddy finds this out…. Do you realize what he has gone through these past six months? I am so disappointed in you."

"I'm sorry, Mommy, I'm so sorry! I ended the relationship. John continued trying to convince me, but I can't go on like this anymore. I want him out of my life, I want to buy my stock back and then go home for a while, but the problem is I don't have money enough, it is a large amount and I'm going to need my broker's assistance for this transaction. I want everything now to be clear and clean. Mommy, could you lend me the money?"

I got up and nervously walked around the room. Katie was in tears!

"What? I never thought that after the most painful and difficult time that I had been going through, you would give me your problem to deal with!

No, Katie, you are not going home for a while, you are coming home for good!

I need some fresh air, I can't think straight right now!"

I left her room and asked Amie to go out with me.

Amie walked with me, knowing that I needed to diffuse my frustration.

"Mommy, it is cold, let's go to The Tea Room."

"Good idea, Amie."

At The Tea Room we talked about Katie returning home.

"I feel horrible that after Katie returns home you are going to be alone in the apartment, eventually Daddy and I will come to visit you, or Gabe when he comes to New York, but we can't always be here with you, *liebling.*"

"I won't be alone, I already thought of that. You know my friend Joy Shu-Fen, she is not happy where she is living, I was thinking of inviting her to share our apartment. What do you think, Mommy?"

"Joy, sure, I like her! I think she would be good company for you, besides you have common interests."

The next morning I told Katie:

"I will lend you the money, and you will pay me back. I hate to hide things from Dad, but in this case I need to protect him, he needs peace of mind to thrive in his recovery.

I can't even imagine how betrayed and hurt he would feel."

I took Katie to Deutsche Bank and made a transfer to her account.

"Don't forget, this is a loan! Buy all of your stock back and be honest to your broker, disclose that John is engaged in fraudulent transactions."

"I'm sorry, Mommy, I am being sincere, I'll fix this and I'll come home. Thank you for not telling Daddy, I can't bear to disappoint him."

"I hope you have learned your lesson, Katie. Now for the rest of my days here, just let's have fun. I don't want to discuss this matter anymore."

The next two days were a holiday celebration, we spent time shopping, going out to Broadway, until the night before my return when I got another unsolicited call from Miguel.

"Clara, I heard that you were spending time with your

daughters, and I came to New York, hoping to see you. I'd like to explain myself."

"This is very troubling, Miguel, as I told you before, we have nothing to talk about. I think I made that clear when you called me in Dusseldorf."

He insisted.

"Please give me the opportunity, listen to me."

I felt uneasy and thought for a minute…

"Where are you staying, Miguel?"

"At the Park Hotel off Central Park, we could have dinner around here or at the hotel, if you prefer. Please, let me come to pick you up, Clara!"

"I know exactly where you are, Miguel. I'll meet you at the hotel in one hour."

I told my daughters, "I'm going out to meet Miguel, he is here and he is insisting to talk to me. A few months ago he wanted to visit me in Dusseldorf, I declined. It is crucial that I put an end to this situation once and for all."

Katie offered to come with me.

"Thank you, Katie, I need to do this on my own. I'll be fine."

Miguel was waiting in the hotel lobby and greeted me with a big smile.

"Thank you for coming, Clara, I have missed you since May, in Milano."

We took a booth at the restaurant.

He wanted to order dinner, I told him, "I'm not staying long, I'll just have coffee."

He started talking about how taken he was by Gabriel and his amazing talent.

"I saw him in Frankfurt and I called him recently again, he told me how hard you were working to take care of your husband. Is he recovering?"

"Yes, Karl is strong and determined! But, tell me why you are really here, Miguel. What do you want to talk about?"

"Clara, it is about my feelings for you. Since we reconnected in Madrid I can't get you out of my mind. All the affection that once bonded us is still alive. Over the years I thought of you with love and much regret, wishing I could go back in time to mend our relationship, to make things right!"

"Miguel, you told me that in Milano, and I told you I have left the past behind. I believe that our encounter brought you feelings of guilt and regret, you do need to let it go and face reality!"

"I can't, Clara, I have looked for you in every woman I have encountered, and in the end it was you, only you, that I wanted in my life. I wish I could have a second chance. Please tell me, do you hate me or are there any feelings in your heart?"

"Miguel, some things do not change. It was, in the past, and still is, all about you! I want to clarify again that I contacted you only to bring closure to Gabriel. I had no intention of reconnecting with you. There are no feelings in my heart for you of any kind, none!"

"Clara, you didn't forgive me, did you? I understand, I can't forgive myself."

"Forgiveness? Let me make it very clear, I let go of the pain and bitterness your evil actions caused me long ago. I set myself free, I had a new life to take care of! I had no time to waste on thoughts of you.

Miguel, I believe you are confusing your feelings of guilt and shame for what you did, for something else. You need to forgive yourself!"

"Clara, I truly loved you and I still do. Please, believe me!"

"Your actions proved otherwise, I do not believe you ever loved me."

"But we have an unbreakable bond, we have a son together, we should be at least friends, Clara!"

"We have no bond! Gabriel is my son! I was the only one responsible to give him life, love, protect and raise him. You are not his father! Karl is his father, the one who nurtured and gave him everything, and taught him to be the man he is!

I don't mean to be unkind, but you and I will never be friends! And remember, only because Gabriel is good hearted, he is giving you the opportunity to be his friend. If you think that maintaining contact with my son you have a connection to me, you are wrong."

"No, not at all. I am in awe of Gabriel and I really want to be his friend. I am amazed to see how you and he speak so highly of Karl. Let me ask you, if he were gone... If you were alone, would you still reject me?"

"That is an outrageous question! Let me make it very clear, I absolutely would never consider having a relationship with you!

I love my husband, I'm loyal to him forever, no matter the circumstances."

Miguel lowered his head. Then he looked at me with endearment and reached for my hand.

"Please allow me to tell you one last time, Clara, I will always love you and I'll regret what I did to you for the rest of my days... If someday you are alone or you need a friend, I'll be there for you."

He was emotional, I saw his sincerity and felt compassion for him, seeing him living in his own emotional prison, making one last attempt for me to understand his profound feelings of remorse.

He lowered his eyes. I saw a tear...

I felt sorry for him and was compelled to say:

"There is nothing you can do about the past, forgive yourself, Miguel! I sincerely hope that you'll find peace of mind. You have a conscience, and I am glad my son had the chance to meet the man you have become."

We left the restaurant and walked to the hotel lobby.

"Thank you for listening to me. I should take you home, Clara! It is getting late."

"No, thank you, Miguel. Goodbye."

I stepped onto the sidewalk alone, certain that this was the end of it. I didn't have any intentions to hurt him, but I needed to be blunt.

I decided to walk home.

The cold breeze of the November night filled my lungs, touched my face and hair, made me feel revitalized and washed away the charged emotions of the evening.

My daughters were waiting.

"What took you so long, Mommy? How are you feeling? Tell us everything!"

"I feel good, it was liberating for me, but I felt sorry for Miguel and tried to free him. He has been chained to his own guilt for too long."

"Do you feel victorious, Mommy? You had the opportunity to reject him!"

"Reversal of fortune! I felt empowered to be on the other side of the situation, with a clear head and a light heart."

"Are you going to tell Daddy that Miguel came all this way to see you?"

"I will someday, for now Dad and I have one goal, get healthier!"

I returned home the next day.

CHAPTER FIVE

GOOD NEWS

*F*ranz was waiting for me at the Dusseldorf Airport. When I got to the car I was surprised to see Karl there.

"You came! I missed you, Karl. You look good!"

"I missed my wife, only five days away, but it seemed like a long time."

Hilda was at our door: "Welcome home, Frau Clara."

"Thank you, Hilda, for taking good care of Herr Weisenwert, he looks good."

Franz brought the luggage inside.

"I just need my suitcase upstairs, all the other boxes go in the den."

Karl was intrigued by the number of volumes I brought.

"All for the holidays! I have so many ideas for Christmas at our home and also some special things for the children at the Hospital. I also thought we should send holiday gifts to the doctors and nurses that took care of you this year."

"I agree, we should do something special while we start organizing the Foundation. I'm also making a substantial donation to the Treatment Center."

"Wonderful, Karl, I support that, our and their holiday is going to be remarkable!"

"What about Katie? Is she ready to come home? What happened with the boyfriend?"

"She broke up with him and resigned her job, she will be coming home for good. She'll fly with Amie. From now until then we have a few busy four weeks preparing everything."

"I'm glad Katie is returning, Erik has been overwhelmed, I suggested that he hire another assistant in the downtown office and a new director at the Industrial Park."

"Well said, Karl, Erik has stepped up, he needs to have more time for himself and his family."

"For now it is just the two of us, Clara, that gives me the chance to have a special birthday celebration for you next month."

"Don't remind me, I'm getting old... Time flies."

"You are not getting old, *meine liebe*, you are forever young!"

"Well, the good thing about getting older is to do it with you, my husband."

The next morning I discussed with Hilda the preparations for Christmas, I instructed her to hire some extra helpers to assist us.

"We are going to start the decorations, our house is going to look magical, like a winter wonderland!"

I called Gabriel and told him about the unexpected visit in New York from Miguel.

"Mama, I'm so sorry I mentioned that you were there with the girls. This time he really stepped over his boundaries, he shouldn't have sought you out. How did you feel about it?"

"I was really upset and at the same time sorry for seeing him tormented by his own feelings. But I believe I gave him the motivation to move on, I sincerely hope he finds peace of mind."

"I do too, Mama, look what he lost..."

"Changing subjects, when are you and Elise coming?"

"On the twenty-third, but we need to leave on the twenty-sixth, we are both performing in Vienna."

"I understand, son, I'm happy that you can both be here, the girls are anxious to see you. Erik and family will be staying with us too. We will have a full house."

Karl went to the Hospital to offer his donation. Dr. Jung was glad to see him.

"I can see you are taking good care of yourself, Karl, you are making progress."

Back at home, he told me:

"I don't feel like going around yet, but there are so many friends, old time employees that have called or sent cards, I would like to see them and say thank you."

I suggested, "Karl, we could have an open house, your friends and business associates would visit you here. We'd schedule one or two afternoons and they would come at their discretion."

"Brilliant, open house! There you go, my innovative wife! I like the idea. Do you think I look presentable, Clara? I lost weight, I am bald!"

"Karl, you are looking better every day, they will be happy to see you."

"The holiday party at the Industrial Park is on the fifteenth, I really don't feel like going, Erik will represent me. And, on the seventeenth is your birthday, Clara, and it is just for the two of us to celebrate. I think we can schedule the open house for the eighteenth and nineteenth."

"Perfect! I also have to attend the Day Care Center holiday celebration at the Industrial Park, it's going to be a circus, with clowns and everything! The children will love it!"

The first weeks of December went by fast with so many preparations. The house was fully decorated, looked majestic, a winter wonderland filled with lights and crystals.

Karl asked me, "Are you sure you don't want to invite anyone for your birthday or maybe go out to a nice restaurant downtown? We haven't been out in so long, *meine liebe*."

"No, Karl. Tonight is just for the two of us."

I set the table beautifully for a romantic candlelit dinner. We had a nice meal, a little wine and a small birthday cake that Hilda prepared. After dinner Karl took me to the den and gave me a folder wrapped in silk paper. He was all excited and kissed me, a long, loving kiss...

"Happy birthday, Clara, this is my gift to you!"

The folder contained a few pages of documents, curiously I started reading them.

"Karl, this is the deed to our house, you put the Weisenwert Estate in my name!"

"Yes, you made this house the most delightful home, filled with experiences and memories of our lives, of our children growing up, you are the heart of this family, the rightful lady of the house!"

"Karl, this mansion, our home, has been the most treasured possession that you inherited from your father. I'm so surprised, what an unexpected gift!"

"From my father, to our family, to our four children, but first to you, the one I treasure the most, my wife."

"Was this what you were doing when you called Scheid, your lawyer, before your treatment started?"

"Yes, it was this and other personal papers, I was afraid I was not going to survive. Now I am happy to be here telling you that all of these months that you stood by me making me stronger just proved I couldn't do it without you, Clara.

Life has thrown me a curveball, initially I felt hopeless, but I found the will to fight because you stood with me. I came to realize that during our marriage I was not always fair or caring enough, how lonely you must have been during many years, getting used to the new lifestyle, the language, taking care of the children while I was focused on work. And yet, you made everything beautiful, Clara, these almost three decades with you have been the best of my life."

He brought tears of joy to my eyes. My husband validated me, once again I felt I was the most loved woman, no one ever made me feel that way.

Once I read somewhere that we never forget how people make us feel. The feelings that my Karl brings up in me are forever imprinted on my soul. His demonstration of love is unforgettable!

"Karl, this magnificent place represents so much to me, it's where we built our lives, raised our children. I am so humbled by your gift, if you only knew where I grew up, in the most poor conditions. This house is nothing but a dream!"

That evening, holding each other, we looked outside through our balcony's glass door, everything was light and bright, covered by snow, but it was warm inside our home...

My heart skipped a beat, I felt so blessed for the life that Karl and I have built together.

"I love you, Karl, I just want you to be healthy and live a long life with me! That's my birthday wish."

The next day Karl was a little nervous but excited, he tried three of his suits. "I want to dress professionally, but nothing fits me right anymore."

I chose a slate gray wool suit, helped him fix his tie.

"You look distinguished as always, your hair is growing back, my charming man!"

Karl enjoyed his first open house. I greeted every single one of his many friends and associates. They had a good time, some were emotional for seeing their boss and friend after so long.

By the end of the day Karl's spirit was uplifted.

"I've enjoyed seeing them all. And there'll be more tomorrow!"

The two open houses were a successful event, Karl started feeling like his old self again, the powerful businessman surrounded by the friendship of longtime collaborators, he was happy for having the opportunity to thank them for their support, personally and individually.

Katherine and Amanda arrived in the early hours of the twenty-first. They brought many volumes. Franz went to pick them up at the airport, alone. We anxiously waited at home.

They were both very warm and loving towards their father who was waiting for them, standing tall and strong at the front door.

"My little girls are home!"

"Daddy, you look so good!"

Katie told him, "I'm here to stay, Daddy!"

Karl was exultant.

"That has been the plan all along, the business girl of the family is finally joining our company. And how is my *little doctor*? I missed you, Amie."

"Daddy you are definitely well, I can see it! And I love your new spikey hair." She touched his new, soft, growing hair, all white! "Daddy you are handsome!"

He laughed. Joy and laughter are back home!

Later Amie told me, "I can't wait to go to the Hospital for the children's holiday party, I brought them so many American goods and I also want to see my friends, I miss them."

"Have you been talking to your friend Alfred?"

"Yes, Mommy, he calls often, and now we will be spending time together here during my stay, if you don't mind."

"I don't mind at all, *liebling*, have your friends over, this is your home!"

I told my daughters about the incredible gift Karl gave me on my birthday. "Mommy, what a nice gesture! A gift of love!"

"He loves us all!"

Gabriel and Elise arrived. That same day I had a lunch party for all the house staff, gave them their bonuses and let them go to celebrate the holidays with their families.

Hilda, who has been working with the cook, told me:

"The refrigerators are full of everything you'll need. Two of the new hires will stay until the thirty-first, for the incentive of getting double pay. I'm staying too, I only need to go to my cousin's for two days. I like to be around here when the girls are home."

"Of course, Hilda, you are their 'Hildie.' You and Franz are part of our family and are invited to join us for Christmas Eve dinner."

Erik, Louisa and the children arrived on the afternoon of the twenty-fourth. Karl was smiling, his cheeks were rosy and his eyes shining, he told our family:

"This is the celebration I was hoping to have, I'm so glad I made it this far, I'm so blessed to have my family around. Merry Christmas, everyone!"

I was grateful, a few months ago I was filled with fear that he wouldn't make it to this day...

After dinner the entire family went to the music room. Karl told them, "Leave all the doors open, let the music echo through the house!"

There was caroling, singing, Gabriel playing his violin, the girls at the piano... Oh, the sweetness of the children's voices, life and joy inundated our home.

I took the opportunity to talk to my daughters-in-law Elise and Louisa.

"I'm so glad you were able to come, Elise, you are like a daughter to us. Does your mother resent that you couldn't make it to Linz?"

"No, during this time of year she is very busy at the bakery, besides she has my sister and the grandchildren. And unfortunately my mother still thinks I'm living in sin because I live with Gabriel, and she never accepted the fact that I moved to Vienna to pursue my dream. She wanted me to remain in Linz and sing at the church choir for the rest of my days."

"Elise, I think you are living in love, but I can't wait to see you and Gabe married."

"Me neither, but we have so many commitments and he travels so often, we haven't found the right time yet!"

"We can make it happen, Elise, we can have a very nice wedding right here, I have experience, I planned Erik and Louisa's wedding! Isn't that so, Louisa?"

"Yes, and my wedding was memorable, Clara did a great job, you should take her up on her offer, Elise."

The Weisenwert family holiday celebration went on, Lili and Will were allowed to stay up until... Grandpa Karl and Grandma Clara retired and brought them upstairs.

Lili and Will were overly excited.

"You go to bed now and you can be the first ones up in the morning!"

I asked my husband, "How is it so far? Is this the family holiday party you dreamed of?"

"Yes and more! It surpassed my expectations! I'm in love with life, with you and our family."

Early in the morning the youngsters ran through the halls, knocking at every door.

"Wake up, wake up, it's morning!"

I met Elise and Louisa in the kitchen to prepare breakfast. Pretty soon the entire family was in the den, sipping coffee or hot chocolate, and the children started gathering their presents under the Christmas tree.

We exchanged gifts and cheers. Karl, sitting in his favorite chair, was observing the children and smiling. I served him a cup of coffee, and he kissed me. Lili and Will shouted, "Grandpa is kissing Grandma!"

Obviously he has mellowed lately, he displays affection openly.

On this note Gabriel got up and announced:

"Everyone, Elise and I have discussed marriage, but I never officially asked her..." He took a little box out of his pocket. "Elise, my love, will you marry me?"

It was a beautiful, large ruby ring. Her birthstone.

"Of course, yes! I love you, Gabe, I'll marry you!"

The family applauded and cheered the young couple. It was sealed, they will marry in the spring!

Katie asked me, "Tell us again the story of how Daddy proposed to you and when he gave you your ring, Mommy."

"Well, Dad invited me and Gabe to come to Dusseldorf, and two days before we were about to return to London he did not ask me, he told me:

'You and Gabe should come and live with me here, let's get married.'"

"Just like that! Oh, Daddy, that was not romantic at all," Katie told him.

"I was shocked, it was totally unexpected, so I asked him, 'Are you asking me to marry you?' He responded, 'I'm saying we should get married, we get along so well. What do you think, Clara?'

I told him, 'In the U.K. usually the man says, 'I love you and I want to spend the rest of my life with you.' Sometimes they even drop to their knee and give the girl a ring to seal their commitment.'

Dad got a little uncomfortable, then he said, 'I'm serious, I'll give you a ring when I go to London to bring you home, and I want to marry you because I do love you.' I finally said, 'I love you, Karl, yes, I will marry you.'"

Karl was fast to say, "Show them, Clara. When I went to London to bring you home, I took you to the finest jewelry store, at Harrods, and bought the most beautiful, classic ring."

"You did, Karl! That day you told me, 'Someday you'll pass it on to our daughter.' That's how I found out you wanted us to have a baby, we were starting our family with two boys and you really wanted a girl."

Erik remarked, "I still remember when Dad told me that you were having a baby and it was a girl! When Katherine was born, Dad was in Heaven!"

Amie asked, "What about me, Daddy? Did you want another girl?"

"Yes, my *little doctor*, girls are sweet! You were a gift from Heaven, that's why we named you Amanda, 'the loved one,' Amanda Grace!"

I told Gabe and Elise, "Dad and I would be really happy to have your wedding here, let me know if you want us to plan it!"

Before they left to participate in Vienna's highlight event of the year, the New Year's Concert at the Wiener Musikverein, Gabriel told us that the best time for the fundraiser concert would be the last week of March or the first of April.

Erik, Louisa and the children left by noon.
The house was quiet again.

The next day Katie went to the downtown office to work with Erik, and he invited her to come with him and the family to a ski resort in the Alps for New Year's.

Amie went to the Hospital to visit the children almost every day. Twice that week she went out with Fred, and he brought her home later. I met him before, but this time Amie had the opportunity to introduce him to Karl.

He started a conversation. "Because of my *little doctor* and personal experience with the doctors at the Hospital, you are very welcomed in our house, I developed a new appreciation for the work you all do."

"Thank you, Herr Weisenwert, what we do is in many ways a work of love, we want to help heal, and when patients recover as well as you, we rejoice, our extensive work, dedication and long hours are all worth it."

Alfred told us that he came from a modest family from Wiesbaden, and he is the first doctor in his family.

"You have that in common with our Amie, she is the first doctor in our family, and we are very proud of her."

Karl and I went upstairs, leaving the young couple alone.

Later Amie told me she would like to invite some of her friends from the Hospital to celebrate New Year's at home.

"The house is so festive, and we have the space, music and a little champagne. Will it bother you?"

"Amie, invite them, Daddy and I will be upstairs anyway, it won't bother us at all. I'll prepare a nice buffet for your guests. How many are coming?"

"It's about eight people, nurses and doctors, the others will be working overnight."

"Let's do this, Amie, tell me how many are going to be working at the Hospital, we will prepare some special baskets and you can deliver them in the afternoon. And here, your guests can come for dinner and stay until... next year!"

"Oh, Mommy, that's wonderful, thank you!"

On the thirty-first during the afternoon, we made and received many phone calls of best wishes. Among them to my dear friend Bertha, my former tutor, I couldn't visit her recently, but I promised I would see her for her birthday in January. She is going to be eighty-nine!

Amie's guests arrived in the evening. Karl and I stayed downstairs until the midnight toast with our daughter.

Before going upstairs we told them:

"Celebrate! Eat, drink, dance, have fun, everyone, and if you want you may stay until the morning… There are plenty of rooms or sofas, don't drink and drive!"

In our suite alone, Karl held me:

"This is truly a happy ending for the most challenging and difficult year, but also a year of gratitude and healing."

We started the new year with a new perspective on how our lives are going to be from now on.

"Aren't you tired of having this old man around the house all day, every day?"

"No, Karl, I enjoy our time together."

"We will have the best times of our lives, *meine liebe*, I feel very optimistic. Remember what my doctor said, to live as normally as possible! I haven't been normal for a while and I feel like it is about time…"

"What do you mean, Karl? You were ill, but now you are recovering. You are normal!"

"Maybe we will do what the youngsters are probably doing downstairs…"

"Karl! How naughty! You are really getting back to your old self… And I like it!"

"You remember us, *meine liebe*? How fiery we were together? I still feel passion for you, can't wait to restart where we left off… I think the only thing I need is to have this port removed from my chest, and I'll be in form again."

Sometimes I miss our passionate relationship, I miss what united us initially, what ignited our love, but I truly enjoy the closeness we have now, the tenderness and true intimacy of a couple in harmony! True love.

Katie returned from the ski trip a little disappointed.

"The resort was fabulous, but I spent most of my time with the children. There was a lot of tension between Erik and Louisa, and I didn't meet anyone interesting, the other guests were all coupled up."

"You need to find new friends around here, Katie. What about your old friends from school? Are you in touch with them?"

"I am, Mommy, but I spent too much time in New York, some people moved away. I am in touch with Julia, she just got engaged, she has another circle of friends now."

"Even if she is engaged, you girls can still get together, maybe she can introduce you to her new friends, Katie. I'm sure that in no time you are going to be readjusted to the Dusseldorf social life."

Amanda left for New York on the sixth day of January. Again I felt sad seeing our younger daughter go.

"Amie, every time you leave I feel this hole in my heart, I understand and I support you in your career, but I can't wait for you to be ready and come back home."

"I know, Mommy, I appreciate your support, I can't wait for my internship to be over, I want to come home." She was teary.

"Amie, are you sad to leave Alfred behind?"

"Yes, one more person that I'll miss... But I'll come back at every opportunity I have, and you and Daddy come to see me, please."

Karl had a new level of energy and decided to resume working in the city office twice a week, but most of our time during January was dedicated to the Foundation project. Peter Scheid completed the legal paperwork. Karl hired an administrator, Martha Kepler, an old employee of the factory's Public Relations Department.

"Clara, I know Martha for a long time, she is very easy to work with and very interested in participating in this project, you'll like working with her. We will see things accomplished soon, she has great connections."

I called Gabriel to confirm that the Dusseldorf Theater was booked for the event at the end of March. Martha was on top of the publicity in newspapers and on TV in all the North Rhine area.

On the last Saturday of the month I went to visit my dear friend Bertha Gjord in a town located northwest of Dusseldorf. Katie volunteered to drive up with me, we had a pleasant mother-daughter day out.

Bertha was a retired schoolteacher that Karl had hired to teach me the language when I moved to Dusseldorf. She was vibrant, enthusiastic and a little demanding. She told me right up front:

"You are my newest project, I am going to teach you to speak German like a well educated person. It is going to be hard work!"

"That's what I want, Bertha, I want to be educated in this language like I am in English, thanks to my late friend and teacher George."

For four years, during which I had my two baby girls, Bertha came to our house twice a week and worked with me, *her project*.

Amanda was just a toddler when Bertha told me I didn't need formal classes anymore, but she suggested that we meet once a month for an afternoon to read and discuss a book.

She formed our own book club, for two, that went on for many years while our friendship grew.

During that time, she told me about her personal life.

Bertha had been married before, never had children, her husband was a nonexistent presence in her life. She said:

"When I met him I thought he was shy, didn't have good social skills, but he was kind and intellectual. Was I wrong!

After marrying him, instead of improving he got worse. His behavior was pathological and he became dysfunctional.

I didn't give up easily, but after many years of trying to help him and spending most of the prime time of my life in that uphill battle, I did the only thing a normal person would do, I left him. The fact that we didn't have children made it easier on me, I had nothing to bond me to him, and I cut him out of my life for good.

Through it all I remained true to myself, living my life with purpose. I didn't feel sad that I didn't have children of my own, instead I became more dedicated to some of the young people that crossed my path, being not only a teacher, but in many ways a mother figure."

Bertha didn't allow the dark cloud of her past experience to interfere with her productive life. She was always happy and energetic, like she didn't have a care in the world. She was a good example to follow.

In the meantime she had a boyfriend Oscar, also a retired teacher. She was happy with him and told me, "It's never late to find love."

When she was seventy-four years old, she announced:

"I'm moving on! With Oscar and some of our old friends we are going to start our own elderly home!"

"You, in an elderly home? I can't see that happening, Bertha."

"It's going to be a home unlike any other, you will see! You are coming to visit me, aren't you, Clara?"

"I will for sure, Bertha, please don't go far…"

They bought a large property outside Krefeld, Oscar's hometown, not far from Dusseldorf. And Bertha told me:

"I don't want to miss the hustle and bustle of Dussel, and I want to be close to my younger friends, and you, Clara, top my list. You were my most successful project, I'm so proud of you, from the ABC's to Goethe you've learned everything about the German language, and you write and speak it beautifully like the classy, well educated *Alemana* you are!"

"I learned from the best, Bertha, and I will always be grateful to you. I had a childhood dream of learning languages, you made my dream come true!"

Bertha started calling me *Alemana*, the word in my Spanish language that meant 'German woman,' since the beginning of our pupil-teacher relationship, even before we became friends! It sounded like a term of endearment to me.

I visited her a few times a year, except last year that was very challenging, but I never missed her birthdays. She is still energetic, bright, funny, I admire her!

Oscar was gone a couple of years ago, and some of her old friends too. There were some new faces around this time, she was not sad.

"I miss them, but I don't mourn them, instead of crying I rejoice for the life we had together, for the beautiful memories… And

102

what is most important:
Remember to live!"

Before we left, Bertha jokingly told us... No, she was not joking, she was serious:

"I'm eighty-nine, how far will I go? I already chose my replacement, she is still young, Ingrid is only seventy-two, she can wait to take my place. When I am gone her only job is to remember that '*Bertha lived here, the one who loved life and enjoyed it until the very last day.*'"

"Alright, Bertha, I'm sure that next year on your ninetieth we will still be talking about this, I'll see you then, my friend."

"Clara, did I ever tell you I love you, like if you were my daughter?"

That brought tears to my eyes.

"And I do love you, Bertha, like if you were my mother, my *Alemana* mother!"

Katie and I had a good time with Bertha and her friends. On the way home we had a conversation about lasting friendships that cross the boundaries of time, distance and generations.

"I want to have friends like that, Mommy, like you are, like Bertha is."

"All you need is an open heart, *liebling*!"

That day with Bertha also made me think about the future. What's going to happen when Karl and I get very old and maybe dependent on others?

I am not scared, aging is a natural process, and I have my family, my loving family. I talked to Karl about it that evening.

"Clara, you are younger than I am, if necessary our children will make the best decisions for us. As far as I am concerned I want to live in this house until the end, like my father did."

"So do I, Karl, I want to be here, until... But for now, what if we do something fun and relaxing like the young people do on Saturday nights? Watch a movie on TV!"

He laughed out loud.

"I thought you were suggesting the other thing young couples do on Saturday nights..."

"Well, husband, some hugging and kissing goes a long way,

and wait until your port comes out..."

Gabriel called in February.

"I have a surprise for you, Elise is pregnant, our unplanned gift! Our baby will be born just around my birthday!"

"This is fabulous, I am so happy! Is Elise feeling well?"

"Yes, Mama, just a little shocked... Because of that we are having our wedding sooner, we are still deciding where. When Elise told her mother, she demanded that we get married in Linz. Elise is upset, that is not what she wants. Would you and Dad come to Vienna if we decide to get married right here?"

"Absolutely, son, I won't miss your wedding! Please tell Elise not to get upset, this should be an enjoyable and stress free time for her, for both of you. And I will help with anything you need.

Remember, Dad's birthday is in March, and with you being here for the fundraising concert I was planning to celebrate it, but now we will have a double celebration, your wedding and his birthday, for the whole family!"

Two days later Elise called.

"Sorry, Clara, I'd much rather have our wedding in Dusseldorf, but my mother compromised in coming to Vienna, she wouldn't travel anywhere else. We are having a simple ceremony for family only, at the University campus chapel in two weeks! Can you come?"

"Of course, Karl and I will be there, he is feeling much better. For now, relax, enjoy this precious time, dreaming of the beautiful baby you are having."

Finally the day to get Karl's last test results arrived. We were both anxious.

"I feel much better, Clara, but I'm a little afraid. What if it is not all gone?"

"Karl, I have faith that you are healed."

Dr. Jung gave us the good news, "Karl, you are officially in remission!"

"Beautiful word, remission! That means I don't need any more medication? Are you going to remove the port?"

"Yes to both, you'll take a chemo pill once a week, it is just preventive. And I'm prepared to remove the port today, if you want."

"I absolutely want this out. Thank you, Dr. Jung, to you and all that helped me on this journey."

"And thank you, Karl, for what you are doing to help the patients at the Treatment Center. I heard that the tickets for the fundraising concert are all sold out!"

Two hours after having the port removed, we came home.

"You need to rest, Karl, the procedure was uncomfortable, you need a few days to heal."

"Clara, I don't feel pain, I feel happy and energetic, I feel like dancing with you! Remember how we used to waltz in the foyer? I can't believe I'm about to be seventy and I am starting over, I feel reborn today!"

He took me into his arms and we swayed and twirled around, tears of joy rolled down our faces.

"Oh, Karl, my Karl, you waltz so beautifully!"

We first told Katie when she got home from work. Then we called Erik and Louisa, Gabriel, and Elise and Amie in New York. The entire family rejoiced.

"Daddy is cured!"

We flew to Vienna. Katie came with us, and we decided to stay at a hotel close to Gabriel's place.

We joined the young couple in their duplex apartment in an old traditional building overlooking the Belvedere Gardens.

"I love this place, Gabe, the view of the snow covered gardens, where the purple lilacs bloom in the spring, it is so beautiful! I'll have many opportunities to see them when I come to visit my new grandbaby!"

"We are counting on that, Mama, our baby will have the most loving Grandma! And I am sorry you had to stay in the hotel because Elise's mother and sister are here."

"Don't worry, Gabe, it's quite alright."

Elise brought her mother Eleanor and her sister Gisele, they were in the kitchen baking the wedding cake. That was the first time we met them.

Eleanor had a severe appearance with her graying hair pulled back, unflattering dark clothes and no smile. Gisele, Elise's older sister, was pleasant and friendly.

Elise asked Katie and me for our opinion on what to wear for the ceremony.

"I didn't buy anything special, everything was so rushed and my mother told me I shouldn't wear a bridal dress."

"I'm sorry, Elise, don't worry, you are going to be a beautiful bride, you are beautiful!"

We looked through her closet and she had a light cream colored outfit that looked perfect for the occasion.

The next morning we reunited at the chapel. Elise and Gabriel invited their close friends Agnes and Wolfgang to serve as witnesses.

The ceremony was simple and short. Elise came in carrying a beautiful bouquet of flowers that her sister had made for her.

Karl held my hand, "I wish we would have given Gabriel a more festive wedding like we did for Erik, with all our family and friends around!"

"We will, Karl. They won't miss out on that!"

Katie went back, but Karl and I stayed an extra day in Vienna. It was our first trip together in almost two years. We strolled through the lovely city.

"I always think of Vienna as a musical, beautiful and happy place."

Karl added: "And sweet with all of these fantastic bakeries! Let's go for coffee and pastries, *meine liebe*, and then take advantage of our beautiful room at the hotel and have some private romantic time."

"Oh, my Karl! Romantic!"

CHAPTER SIX

CELEBRATIONS

*T*he end of March came fast. So much happening at the same time!

Amie was coming home on her spring break, just in time for the concert and celebrations!

I had asked Katie to help me surprise Elise, "Let's give her something bridal to wear to the party on Saturday!"

I also asked our old friend Pastor Meyer from our neighborhood Lutheran Church to join us for a special blessing for the newlyweds, and also to give thanks for Karl's recovery.

I told Gabriel and Elise to invite as many friends as they wanted for the reception. He invited a few, including his friend Gunther from Frankfurt, and Elise invited a couple from the Dusseldorf Opera House. She did invite her mother and sister, but they were not coming. Her mother doesn't travel far, and Easter is a very busy time at the bakery that she manages.

Karl invited our old friends.

Hilda helped tremendously, she was excited about everything: "What a difference one year makes…"

Gabriel and Elise arrived two days before the concert for his rehearsal with the orchestra. Martha had been working tirelessly promoting the event, she asked Gabriel to participate in an interview with the local TV station. *'The son of Dusseldorf,'* as he is known in the North Rhine area, is performing in town!

In the TV interview Gabriel talked about the purpose of improving the lives of the ones afflicted by cancer, and their families.

"Let's join my father in this endeavor, helping in any way we can, many of our friends and neighbors. Our community will benefit from it."

Amie arrived, to our delight! "Now our family is complete!"

The fundraising event was magnificent!

The public's response was enormous. Martha told us that so far thousands of people have signed up for monthly contributions, and many did right there at the theater, as they arrived.

The next day 'The W Mansion' was fully prepared for the reception.

In the morning Katie and Amie took their new sister-in-law upstairs.

"Come, Elise, let's dress up."

They showed her the dress.

"This is what you are wearing this afternoon, it is a gift from Mom, it is your wedding celebration, after all!"

Elise was surprised and emotional. The delicate empire waist dress fitted her so well!

While the girls were getting dressed up, I spoke to Gabriel:

"We have a surprise for you and Elise, this is your wedding celebration too. Remember Pastor Meyer? He is going to give a special wedding blessing, and wait until you see Elise, she will be wearing something beautiful, like she deserves. Today I only want to see a smile on your faces! Prepare your vows. Later there will be wedding cake and champagne!"

"Oh, Mama, it is wonderful. I bet Elise is in tears right now. She was sad about the way we ended up in a rushed wedding. Thank you for making it all better."

Karl thanked him for his participation in the first event for the Foundation. "We couldn't have done it without you, son."

Gabriel told him that he is committing to fundraising, one concert a year, from now on.

"It can be here, Koln, Bonn or Frankfurt, any city around this area, the entire proceeds are yours! And Dad, I would love if you could attend one of my concerts on my next tour."

"I will, Mom and I will be there."

The house was full of friends, the ceremony was performed, the bride was beautiful!

Karl was all smiles. "My family is happy, I'm happy!"

Our family and guests had a good time interacting in animated conversations, eating, dancing.

Amie brought some of her friends from the Hospital, especially Alfred! We are getting used to having him around. It's obvious they are in love!

We finally met Gunther, Gabriel's friend, he was hilarious, sometimes self deprecating.

He is in his late forties, maybe fifty, short and a little pudgy, with a great appetite for good food. He told the girls to call him Uncle Gunther.

Katie laughed at his jokes and told him she was bored in Dusseldorf, he told her to go with Gabriel to Frankfurt, he has many social friends, she could have fun there!

On a sour note it looked to me that Erik and Louisa were not enjoying themselves like the rest of us. I asked Louisa if she was alright. She apologized:

"I'm sorry, Clara, I'm not my best lately, but I am trying..."

"Louisa, if you need to talk I am here for you, call me."

I didn't mention anything to Karl, he was having a happy day.

Two days later, after meeting with Martha and confirming the proceeds from the fundraising event, Karl went to the Hospital and made a donation for new equipment for the Treatment Center.

He also met with Dr. Altmann, the Children's Infirmary director, and told her that by suggestion of our daughter and her friend Dr. Alfred he was considering to buy a house to lodge families of the children in treatment at the Hospital.

Amie and Alfred have told us that many of the parents can't afford to stay with their children for lack of affordable accommodations.

Dr. Altmann immediately agreed.

"That will be a significant contribution to the children and their parents, the little patients benefit much from having a parent with them throughout the treatment."

"I can imagine quite well, the young patients will have that comfort, we are going to start looking for a house immediately."

Karl instructed Martha to work with a realtor to find a large home in the vicinity to accommodate those families.

Amanda returned to New York.

"I'll try to come again, Mommy, it is very difficult to arrange time off. By the way, Fred is coming for a week sometime in the summer, that will be his first trip to the U.S."

"I'll miss you too much, *liebling*. Daddy and I will plan to come and see you."

Karl has been going to the office twice a week and he works from home the other days, he is getting back to normal, but it will never be like before. Now with Katie being Erik's right arm, he feels more comfortable delegating.

Louisa called me and asked me to come and see her one morning while the children were in school.

From the moment she opened the door I could see her teary eyes and that something was wrong.

"How can I help you, Louisa?"

"Clara, this is going on for a while, I have been very conflicted, I don't know what to do, there are days when I think Erik and I should get a divorce."

"What happened to both of you, Louisa?"

"Straight to the point. Last year when Erik was stressed out, working late hours, he had an affair! I confronted him, he confessed, he said it was inconsequential, it was a misstep, he would never do it again. Now every time I want to vent about it, he doesn't listen to me.

I can't get over it, and he doesn't want to talk about it anymore. Do you understand how I feel, Clara?"

"I understand completely. Just let me ask you, do you love Erik? Does he tell you he loves you? Does he want your marriage to be saved?"

"Yes and yes, I love him but I can't pass through what he did, I feel angry, sad and betrayed, disgusted! I have withdrawn from him."

"Louisa, I love Erik, as you know we are more like older sister and younger brother, I believe I know him well. He is pretty much like his father, he means what he says and he has a hard time dealing with anything that represents failure to him. He failed you, and that is very hard on him.

There are men that are serial cheaters and they can't be trusted, and there are others that have integrity and respect their marriage, but they are not perfect, they make mistakes… I truly believe that Erik, like his father, is in the second category."

"I agree with you, Clara."

"That said, if you love him you need to forgive him, renew your trust in him and rebuild your marriage. I know how hard it is, but when we have a husband like Karl or Erik, that is all possible. I am speaking from experience, Louisa."

"Are you telling me that my father-in-law cheated on you? I can't believe it, he loves you so much, you are bonded, we can see it."

"That's all true, but there was time when Karl stepped out of our marriage, his reason was because I was not supporting him, he was against Gabriel's decision to go to school in New York, and I stood up for my son.

He became frustrated, got cold and distant, and he felt for someone from his past who was around and available. He told me that he regretted his inconsequent and foolish action.

I was devastated and heartbroken. I thought our marriage was over. I took Gabriel and the girls to New York, and we spent the summer there. When I returned home, we had one final conversation about that issue. He listened to everything I had to say and asked me to trust him again, made promises and amends, and he told me that after that day he would never want to talk about that anymore because that reminded him of his failure.

He devoted more time to me, arranged for some romantic getaways for the two of us. I saw his sincerity, his actions meant more than words, I loved him, I didn't want our marriage to end and I worked on myself. It did take me a while to get over, but eventually I did."

"So you are telling me that the anger, the resentment and mistrust, it all will go away?"

"You can forgive and let go, but before you do that I would recommend that you talk to Erik one more time, he has to give you the chance to tell him how you feel, ask for his acknowledgment of your hurt feelings, ask him if he wants to save your marriage and what he is willing to do. After that, if you are satisfied with everything he tells you, don't go back to it. Start anew!"

"Just for the fact that you have gone through this and you have a great marriage, I believe there is hope for me and Erik."

"There is hope, Louisa, and if you decide to reconcile, take some time away only the two of you, I'll take care of Lili and Will."

Louisa embraced me and sobbed.

"Thank you, Clara, it is so good to take this off my chest, I should have talked to you before. I couldn't talk to anyone, not even to my own mother."

"Don't tell Erik I know, he would feel humiliated. And please don't comment about his father either. That is all in the past, and I gave you that information only as corroboration of the 'like father, like son' behavior. Remember, both of them were scarred by mistrust, by the cheating of Erik's mother, neither one of them wanted to be like her…"

"I have a new perspective on this now. What he did was not really against me or because our marriage was stale. I have to admit that it has been cold, but it is worth fighting for."

"I'm glad you are feeling better, Louisa, fight for your marriage!"

She smiled.

"It's good to see you smiling, Louisa, no more tears!"

A few days later Erik told his father that he was taking time off to take Louisa on a little vacation. Louisa brought Lili and Will to spend time with us. They reconciled!

Two weeks went by, Martha and the realtor were having difficulty finding a house close to the Hospital, until she told me:

"I was discouraged, there is nothing available in the area that fits our plan, but something came up. Do you want to see it, Clara? It's two attached three bedroom houses, one has been for sale for a long time and needs work, the other was just listed. The realtor suggested that we demolish some walls, renovate and make a whole large home. The location is perfect, it is walking distance from the Hospital!"

I went to see it and got very excited! I could see the potential for the house and I loved the yard, we could build a playground for the children to enjoy on their better days.

Karl was in the office, I called him.

He told Martha to make an offer.

"And if the money we have is not enough for the purchase and renovations, I'll pitch in," he said.

They closed the deal, and Karl was satisfied. Martha hired a contractor to start working on the house immediately.

"After this is all done we should go away, just you and me, *meine liebe*. Every couple needs a break from daily life. Did you see Erik and Louisa? They were grumpy before, but since they took vacations they are both relaxed and smiling. I think they had a little honeymoon!"

"They look happier now. By the way, I was talking to Gabriel about the concert tour and he asked if we can meet him for the one in Stockholm. For two reasons, first there'll be a reception at the Royal Palace and he wants to introduce us to the monarchs. Second he would be alone there, Elise will be with him in Amsterdam, but she needs to return to Vienna for her opera performances."

"I like Stockholm, I do business there and we might stay a little longer and find a place to retreat. I'll check that out. Do you like the idea, Clara?"

"Absolutely, I would love to see Elise too, but there is a good reason that I don't want to go to Amsterdam. Miguel is going to be there with his son Fabio."

"I see, you are avoiding him, but it looks like Gabriel sees him once in a while."

"He will not go out of his way, when Miguel comes around he treats him with courtesy, like he does with any other friend. And it is true, Karl, I am avoiding him. Last year when I was in New York, he showed up uninvited to meet me. I was shocked! Prior to that he was in Frankfurt and called me asking to meet me here. I said no! I had nothing to say to him."

"What did he want to talk to you about?"

"He spoke about his feelings and asked me to be friends. I was very blunt telling him never, and I made clear that I had absolutely no feelings of any kind for him. I didn't tell you when I returned home because we were facing many important issues."

"Alright, I don't know if I am feeling jealous or flattered. Clara, let me ask you, if I hadn't survived the ordeal, would you consider another companion?"

"He asked me the same question and I told him, 'No! I love my husband in any circumstance, I am and will always be loyal to him.'"

"Thank you, Clara, I didn't expect any different from you, I think I'll choose to be flattered. Maybe someday, somewhere, we'll meet this man, and he will see who's the one that really loves and deserves you."

Together we visited the Children's Home now under renovations, we appreciated how it's coming out, it is a very large house with accommodations for many. Two dining rooms in the downstairs area were converted into bedrooms for a total of eight bedrooms, and there was a large recreation room in the basement.

The fence between the original two houses was demolished, the yard was cleaned and a playground was being set up.

"It's wonderful! In no time the families and children will be able to enjoy this space."

Karl told Martha not to spare any funds, and after we return from our trip to Sweden I will help her acquire all the necessary furnishings. He wants the house to be finished as soon as possible for full use.

We invited Katie to come with us to Stockholm for the concert and the reception at the Royal Palace. She accepted, of course, but she will return home immediately after. Karl and I will stay to go to a resort in Borgholm.

Before leaving I called our younger daughter in New York City to tell her about the Children's Home.

Amie was excited. "It's so good to know that Daddy has all that disposition and he is invested in the project. I can't tell you how much that means to many families. I also want you to know that Fred is coming in June for a week, and if I can take time off I might return with him to see you and to visit the Children's Home."

"It will be wonderful, *liebling*, maybe it will be possible to coordinate the dates for you to be here for the inauguration."

We met Gabriel in Stockholm on the eve of the concert.

The next morning he had a little time for us before going to his rehearsal at the Royal Swedish Opera Theater.

"Thank you for being here, Mom and Dad, and I'm so happy you came along, Katie, it means so much to me that my family is here, this concert is unlike any other you have seen before, it is very regal!"

I asked him about Elise and his performance in Amsterdam.

"Elise is doing very well, she was sorry she couldn't come, and tomorrow I'll tell you more about Amsterdam."

Karl, Katie and I spent a few hours sightseeing, and later we got ready for the gala.

The concert was grand and sophisticated, rich and beautiful music, and as Gabe said, it was regal. The Royal Family attended. Limousines were waiting to take us to the reception at the Palace.

Katie and I had practiced bowing for the Queen. We were surprised to see how down to earth and very welcoming the royals were. We absolutely enjoyed meeting them.

Her Majesty gave me compliments: "From one mother to another, congratulations, you have a magnificent son." I was humbled. I told her I loved Stockholm and we were going to extend our trip for a few days, going to Borgholm, and she told me:

"We have a summer home there, Solliden Palace, you should see it, visitors are welcomed."

The next day Katie took an early flight to Germany.

Karl and I spent a little more time with Gabe before he went to Oslo. He told us, "Miguel came to Amsterdam with Fabio, I liked seeing him, we became instant friends! Miguel brought me a gift, an old home movie reel about his grandfather, he got it from his great-aunt. He was really happy to give it to me, he said that now I'll have the opportunity to see and listen to his grandfather playing the cello and I might see something familiar in him...

I appreciated the gift, I'll be watching it next time I go to the studio in Frankfurt, I'm sure Gunther has the right projector."

Karl told him, "We have an old projector in our house, somewhere in the basement, you might be able to watch it at home with us."

After Gabriel went to the airport Karl and I went on a tour and truly enjoyed it.

Stockholm, the capital of Sweden, combines modern attractions with historic charm. We already had been to the Palace the night before, which is the official residence and principal workplace of the Swedish Monarch, but I learned that the Drottningholm Palace is the Royal Family's private residence.

The tour took us to Old Town and over the picturesque bridges that connect the city's canals. It was interesting to learn that the city was spread across fourteen islands in Lake Malaren, stretching out east to the Baltic Sea.

Stockholm is the cultural, media, political and economic center of Sweden. It also houses some of Europe's high ranking universities.

I was very impressed with its beauty, grand public buildings and palaces, rich history and culture!

Returning to a café close to the hotel, there was a quartet playing at the square. People were gathering around, they were playing a waltz, and Karl unexpectedly held my hand, "Let's dance, *meine liebe*."

"Right here in the street with everyone looking at us?"

"Yes, we are ordinary folks and we love to waltz!"

We danced! And it was fun!

My Karl is so much more relaxed now, what happened to him changed him for the better, he enjoys the little pleasures of life more than ever.

The next day we took a ferry to Borgholm, on the island of Öland in the Baltic Sea. The ride was spectacular!

Arriving at the site we were directed to a fabulous resort hotel by the water, close to a marina. Karl was in Heaven, he loved water views, sunsets, nature!

Borgholm is one of Sweden's historical towns. The city is known for its once magnificent fortress, which is now a ruin located north of the Öland Bridge which connects the island to the mainland.

We did not miss the chance to see Solliden Palace, surprisingly the architecture and the gardens resembled ours in Dusseldorf.

After three lovely days of sharing that new experience together, we came back home refreshed and more bonded, if that is possible!

"I'm so glad we did this, Karl, you were motivated and in good health. Do you feel tired?"

"No, *meine liebe*, I feel brand new. We might still go on another trip to our romantic place in the South Alps, before the summer is over…"

Martha and I worked together, furnishing and decorating the Children's Home.

Karl set the inauguration day, June 30th! Dr. Altmann had a list of names of eligible parents to occupy the house while their little ones were in treatment.

Good news! Amanda came home! She arrived with Alfred.

Our daughter told me that she had a wonderful time with Alfred in New York and they are taking their relationship to another level, they are committed. And he has applied for a fellowship in nuclear medicine there.

"If he is accepted next year, we might be together in New York! Do you mind if he stays with me in our apartment, Mommy?"

"I don't mind, if you are absolutely sure you are committing to this relationship. I trust your judgment, Amie. But Joy is living there with you, is there any conflict?"

"No, we all get along well. And yes, Fred and I are very serious about our relationship. Don't worry, we are not going to do anything rushed. He wants to come here tomorrow to talk to you and Daddy about us."

"Alright! Something serious is happening with my baby girl! I just wish that he deserves your love."

Alfred came. During dinner we had a light conversation about his impressions of New York City and his interest in nuclear medicine. After dinner Amie invited him to the den for coffee, and he talked to us.

"Frau and Herr Weisenwert, meeting your daughter changed my life! I was not planning to be in a committed relationship anytime soon, before I complete my training. But I love Amanda, and I want you to know I am in this relationship for the long run.

I came from a very modest family, as you know I don't have any material possessions to offer her, but working hard I will be able to offer her a very stable life in the future. We have the same common goals, we are both planning to finish our training and start our careers first, but I would like you to accept me as part of Amanda's life."

Karl responded:

"Thank you for the consideration, Alfred. Our daughter is the most good hearted, caring person, she deserves the best, she deserves to be loved. I am happy for both of you. I don't care if you don't have the financial power, it doesn't define who you are, you have the potential, it will come in time.

You are both doctors, you have a bright future ahead. I admire and respect the work you do and sacrifices that I'm sure you have made to come this far. I support both of you."

I told Alfred, "One of these days I am going to love you as a son. Just be good, fair and honest to our Amie."

On the last day of June, members of the Hospital's Treatment Center, and Karl and I as the Foundation representatives, officially opened the Children's Home.

Amie and Alfred were present! That same day, parents of some of the children moved in. They were from towns or villages distant from Dusseldorf and did not have the financial means to afford lodging while their children remained in the Hospital. They were extremely grateful.

Our hearts were joyful knowing that those children would have the love and support of their families every day, until they could return to their homes!

Amie returned to New York, too soon!

In the beginning of August, Gabriel went to Frankfurt and invited Katie to meet him there.

"I'll be here only for two days. Gunther is having a promotional cocktail, it should be fun! Get on the train and come, I'll come back with you to Dusseldorf to see Mom and Dad."

Katie, who has been complaining of boredom, did not miss the opportunity and joined her brother.

They returned home together on a Sunday afternoon, and Katie was radiant. "I'll tell you what happened there later, Mommy."

Karl told Gabriel that he and Erik had found an old projector, tested it and it was working. "Did you bring the reel, Gabriel?"

"No, Dad, not this time, but thank you!"

Later Gabe told me that he brought the home movie from Miguel and he watched it at the studio.

"I was a little afraid of showing it here to Dad, I didn't know how much he would appreciate seeing Miguel's family, and I also didn't know how I would feel watching it. But I wish you were there to translate all those Spanish conversations..."

"How was the experience, Gabe? How did you feel watching it?"

"It was black and white, but in very good shape. A large family gathering, talking, laughing, children running around, mothers screaming at them to be quiet, the old grandfather holding his cello.

At one side of the room I immediately identified Miguel, a teenager, rolling his eyes, looking totally uninterested. His grandfather started playing, and even with the rusty sounds of the old reel, it sounded wonderful, I observed him closely, the way he ran his fingers on the strings, the way he tilted his head, even his facial expressions when playing, like he was feeling the music. I could see his artistry... He played with his heart, Mama. I felt right then that my musical gene came from Antonio José Terrades."

"Gabe, now you can close the circle. Did you feel more connected to Miguel?"

"That didn't change, I still see him as a friend."

After Gabriel left, Katie told me, "I met someone very interesting at the party. He is a baron from Bavaria and he is single! Gunther was saying that he lives the playboy lifestyle, but he was very engaging and fun!"

"What's his name? Where does he live?"

"Leopold, Baron Von Lesch, lives in Frankfurt, he has a building restoration business."

"Why did they call him a playboy?"

"Because he is mature and single, always in the company of beautiful young women. He was very interested in me."

"Of course he was, you are young and beautiful. Be careful, Katie, men like that sometimes just come and go. How old is he, anyway?"

"Soon to be thirty-nine. But he is so charming."

"Kind of old for you, Katie, you are only twenty-six. Are you planning to meet again?"

"Yes, we are in touch, he said he is coming to Dusseldorf to visit me."

"I really have mixed feelings about you dating an older guy."

"You shouldn't, Mommy, Daddy is older, and he is a pretty good husband. Did you have any doubts when you met him?"

"Dad was never the playboy type. When I met him he was a serious man raising a son by himself, he didn't want me only for fun, he wanted a committed relationship. So did I. Be careful, Katie."

The relationship between Katie and Leopold was heating up, our daughter seemed pretty happy. For the rest of the month he came to Dusseldorf twice and she went to meet him in Frankfurt a couple of times, but we hadn't met him yet.

I spoke to Elise and confirmed that I would spend a week with her when the baby arrives.

As the end of September approached, Gabriel called me: "The baby will come anytime now."
I went to Vienna alone, Karl was home and working at the office now three times a week, but he was anxiously waiting for the news.

Exactly a week before Gabriel's birthday, Marie-Claire was born! I loved her name! My beautiful granddaughter, it was very emotional to hold her for the first time, and secretly I liked that Elise's mother couldn't come, I could pamper my granddaughter all by myself!
Gabriel was very emotional holding his baby girl!
"This is how it feels to be a father! It's magical, like a miracle!"

Elise and Marie-Claire did really well. After we celebrated Gabriel's birthday, I got ready to return home.
"Mama, having you here is so good, I love the way you take care of our baby, I wish we lived closer, Marie-Claire would have the best grandmother always around."
"I know, son, I would love to pamper her, see her growing up, but I'll come to visit, and you and Elise come as often as you can, and when you go on trips you can leave her with me, your father and I would love to have our granddaughter at home."
"I do too, if Elise didn't have her permanent position at the Opera House here, we would be living in Dusseldorf, close to you."

The day I was leaving, Gisele arrived to meet her new little niece and help her sister for a couple of days. It was nice seeing her again.

When I returned from Vienna I was a little down, sad for leaving my baby granddaughter. The magical feeling of holding a newborn reminded me of my own babies, all grown up now. I'll be looking forward to have them over for the holidays.

This year was going by fast, I hadn't seen my dear friend Bertha since January. I invited Karl to come with me.
"It's beautiful out there in the fall. The golden, warm colors of nature on and around her property, the crisp air... Autumn is a poetic season and I love to share it with you!"
I asked Hilda to prepare some strudel, Bertha and her friends' favorite.
Karl and I drove away in a sunny, almost warm afternoon to Krefeld.
As always, Bertha was very happy to see us.
"I love surprises and your apple strudel!"
This time Bertha looked frail.
"I am aging, now I can really feel it."

Karl was impressed with the walls of her living room. Bertha had someone stencil a few of her most favorite Goethe verses in very large black letters. She told him:
"You don't need glasses to read them. Please read them out loud, Karl, I like to listen to your strong and impressive voice."
I thought to myself, no one likes his voice more than I do. It was the first thing I noticed when we met, his commanding, and at the same time, melodic voice.

Bertha's friends sat all around. Karl started reading out loud:

'Nothing is so strong as gentleness, nothing so gentle as real strength.'
'Dream no small dreams, for they have no power to move the hearts of men.'
'Nothing is worth more than this day!'

'Every day we should hear at least one little song, read one good poem, see one exquisite picture, and if possible, speak a few sensible words.'

Our afternoon gathering was very pleasant, I told Bertha that I would be back for her birthday in January.

"Maybe before that, Clara, we are planning to go to Dusseldorf for the ballet in December, we don't know the day yet, we haven't bought the tickets. Kurt, our roommate, is in charge of everything. He said he had transportation lined up, but he didn't find the tickets for a matinee."

Karl was fast to reply, "Clara and I will take care of the tickets for the ballet. Do you need anything else, Bertha?"

"I was thinking of going in the morning, touring around the city for a little while and having lunch at a good restaurant close to the theater before the spectacle."

"All done! We will take care of the restaurant reservations, too."

"Karl, I always thought of you as a very smart and lucky businessman that married the sweetest Spanish-Alemana girl, but you are gentle and kind too, you make the perfect couple, you made my day! Thank you for taking time from your busy life to come and see us."

"Thank you, Bertha, I learned much from you. It was a real pleasure being here."

I told Bertha I will call her soon to confirm everything.

While on the road Karl repeated:

"*'Nothing is worth more than this day...'* That's what I learned after battling cancer, and I really appreciated today. Being around those old folks made me feel that we still have time ahead, but someday we will get there..."

"We will get there together, Karl."

With so much going on, we have postponed our trip to the South Alps for next spring. We were deciding if we should go to New York to see Amanda, or Vienna for Karl to meet the baby.

We called Amie, she said she was very busy, working around the clock on her hospital shifts, she hardly would spend time with us. She confirmed she is coming home for the holidays. We can't wait!

Karl and I went to Vienna, our granddaughter was eight weeks old and Karl hadn't met her yet.

We had two glorious days, holding our grandbaby reminded us so much of our little girls...

Gabriel and Elise were very happy that we came, we gave them a night out alone, their first after Marie-Claire's birth.

My son gave me a DVD. Gunther had Miguel's old home movie edited and copied.

"It came out very good and clear, Mom. If you think it's appropriate, you can show it to Dad."

"I will, I'll watch it with Dad."

Karl and I did some Christmas shopping in romantic Vienna and returned home to start preparing for the holidays.

As a tradition the whole family will reunite again in our house.

During all this time Katie has been very involved with her baron, numerous trips to Frankfurt and many nights out. I started getting concerned about their relationship that was going too fast...

Karl asked: "What is going on with Katie and her new boyfriend? Why didn't we meet him yet?"

"She said she is having a wonderful time, he is great company and she is falling in love. Leopold, the baron, is very seductive and he is crazy about her."

Like any protective father, Karl reacted, "Seductive! One more reason for her to bring him home."

I discussed with Katie inviting him home next time he comes to Dusseldorf.

"Mommy, I really like him, but for now I am just having fun and I am taking my time, I don't want to be in the wrong situation again."

In December I met Bertha and her friends at the traditional restaurant Altstadt for lunch. I was surprised to see Bertha in a wheelchair.

Karl and I offered them the lunch and the tickets as a Christmas gift. She was delighted.

"This is my last time in the city, my dear, better make the most out of it!"

"Happy holidays, Bertha, I'll come to see you next month on your birthday!"

The holidays are here! Louisa came home a few days in advance to offer her help with the decorations and the menu.

"But the real reason I am here, Clara, is to tell you, secretly, that I am pregnant! Erik and I are going to make the announcement on Christmas Eve. Can you imagine? I'll be forty when our baby is born!"

"Congratulations, Louisa, I'm happy for you and Erik, that is a sign that your marriage is back on track, isn't it?"

"It is, as you said, it is hard, but I am getting over it. Erik and I are stronger than ever and we feel that we are starting again."

"It's wonderful, Louisa, and I'll keep the secret."

Amie came home again, there will be just one more year in New York. The day she arrived, she and Katie prepared a special celebration for my birthday.

"Don't tell anyone, girls, but I am getting to the end of my fifties…"

Gabriel and Marie-Claire arrived. My three month old granddaughter was so cute and beautiful!

Karl was delighted with our growing family around.

I asked Katie about her plans. She said Leopold is spending the holidays in Frankfurt, but he will come to Dusseldorf after Christmas, and they will go back together to Frankfurt to celebrate the New Year at a masquerade ball, an event that attracts hundreds.

"Sorry, I won't be here for New Year's, Mommy, but you might meet Leo this time."

Amanda stayed home like she did last year with Alfred, they invited their friends from the Hospital. They also had an announcement, Alfred got the fellowship in New York, they are going to be together for the entire next year!

Erik, Louisa, Lili and Will arrived for dinner, and after the celebration, while we were sharing sweets and drinks, they announced:
"Our new, unexpected baby will arrive next summer!"
We rejoiced.

This was one more delightful evening with our family and one more magical Christmas Day.

The next day Gabriel and Elise returned to Vienna.

Katie brought Leopold home, and we invited him to stay for dinner.
The baron looked very self-assured, but lacking in maturity, bragging about his deals, his boating interests, it looked to us that he was not a man of substance, but a *bon vivant*.
He treated Katie with affection, but in a manner like she was under his spell, and to top that he demonstrated a propensity for drinking too much.
He was cordial, so were we, but he mentioned his title and his royal lineage a few more times than we cared for...

After they left, Karl commented: "He impressed me, but not in a good way. Katie should be cautious, I don't want our daughter to be disappointed."
"I know, Karl, I tell myself, as a mother it is very difficult not to cross that line between feeling we are losing our daughter to someone else or if that man is really right for her. I have doubts too. I thought he was pretentious!"
"I don't want to end this year worrying, I count our blessings, starting with my recovery, the creation of the Children's Home, and donations pouring in to help patients at the Treatment Center. This is the minimum we can do for another human being, and it is so rewarding."
"Yes, *liebe*, we have many blessings to count, including another little Weisenwert on the way."

We always start a new year hoping that this one will be better than the past for all humanity! But at home it started on a sad note when Amie returned to New York. This time she won't be alone, Alfred will follow her soon.

Our family has been divided, I know it is temporary, I would love to have her always at home.

Katie is very dedicated to work, Erik and Karl are very proud of her. But now that she has this boyfriend in Frankfurt, she doesn't spend much time at home with us.

She came back after her New Year's celebration with Leopold, saying that he introduced her to some new friends as 'his baroness.'

"Katie, is he talking about a serious commitment?"

"He has said that I am the one, now he calls me 'baroness,' I think we are heading in that direction."

Karl was about to have his tests done. He didn't talk about it, but he was apprehensive. He paced back and forth, sometimes he sat in his lounge chair, pretending he was reading, but his mind was wandering.

"Karl, are you worried about anything?"

"No, *meine liebe,* I'm not."

"I think you are. Is it about your next appointment with Dr. Jung?"

He looked at me with anxiety in his eyes.

"Once you have cancer there is always a risk...."

I knelt down close to him, held his hand.

"Karl, you are alright, you had your share, it is over, *liebe.*"

"Life is not fair, just look at those little children at the Hospital, they are having a share of suffering much bigger than they can carry."

"Yes, it is unfair and undeserving, and you are making it a little easier for them, that is what the disease did to you, it opened your heart wider to others. I'm so proud of you."

I was there at Dr. Jung's office, and the results of Karl's tests were again excellent! We sighed in relief!

Karl asked him if they had any immediate need to provide for the patients.

"As a matter of fact, Dr. Altmann and I were talking about the iPads and video games that your daughter Amanda brought to the children and how much they help the little patients, distracting them from pain. Some of our adult patients also own those devices, but others can't afford them. Is your Foundation able to provide them to the adults too?"

"Absolutely, Doctor, we will get them right away."

When we returned home, Karl immediately called Amie and told her how much her gifts to the Infirmary were appreciated, and they were extending them to the adult population.

"I am happy your Foundation can help so many, Daddy!"

"It's ours, 'The W Family Foundation,' you are part of it, my *little doctor*!"

This is Karl! My Karl! Generous heart!

"Karl, this is what gratitude is, you personify it by giving!"

"My test results were one of my concerns, the other is at work. Otto, my long time collaborator and friend, is retiring this year, he has an enormous responsibility in his hands, it won't be easy to replace him.

The second man in line is about his age and is also contemplating retirement soon. This won't happen until the fall anyway, maybe he will stay until the end of this year while he is preparing someone to succeed him."

"Don't start worrying now, Erik can also help with that."

"Erik is in the clouds with the new baby coming, he said they didn't plan to have a third child. Did you know that Erik and Louisa hit a hard patch last year? This baby is the result of their reconciliation."

"I knew, but she loves him, he loves her, and where there is love everything is possible!"

CHAPTER SEVEN

LIFE GOES ON

I went to visit Bertha for her birthday, this time Franz drove me.

When we arrived, I saw her sitting quietly in her chair with a blanket warming her legs up, but smiling as always.

"I am glad you brought me my strudel, at this age I allow myself to eat all the sweets I want! Isn't that great?"

"I think it is, Bertha, you make me laugh. Look at us, we have been celebrating your birthday for almost three decades. I was thirty-two and look at me now, I'll be sixty this year! Can you imagine?"

"You're a young lady! Just to remind you I found true love at sixty-four! And pretty soon I am reuniting with my Oscar, he is waiting for me... It is about time!"

She pointed to a brown paper wrapped package tied up with string on a side table.

"Please get that package, Clara, it is a present for you. I can't carry them where I am going, but if I could I would... They are my most treasured possessions, but don't open it now."

"Bertha, why are you giving it away?"

"Because I am lucky to be able to say goodbye to my dear friends, most people are not, they just leave a void, an empty space..."

In that moment I felt that I was looking at her face, into her shiny, lively eyes for the last time.

My eyes welled up, I held her small, soft, white as cotton and wrinkled hand.

"Bertha, you made such a mark on my life, you taught me every word I speak, write or read, you are unforgettable. I love you!"

We spent the next hour drinking tea and reminiscing about our long history as teacher and pupil, the books we read and discussed together. Bertha got very tired.

I left her with a knot in my throat. My bold, strong, full of life friend was frail, she was fading away, the light was dimming.

I brought the package home and was afraid of opening it, it was like if I opened it I would be letting go of her and she wouldn't be there anymore...

That was our last time!

By the end of February I got a call from her roommate Kurt. Bertha had died peacefully. She left her place reserved in the local cemetery beside Oscar, the man she loved the most, and written instructions for her funeral.

She wanted no viewing, no religious service, a simple casket covered with flowers, many flowers, asking us, her friends, to gather together, listening to good music, reading poetry, and no tears, only smiles. With a message for all of us, her favorite Goethe quote: *'Remember to live!'*

Karl held me.

"I know you loved her, but just think of the incredible, long life she lived and the legacy she left. She educated hundreds of people, but if she had just one, you were her highest accomplishment. I'll come with you to her funeral."

I opened the package she had given me, it was her collection of the oldest editions of Johann Wolfgang Von Goethe books! With a note:

'Alemana, you are the young friend that I treasured the most! With love, Bertha.'

I sobbed in Karl's arms.

The way she lived her life, savoring every day, not looking back, not getting wrapped up in sadness, she was such an example.

Karl and I bought all the flowers we could find at our local florist, in the dead of winter that was not an easy task.

We asked Franz to drive us to Krefeld with the car full of bouquets of flowers. Hilda came along to pay her respects, and brought apple strudel and cake for Bertha's friends.

We brought one of her Goethe books, and after she was laid to rest we went to her house. Hilda served strudel and cake. Bertha's friends and some others who came from Dusseldorf sat all around.

Kurt asked Karl to read.

"She liked your voice and the way you read the writings on the wall."

Then at the sound of music, each one of us said farewell to Bertha in our own words.

I read one of her favorite lines from the book and said, "Goodbye, dearest friend and teacher!"

Spring came soon and Katie asked for time off from work.

"Leo invited me to go Bavaria, to Munich and then to his village to meet his parents!"

"Aren't you going to celebrate your birthday with us, Katie? Is he coming to meet you here?"

"Well, I thought you wouldn't mind, Mommy, if I go away for my birthday."

"I mind, Katie, I had plans to celebrate it here, but I understand."

Katie was in love, and to Bavaria with her prince, I mean 'her baron,' she went.

"You are not happy with that, are you, Clara?"

"I am not, Karl, I wish she would spend her birthday here with us and then go on the trip."

"Let's trust that our daughter knows what she is doing. In the meantime we should go on a short vacation ourselves! We had an eventful winter, we need to relax!"

"You are right, I was thinking of going to New York to see Amie, but Alfred just moved there, she is not alone. I know you were planning a trip to the South Alps last year and we didn't go. Or maybe we could go to Vienna to see our granddaughter, we haven't seen her since the holidays, and Gabe will be playing at a festive spring concert, Elise will be singing."

"That's where we are going, to Vienna. The Alps are better in the summer, and I understand you need to see the baby. It will be a few days away, just the two of us, I want to stay in that hotel near their place, we'll relax, have privacy... I love Vienna."

Gabriel and Elise were very busy with the spring concert that turned out to be a happy and colorful event. We loved it!

Elise hired an *au pair* for Marie-Claire, Helene, she was very gentle. Our granddaughter has grown beautifully, she's adorable and cuddly. We were delighted with her. "I wish I could cherish her more often."

Gabriel told Karl he is performing with the Berlin Symphony Orchestra by the end of the spring, it will be a major concert, and all his profits will be donated to the Foundation.

"It would be nice if you and Mom could come."

"We will, Gabriel, I promised I would not miss your concerts, I'll be glad to be there, and thank you very much for the donation!"

Karl reported to Gabriel what was being done with the donated money, how many lives would be impacted, providing not only treatment but comfort.

"Our family is giving back to others, we are in this together!"

Karl and I had the time and opportunity to take long walks at the Belvedere Gardens where the purple lilacs were in bloom.

"Vienna is so beautiful, it makes me feel like going around Austria, visiting other cities, like Salzburg, we have never been there!"

"I like the idea, Clara, Austria has much beauty to be appreciated."

We had the most pleasant time and returned refreshed, hoping that Katie's trip to Bavaria was successful, too.

But something happened. We were not quite sure, she didn't want to talk right away. Katie only spoke about Munich, the splendid venues, how entertaining and lively the city is, attracting visitors from all over the world.

"Yes, Katie, we know, it's a fabulous city, but did you meet Leopold's family? In Landsberg, isn't it?"

"We did. I'll tell you about that some other time, Mommy."

"Katie didn't sound happy, Karl, I'll give her time. I believe something went wrong."

She didn't look happy anymore, she has been stressed out. When she came home from work, she went straight to her room after dinner. We hardly saw her.

After a few days, I caught her crying.

"Katie, are you ready to tell me what is going on? You are spending hours on the phone with Leopold, you have been crying, avoiding talking to me."

"I am conflicted and I don't know what to do yet, Mommy."

She asked me to come to her room, and showed me a ring.

"Leo gave me this ring in Munich on my birthday, it was his mother's, it's a family heirloom, but I am not sure I want to keep it.

Everything was fine in Munich, although I had already heard some things from him that didn't sit right with me, like if I gave him an office in our company's building downtown he would move his restoration business to Dusseldorf."

"What? He can't afford his own office space?"

"From then on I realized that his business comes far in between, he is not really invested in it, he doesn't do any restorations, he hires people to do it, when and if he gets a deal, he is the middleman. His office in Frankfurt is a room in his apartment.

Well, I kind of turned a blind eye to that. When we got to his village, at his family's old castle, I was shocked. The so called castle was a very old, run-down property in serious need of repair, they use only a few rooms, and still they are not well kept.

His mother and father are in their seventies, but they look older, they don't take care for themselves and they drink, they love to drink… I was horrified to see his mother, laughing one moment and falling asleep the other in the chair, drunk.

He introduced me to them as the heiress. Money was the topic of our conversation, and on the second day his mother told me that with my money and their title we could make that castle a palace and the village would prosper.

I understood that they had talked about using my money to renovate their place. I told her:

'I have no money, my father owns the factories that my grandfather worked very hard for, and I'm not the heiress, we are four, brothers and sisters and respective families, and I work very hard for the money the company pays me, I am an employee.'

The conversations between me and Leo continued being about money versus title. I told him that I had no interest in any title. I couldn't stay there for more than a few days.

We returned to Munich, and he tried to appease me, saying his parents didn't know what they were talking about. They were drunk.

Now I know that his family is bankrupt and they expect that Leo find someone rich to rescue them. He says no, that is not it, he truly loves me, but I am doubting."

"What about your feelings, do you love him, Katie?"

"I don't know, I thought I did, but maybe this was all an illusion. Again, here I am, being lured into a situation by a charming guy. What's wrong with me, Mommy? Why can't I find someone who means what they say? Why can't I find someone who loves me for who I am, not for what I have?"

"The only thing that went wrong is that you rushed into a situation without knowing exactly who you were dealing with, Katie. There is nothing wrong with you, you are deserving of being truly loved by an honest man. You'll find that man, just take your time, make your best decision now."

"He keeps repeating that he loves me, that he is crazy about me, that it has nothing to do with money, but I am not sure, I am confused, Mommy."

"Do you want to talk to Dad about this and get his perspective? He knows what a man with integrity is like, he would help you."

"No, I am embarrassed. I need to make a decision on my own. If I break up with Leo I am going to be alone and I'll miss him, if I stay it might be the biggest mistake I ever made in my life, besides the other one…"

"Katie, you are young, intelligent and beautiful. You have your life ahead, *liebling*. Don't let this bring you down. Leopold is charming and seductive as you said, but is he the right man for you? When you met him you told me you heard he had a playboy reputation. Who told you that?"

"Gunther, I remember he said he didn't know Leo very well, but he had a playboy reputation."

"Katie, when I hear 'playboy' I think of an inconsequential man, a player, just living in the moment, a *bon vivant*. What do you think?"

"You are right, Mommy. I think I missed that warning. The thing is, if I were sure about him and his intentions I would not be feeling this way, I would be happy to have this ring!"

I felt sad for my daughter. She is facing another disappointment, but she is very smart, she can make the best out of her life. I am praying that she does. I told her that by the end of May we are going to Berlin for Gabriel's performance, and she should come with us. She declined.

Gabriel called me two weeks before the concert to tell me that Miguel was going to be in Berlin.

"He is coming with Fabio. What do you think, Mama? Are you and Dad going to be annoyed seeing Miguel there? I didn't invite him, he found out and bought the tickets and he is all set to go."

"Thank you for telling me, don't feel bad, your events are advertised all over. I have no problem seeing him, but I am going to tell Dad, I believe he wouldn't care either. We are going to be there for you, son. Is Elise coming too?"

"Yes, Mama, we are very comfortable leaving Marie-Claire with Helene for a few days."

I told Karl, that didn't faze him at all.

He said, "We are staying at the Grand Hotel, it is a traditional place in a very convenient location. It has been a long time since I have been to Berlin, I'm looking forward to it."

Since the reunification of Germany in 1990, Berlin has become a popular destination for visitors. There are many places of interest, both in the town center and the outskirts, including historic monuments, museums, modern developments as well as places for recreation and amusement.

We arrived in Berlin the day before the concert. Elise spent the day with us while Gabriel was at the Konzerthaus, the concert hall.

Karl decided to rest, and Elise and I went to visit the Holocaust Denkmanl, the National Holocaust Memorial. We were impressed and saddened by the representation of a dark time when millions of lives were taken. No matter how much we know, it was devastating to see and learn more about it. We prayed!

We returned to the hotel, and Karl told us, "I made reservations for a late dinner after the concert tomorrow night. If Gabriel wants to invite his friends, they will be welcomed."

"Are you sure, Karl?"

"I am quite sure. They are Gabriel's friends, they came this far to see him, and I have to confess that I am a little curious..."

The next day Karl, Elise and I went out for the morning, but the afternoon was dedicated to getting ready for the gala event.

We arrived at the Konzerthaus, a magnificent theater building. We had special seats reserved for us.

The concert started and it was stunningly beautiful.

We didn't see Miguel and Fabio until intermission, when Elise and I went to the atrium for some refreshments.

Miguel approached us, "Nice seeing you ladies, you both look wonderful." Standing beside him was a young man, so identical to Gabriel that I knew immediately that was Fabio.

Miguel introduced me to his son. Elise had met him already in Amsterdam last year. Fabio was very pleasant.

"This concert is even more magnificent than the one I saw last year. I am glad to be here."

Miguel told me, "Gabriel invited me and Fabio for dinner at the Grand Hotel Esplanade, I hope that it is not an inconvenience."

"It is not, the invitation came from Karl. I need to return to my seat now. See you both later."

"Karl, I just saw Miguel and Fabio, they are coming for dinner."
"Alright," he smiled.

The concert continued. We felt proud of Gabriel standing tall and handsome with his violin, being accompanied by the symphony, he was at the peak of his career.

When it ended we met him at a side door where a car was waiting to take us back to the Grand Hotel, where Miguel and Fabio were waiting for us.

Gabriel introduced Karl:

"I have the pleasure to introduce you to my father, Karl Weisenwert."

The men shook hands in a cordial manner, Miguel thanked him for the invitation for dinner.

There was a large round table reserved for us.

Gabriel was relaxed. Karl observed him closely, how he was interacting with Fabio and Miguel. Gabriel never demonstrated any special closeness to Miguel, but he was friendlier with Fabio.

Karl whispered in my ear, "The boys look alike, but Miguel can't take his eyes off you..."

"That's why you are keeping me close and your arm around me, *liebe*?" I kissed him on his cheek. "I'm yours, don't worry."

Dinner was pleasant. Miguel didn't miss the opportunity to tell me a few words, "I am glad to see you happy, Clara, and Karl, as I expected, looks like an outstanding man."

"He is, Miguel. What about you? Are you happy with your life?"

"I am alright, I found peace."

"I am glad, Miguel."

Fabio told me: "I was looking forward to meet Gabriel's mother, he talks so much about you, so does this one here," he pointed to his father. "And you are everything they say."

"Thank you, Fabio, I am glad we had this chance to meet."

Karl signed the restaurant bill, and we excused ourselves.

Gabriel told us, "Mom and Dad, we will talk more in the morning before our flight."

Karl hugged me when we got to our suite.

"Now it's just the two of us, I liked the way you were around Miguel, totally unaffected."

"The way it should be, I feel indifferent about him."

The next morning Gabriel and Elise told us they stayed up for a while talking, then Miguel and Fabio went to their hotel, but Miguel told him:

"I appreciated meeting Karl, you have the father that you deserve."

We returned home feeling good about the experience.

"It was marvelous, Katie. How is everything with you?"

"Mommy, I broke up with Leo and returned his ring. But before I did that, I talked to Gunther and asked him what he knew about Baron Von Lesch. He said the rumor in their circle is that Leo is getting on with the high life without working hard for it, mostly depending on others' money or prestige. There goes eight months of my life that I can't get back..."

"Just move forward, Katie. I was thinking I want to visit Amie in New York, she is not coming home this summer, do you want to come along? Dad is not up for a long trip, we have travelled too much lately, and there are things at work that he wants to take care of."

"I miss New York, yes, let's have a shopping trip and see my little sis."

Summer in New York was hot! Very hot! Nevertheless the girls and I had a good time together. We briefly saw Alfred, he was mostly working at his fellowship, sometimes for twelve hours straight.

"Amie, I couldn't wait until the end of the year to see you!"

"Likewise, Mommy, I am so happy you are here."

Together we did some shopping for our Marie-Claire and Erik's baby, it's a boy to be born by the end of August! We also got some special requests from Lili, now a fashionable preteen.

When we returned, Karl was ready for his delayed visit to the South Alps.

"We will go by train, it is all reserved!"

"I am glad, enough of flying for a while."

Karl told me he spent a day at the Industrial Park, saw his old friends, and Otto introduced him to the young man he thinks is ready to replace him.

"Thank goodness Otto decided to stay until the end of the year."

"How young is his replacement?"

"He is thirty-two! He has been working with us since he graduated. He is a mechanical engineer, and we need more of those in the company, he is Herman Kiedrich's son.

Years ago we merged with his small brake factory. One of his requests was that we employ his son after graduating. I agreed, Kiedrich was a good and honest guy, and I hoped 'like father like son.' Since then he has been Otto's right arm."

"He is not too young for the job, you were the head of the company at that age, Erik was the V.P. at that same age, it's all relative!"

In the beginning of August, we went to the chalet in a resort in Bodensee, Lake Constance, and again Karl enjoyed the serenity and natural beauty of the surroundings, the simplicity of everyday clothing, hiking along mountain streams, fishing, and breathing that air… "The purest air in the world!"

It was a place where we felt totally in tune with nature and each other.

Two weeks later Erik and Louisa's baby boy was born! Maximilian Karl, Little Max, was not so little, he was a big, healthy baby and brought much joy to our family.

"Another grandchild, I already have four, two boys, two girls, the family keeps growing, and I love it!" Karl said.

I helped Louisa for a few days, mostly entertaining Lili and Will. She was doing really well.

Katie was getting more motivated, her friend Julia is getting married in September, before the summer is over, and invited Katie to participate in activities and preparations.

"I am involved! It's good to have my mind somewhere else. Julia is the only friend I have left here from my time in school. I also like her future husband, he is a nice guy. She is lucky!"

"You'll find your nice guy too, Katie!"

Occasionally I spoke to Gabriel or Elise, Marie-Claire is doing wonderfully and they will come for the holidays. Can't wait!

Elise told me that they see Fabio often, he visits them every time he flies to Vienna.

"Gabriel has an infinite number of friends all over Europe, he didn't have one in Spain. They have a connection, and I believe they have much to talk about."

"I am coming over to celebrate my granddaughter's first birthday! I can't believe she'll be one already! This first year went by too fast."

Katie attended Julia and Ernst's wedding in mid-September. There were several occasions, pre-wedding parties, the ceremony and reception were at the beautiful garden of her father-in-law's residence!

For a few days Katie was busy and happy. She was not talking about the Baron anymore.

After the wedding, she told me she had a great time.

"I met someone at the wedding reception, one of Ernst's friends from college, and he was really nice, I thought he is someone that I want to know better, I am going to see him on Sunday again."

"That sounds good, Katie, but take your time. Is he from Dusseldorf? What is his name?"

"Yes, but he lives on the west side, he has a job outside the city. Viktor and I danced all night. We exchanged phone numbers and we'll talk again, I hope. And yes, Mommy, I'll take my time, lesson learned."

On Sunday afternoon Katie went to meet Viktor at a café by the charming park of Hofgarten. She came back home around dinnertime, and she didn't look happy!

"What happened, Katie? Did you have a bad impression of him?"

"On the contrary I liked him, but there is a problem, he works at the Industrial Park!"

"Oh, he works for Dad's company!"

"Yes, the conversation about work came later, when he told me he lives outside the city on the northwest side to be close to his job at the W Industrial Park. I froze, I had told him that I work downtown as a financial analyst, I never mentioned I worked at Dad's company, he doesn't even know my last name. He is a mechanical engineer, he has worked there for eight years.

He loves his job and the people he works with, and he has a future there, he is in line for a big promotion... How could I ever tell him that is my father's company! Oh, Mommy, I am out of luck!"

"If he really doesn't know who you are, he did not have second intentions approaching you."

"I feel that he is sincere, but I couldn't tell him just yet, I like him. What do I do? He might run away when I tell him, 'by the way, you work for my father.'"

"Do you know his full name now?"

"Viktor Herman Kiedrich."

"Katie, I heard that name before from Dad. Do you want me to ask him? Or better, why don't you talk to Dad, he will shed some light. Are you planning to see Viktor again?"

"Yes, he said he'll call me and we'll meet after work one evening this week for dinner. Thank God I gave him only my cell number. He has no idea where I work."

On Monday evening Katie got the courage to tell Karl about her new friend.

"Viktor Kiedrich! He is the young man that Otto recommended as his replacement. I knew his father, I did business with him for a long time until we acquired his company. He moved out of town, I haven't seen him in years."

"He is in Bonn now, Viktor told me his mother always wanted to go back to her hometown."

"I know Otto likes Viktor, he spoke highly about his professional skills. But we never know how he is as a man until we get to know him better. If you want to continue seeing him, tell him the truth, Katie. Take your time getting to know if he really deserves you. I don't want to see you hurt."

"Daddy, don't you mind if I see one of your employees?"

"Of course not, we have over a thousand employees, how can we avoid people crossing paths, just don't dive into a relationship without knowing him well."

"I feel better, Daddy, I thought you would oppose for conflict of interest."

"I do not oppose it, just don't disclose classified business information, that applies to everyone."

A few days later, Katie had a dinner date with Viktor, and she went prepared to have an open talk with him.

Later when she returned home, she came to talk to me.

"Mommy, Viktor started out telling me that after a broken engagement a year ago he thought he would not be getting romantically involved anytime soon with anyone, but I made him change his mind and he wanted to pursue a relationship with me. He asked me what I thought, if I was up to see where life would take us. He said he likes me and that he is very attracted to me.

I told him I liked him too, and I would like to continue seeing him, but there was something I needed to tell him. And I went straight to the point and told him that I also work for the Weisenwert Industries!

He thought that was just a coincidence and asked me why I didn't mention it before, he was concerned about any company's policy that employees can't date.

I said there was not such a policy, and our work should not interfere with our personal relationship because we work in different areas and locations.

He agreed and then asked me, 'If you are in the central office you probably have met Erik and 'The Boss,' haven't you?'

I took a deep breath and told him straight up, 'Erik is my brother, and 'The Boss,' Karl Weisenwert, is my father.'

Mommy, Viktor got so pale I thought he was going to pass out. He became very concerned about me being 'The Boss's daughter! 'This changes everything for us!' he said.

I asked him if it would change everything just because he works for my father's company. And also, when he met me, if he had any idea that my last name was Weisenwert.

He guaranteed he had no idea and that he meant it when he said he liked me, and he was looking forward to see me again. 'If your family doesn't have any restrictions on you dating an employee... What do you think your father would say?'

I told him not to worry and 'let's see where this will take us...' And my father always said the same thing to me and my sister, he wanted us to find a man of character and integrity, who will love and respect us for who we are, and if not, we should let them go before anyone gets hurt."

"Katie, it sounds like he is invested in you. The only thing you should do, for now, is to not bring him home until Dad makes the decision about Otto's replacement. The fact that you know Viktor personally should not influence Dad's decision."

"I respect that, I am going to take my time, Mommy. I think I am on the right track, I really, really like him."

The next couple of months went by in a flash. Erik assigned more responsibilities to Katie. We hardly saw her, many times she came home later, after having dinner in the city with Viktor.

They also went out together every weekend, the only comment she made was that things between them were going pretty well.

From my side I divided my time between visiting Louisa and my new baby grandson Max, working with Martha on the Foundation, and occasionally visiting the Children's Home.

The other day Karl complained a little:

"You are getting too busy, I want to spend more time with you when I am at home, *meine liebe*."

"With the holidays approaching, there is much to take care of, but you are always my priority, *liebe*."

Karl asked me to prepare a festive dinner party to celebrate Otto's retirement.

"I am inviting Otto, Heinrich and their wives. Heinrich will be retiring next year and graciously he told me to promote new blood to the director's position, but while he is still there he'll gladly assist the new director.

Erik and I agreed, and we are offering the job to Viktor Kiedrich, he has proved that he is qualified and he is not going to retire anytime soon…"

"I'll prepare the best reception for them, is anyone else coming?"

"Yes, Erik is going to give you a list of Otto's friends, they are directors for other divisions of the company. I will personally call to invite them. I think we will have about eighteen to twenty guests."

"Alright, it is a bigger number than I thought, but it will be done. Are you inviting the new director too?"

"Not this time, this reception is a farewell for Otto only and the old timers. Is Katie still seeing Viktor?"

"Yes, Karl, she is and she likes him very much."

"In that case tell her that after I make the official announcement, she can invite him to our home. I didn't want to mix personal and business before that decision."

"Our daughter will be thrilled, *liebe*."

I organized a sumptuous dinner party for Otto, his wife and their friends. With Hilda's help, everything came out excellent.

Karl was actually happy seeing Otto starting his new life.

"It's good when I see my friends embarking on a new venture, healthy and with disposition to enjoy it. I wish a good new life to you, Otto, and thank you much for your contributions. Hope our friendship continues for many years to come!"

Otto will continue being part of the board of directors and he will join Karl and Erik in meetings at the central office.

Our Amie is back home for the holidays. Arriving, she told me that Alfred invited her to meet his parents in Wiesbaden, she won't stay with us for the whole week.

"It will be only for two days, Mommy. I will be here for Christmas and also for the New Year. Then Fred and I will have one more semester in New York City, we will be back for good in the summer."

"I like the sound of that, *liebling,* you will be coming home soon."

"I will, Mommy, and I will not go anywhere else, I never want to be away from you again, I'll be living right here at home."

Karl and the girls surprised me with a birthday celebration. "Please everyone, forget how old I am, I don't feel old yet, it was just the other day when I was young!"

This holiday season was even more beautiful than the past, now with the addition of our two new grandbabies. Marie-Claire, a toddler, is all over the place, running, talking, she is delightful. Max is the happiest baby.

We have a beautiful family! I love my family!

As usual Erik, Louisa, Lili, Will and Max left for a ski resort. Gabriel and Elise returned to perform in Vienna.

Amie went to Wiesbaden with Alfred to meet his family, and returned the next day.

"I was very welcomed in the family, they are very nice people, father, mother, sister and brother-in-law. I liked them all."

Katie was alone with us. Viktor went to Bonn to see his parents, but they have a planned, end of year party with their newlywed friends Julia and Ernst.

The year started out cold, extremely cold and snowy. Karl was apprehensive about his upcoming annual check-up. Like every year we felt anxious, but luckily everything was alright.

I wish we could forget he had cancer, I wish we never had to revisit that again, it is like a cloud hanging over us. On those tense days I reminded him:

"Live in the present, let's not worry about tomorrow…"

Katie finally brought Viktor home. It was an unscheduled occasion, they showed up for dinner.

The first thing he told Karl was that he wanted us not to have any doubts about his intentions. He seemed sincere, I liked him and I could see why Katie was in love with him. I thought she found her match.

Karl told him he was welcomed in our home and asked about his father. "I haven't seen your father in a long time. Is Herman happy in Bonn?"

"My father is fine, but my mother has been ill for a while, and he is very worried about her. She had emphysema for a long time, but now is getting worse, it doesn't look good."

"I hope she recovers, it is very depressing to go through a chronic illness, I wish your mother well."

After Viktor left, Katie thanked us for being welcoming to him. "I was thinking for a while that there was no hope for me, all my friends and even my little sister, they are all coupled up, and then Viktor came into my life, and I feel I found my better half. I love him."

She believes that the romance between them is promising.

Hilda and Franz had gone to Koblenz. Franz came back alone, Hilda stayed a little longer. When she returned, she was distressed and talked to me in private.

"I was taking care of my cousin, and it is very serious. Years ago we became partners buying a bed and breakfast, the business is doing well, but she can't manage it alone anymore. Her daughter, my niece, has two small children and another on the way.

I am sorry, but I need to leave. I need to go to Koblenz to help Erma and take care of our business."

Hilda broke into tears. She couldn't continue talking for a while.

"Hilda, I understand your need to help your cousin. Maybe if you take a leave of absence, for whatever time you need, that might be enough. You won't have to quit your job."

"No, Frau Clara, she is not the only reason I'm leaving Dusseldorf, it is also about me and Franz. We are going our separate ways."

"This is shocking! You and Franz separating? You have lived here with us for more than twenty years and I never noticed any problems between the two of you... What is happening?"

"Frau Clara, I could never forgive him, and with time our relationship became distant, now I have the opportunity to start a new life away from Franz.

In this house I was always treated like family, I love all of you, but please understand that there is a time in life that we need to break away. I am getting older and I feel like there is not much left for me."

"Hilda, I support you in that. You have your business and your family in Koblenz, but I can't understand, what did Franz do that you can't forgive him?"

"When we came to work for you, we had lost our little daughter Helga. She was born with muscular dystrophy and lived only four years, always sick, she didn't develop like a normal child.

My heart was ripped out of my chest when my daughter died. Then I came to your house, I gave your children all the love I had, and that helped me survive my loss.

It was not until years later that I learned that two other people in Franz's family had perished of the same disease. Franz never told me, not before we got married, not even when our Helga was born. When I found out, I couldn't forgive him for not telling me, we could have prevented it. I love children, I was meant to be a mother. After my Helga died I felt guilty and I could never try to bring another sick child into the world. He robbed me of my daughter's life!"

"Hilda, maybe he didn't tell you because he didn't know he was at risk of having a child with that condition, maybe he has suffered as much as you with the loss of your child."

"That's what he always said, but no matter what, my heart closed off to him."

"Hilda, I am not going to tell you how you should feel, but harboring bitterness makes you suffer more. Losing a child is the worst that can happen to a mother, and I am very sorry that happened to you, and I understand why you want to go away. I do wish that you may overcome those feelings and your heart lightens."

"Frau Clara, you have given me the best life here, I love you and your family, and I will miss you all."

I embraced her, "You have been a friend to all of us, you are like family, we will miss you, Hilda. Come back to see us whenever you can."

I told my husband: "Karl, I didn't see it coming and I can't understand why a person like Hilda has harbored ill feelings for so long. I truly wish her well. She was wonderful with us and our family, we will all miss her."

"That means that Franz is staying with us? Are you letting Hilda go just like that, with no notice? Who's replacing her?"

"She is in a hurry, Karl, her cousin is ill. Franz is going to talk to me tomorrow, today when I tried he became emotional. And among our maids, we have Doris, she is with us for years, she is reliable, very organized, she has spoken to Hilda before, asking for more responsibilities. I'll talk to her on Friday."

The next morning Hilda left the house sobbing, I was heartbroken to see her go. "Hilda, our door will always be open for you."

After Franz dropped Hilda off at the train station, he returned home and spoke to me.

"I'm sorry I couldn't talk to you yesterday, Frau Clara, I was broken but not surprised by Hilda's sudden decision. She had threatened to leave me, but I thought she would never do it."

"What is going on, Franz? We need to know if you are staying with us or if you are going to follow her to Koblenz."

"I am not following her, this is more than a job to me, it's home! To be honest, I am relieved Hilda is leaving. She has blamed me for our daughter's death all of our lives. I never expected to have an ill child, our little one suffered so much throughout her short life. It was devastating. Hilda blamed me, and as she continued accusing me, I gave up. For many years both of us have been living a very lonely life.

Frau Clara, I truly believe she will be happier without me."

"Franz, I am sorry for what happened, I do accept she has the right to live her life the way she chooses, and I am glad you are staying with us."

"Thank you, please count on me."

"Franz, please tell me what you know about Doris. She had asked me for a full time position and eventually she could be a possible replacement for Hilda."

"I think she is very responsible and hard working. She lives in the city with her in-laws and her two children. She has told me that the conditions she lives in are precarious, and all the money she makes goes into the household. Many times she asked Hilda for leftovers to bring to her family. She struggles."

I spoke to Doris on Friday, and offered her the full-time position along with more responsibilities.

"Where do you live, Doris? Is it easy for you to come this way every day?"

"I live on the far west side of town, I take two different buses to come here, but working in your house is a privilege. I thank you for the offer, I desperately need to earn more money for my family."

"Tell me about your family, Doris."

"Since my husband left, my in-laws allowed us to live with them. I have a son and a daughter, ages thirteen and eleven. They are in school all day. The grandparents don't have much, and I am responsible for providing food for all and the extras that the children need. My dream was to have a job where I would be able to support my children and myself without depending on them.

I'll work as long hours as you need, I'll meet all the needs of your house and your family. You'll not be disappointed, Frau Clara."

"Doris, for now I'll be managing the house staff and you'll work longer hours, as time goes on and we need more of your collaboration I'll discuss it with you. To start, I am going to ask Franz to drive you to the supermarket to pick up a few items."

For the next months, Hilda did not contact Franz or us to say how she was doing in Koblenz, but things were well taken care of at home.

I saw Karl becoming somehow withdrawn. From his conversations with Erik I understood that there were problems with the factories.

"Karl, please, you need to tell me what is going on, it's clear that there is a problem. Don't shut me out."

"I don't mean to shut you out, Clara, you are right, I am very concerned and I think it's crucial I go with Erik to New York City for a meeting with our old customers. They told Erik that they are moving out of state, reducing costs and planning to produce their own engines.

That is very bad news, if they discontinue the use of the genuine engines that we provide, we might lose a considerable volume of business, and eventually we will have to lay off employees or close one of our factories."

"Karl, that is serious, but I am more worried about you, this stress can't do you any good. What can I do to help you?"

"I do not mean to worry you, Clara."

"Do you really need to go with Erik to New York? Remember that when you were Erik's age you were there negotiating this same deal. Don't you think he can handle this business by himself? You taught him well!"

"I trust him, but this situation needs a reinforcement, and you are right, thirty years ago is when I started this trade, and we can't lose it now."

"In that case, Karl, I'll go with you. I'll spend time with our daughter, and I will watch after you. I'm coming!"

We flew to New York City, Karl, Erik and I. Amie was waiting for us.

"I am so glad to see my family here! I am alone most of the time."

Amie's roommate had moved back to Seattle, and Alfred was always busy with his internship.

The first round of meetings was grueling. They were ready to move out of the State of New York, and invited Karl and Erik to visit their new car assembly line in Texas.

"As a gesture of goodwill we are flying down to Texas."

"Are you sure, Karl? Are you up for it?"

"Yes, I am feeling alright and I believe we are going to come to a beneficial compromise."

While Karl and Erik went to Texas, and my daughter was at the hospital, I spent a delightful afternoon with my only American friend Caroline, who lives in the same building. She is a lovely woman, and now that she is also a grandmother we have more to talk about.

Amie came home, "Mommy, can you believe I'll be done in a couple of months and I'll be coming home, this time for good!"

"Oh, *liebling*, it will be like a dream, my two girls living at home..."

"How is Katie doing with her new boyfriend?"

"She is happy, it does look like this is the one she is going to marry. Viktor is very serious about her.

But I have some other news for you, Amie, I told you Hilda went to help her cousin, she is not coming back, she moved to Koblenz permanently."

"Why? She is not at the age of retirement yet!"

"The truth is she left Franz and decided to start a new life managing her bed and breakfast with her cousin."

"What a shock! I'll miss Hildie, she was so sweet! How is Franz? Is he going to move away too?"

"He is fine, he is staying with us, and he has helped me quite a lot after Hilda left."

Karl and Erik came back from Texas.

"We are alright! We have renegotiated our contracts and it is not going to affect our production, consequently we won't need to cut any jobs in Dusseldorf!"

"That's wonderful news, you are still the master dealmaker, *liebe*."

Erik returned to Dusseldorf immediately, but Karl and I stayed a couple of days longer with our daughter, out and about the city.

On our last day Karl told us, "I feel like celebrating and getting something special for our girls. Let's go to Fifth Avenue, to that famous jewelry store!"

"Jewelry? That's so unlike you, Karl."

Amie quickly responded. "Let's go, Daddy!"

The three of us walked down the Avenue, Karl made some extravagant purchases, two diamond bracelets.

"To celebrate the best gifts of our lives, our two beautiful daughters!"

CHAPTER EIGHT

BEAUTIFUL FAMILY

*W*e returned home to Dusseldorf. Good to be back!

I called Gabriel, it had been a long time.

"We just came back from New York, and I was thinking of visiting you now, but it might be better to come in the fall for Marie-Claire's birthday!"

"Mama, Elise and I are planning to come and see you before the end of the summer, after the concert in Kohl."

"That will be wonderful, son! It looks like our family is going to be all together this summer, we will celebrate Amie's return home in style!"

I asked Franz if he had heard from Hilda recently.

"As a matter of fact I did. Erma passed away and Hilda is definitely not coming back, but she told me that she misses you and your daughters and she'll come to visit you someday."

"What about the two of you, Franz? Did she ask you to join her?"

"On the contrary, she wants our situation to be official, I am ready for it. I'll sign the divorce papers anytime."

"You and Hilda divorced! Life is full of surprises, Franz. But let me ask you about work. How are you and Doris getting along?"

"She is an easy person to get along with. I always drive her to pick up groceries. And the other day when you were away, I drove her home, it was raining... I was sad to see that she lives in a small house. She said she doesn't have a room there, she sleeps on the sofa. Imagine, after a long day of working, she takes two buses and doesn't have a decent place to rest.

Excuse me for asking, are you considering offering her the house management position?"

"I had thought of that, Franz, but she has two children in school, I don't know if she would move, and I only have one room available downstairs in the employee quarters, the butler's suite, we never had a butler."

"Frau Clara, allow me to suggest if you bring Doris and her children here, I'll move to the butler's suite and you can place her in my apartment. There is space enough for a family there."

"Are you willing to forgo your apartment, Franz? You really like Doris!"

He blushed! Something is going on...

"She is a very nice person, she had her share of suffering, and I would like to help her."

I called Hilda in Koblenz to offer my condolences. She told me she is invested in the bed and breakfast and also helping out her niece with the children.

"I live for others, I feel like I am doing my best for them and that makes me happy."

I asked if her mind was permanently made up, if she is not planning to return to Dusseldorf or to her husband.

"My relationship with Franz was over a long time ago, but I'll come to visit you and the girls, I miss you all!"

Knowing that Hilda's decision is permanent, I told Doris that my younger daughter is returning home in June, and with her around, with her boyfriend, plus Katie and her boyfriend, plus Erik's family and my son Gabriel and family coming this summer, we are going to have a full house and we definitely need more help.

"You have been doing a great job, Doris, therefore I am ready to offer you the management position, and with that comes housing. Are you willing to move to our estate?"

"Move to this wonderful property, it is like a dream! But my children are in school, I don't know if I can. Maybe the grandparents won't approve of that, I need to talk to them."

"Doris, if you move here, transfer the children to the school in our area, I don't believe that is your in-laws' decision."

Doris started crying.

"Please don't cry, this could actually be very good for your children, they will have better education and would always be close."

"Frau Clara, I thank Heaven for the day you hired me to work in your home. Yes, I'll move as soon as the school year is over. Would you please help me with the school transfer? What do I need to do?"

"I'll call our school tomorrow and I'll give you the information. There is more, Franz is willing to move into the butler's suite to give you and your children the apartment over the garage."

She cried even more. "I'm sorry, I can't stop crying. I never cried happy before in my life."

I told Karl in the evening:

"Giving the job to Doris, we are helping her raise her two children. I feel good about this decision."

Louisa brought to my attention that she is having problems with Lili.

"My teenager needs more of my attention than my baby. As a matter of fact she is jealous of the time I spend with Max. She is asking me for mother-daughter time alone, like a shopping trip. Imagine if I can do that!"

"Louisa, you can do it, you should go on a trip with your daughter, you will bond together and she'll have a lasting memory. Where does she want to go?"

"To New York, Tante Amie is there, and you know how Lili idolizes her, she wants us to go as soon as school is over."

"If you decide to go, leave Max and Will with us, I'd love to have them here, and Grandpa Karl too."

"Oh, Clara, you always have the best advice! When I told this to my mother, she responded, 'Don't spoil her!' I see your point and thank you for the help."

Louisa and Liliane went to New York City. They spent five days with Amie! And had a great time!

Amie came home with Alfred by the end of June! They completed their fellowships, and they are now ready to start working.

Alfred went right back to the Hospital, where he resumed his position. Amie was in negotiations with a pediatric practice, she will do turns at the Hospital, checking on her patients. Her new job will start in the fall. She had some well deserved vacations until the end of the summer.

"I am so glad my *little doctor* is home again!"

Katie is going steady with Viktor. He took her to Bonn to meet his parents.

His father was delighted to meet 'Karl Weisenwert's daughter.'

"But it was sad to see his mother, she is on oxygen, didn't look good at all. Viktor thinks she won't live long, that's why he goes constantly to visit her. I felt sorry for him, I could see he is a good son, he loves his parents."

Doris moved into the guest house in August. She had a hard time convincing her in-laws she needed to move out for her new job.

"They made it difficult and made me promise I'll bring the children to see them every weekend. I'm sure they were more concerned about me not being there, providing for everything. They have their retirement, which should be enough."

Gabriel, Elise and Marie-Claire showed up in September. Our granddaughter is a doll. So cute! She is fluent in her own way. She went around talking to everyone: *Tanti Kat, Tanti Am, Popa Karl, Moma Clara*. She also mentioned her *Onk Fabo*.

"Do you see, Mama? She made up special names for everyone and she can't pronounce 'uncle' and has a hard time saying 'Fabio,' he is a very fun uncle. As a matter of fact we see him often, he visits us every time he flies to Vienna."

"Gabe, I like that you have a connection with a Spanish relative about your age, and through him you are learning more about your heritage."

"Talking about heritage, Mama, I was thinking that you never had the interest to find your father, you really don't know who he was. I tend to believe that was one of the reasons that you agreed with me to meet my biological father, for which I am grateful. I have no unanswered questions."

"I didn't miss having a father, Gabe. Growing up I had a loving mother, and in a twist of fate life brought me validation, love, friendship, support from wonderful men: George, who I will always consider my brother; Karl, my husband; and you, my beloved son!"

On Saturday Katie and Amie were very excited, running around, preparing the house for our family reunion.

"Girls, what are all of these flowers for? I thought we are having a pool party!"

They just smiled.

In the afternoon we got a surprising visit: Hilda!

"Hildie!" The girls ran to her. Amie whispered something in her ear. *'What is the secret?'* I thought.

I embraced her.

"Hilda, I didn't expect to see you today, but I am happy you are here."

"Katie invited me and I couldn't miss the opportunity to see the girls and you, I missed you all."

"We missed you too, Hilda. Are you happy in Koblenz?"

"Yes, the family and the business are all doing very well."

She went to talk to Franz.

Erik, Louisa, Lili, Will and Baby Max arrived.

Katie and Amie brought me upstairs.

"Mommy, come, Daddy wants to talk to you, he is waiting in

your suite. Then come to my room, Amie and I have a surprise for you."

"What's going on? Everybody is so mysterious today."

"Karl, why are you formally dressed up, it's just the family!"

"No, *meine liebe*, it is our wedding anniversary celebration! That's why the whole family is here. That day in New York when we were walking by Saint Patrick's Cathedral I remembered that we never had a proper wedding. So, I thought of making a great celebration on our anniversary by the end of the year, but why wait? *'Nothing is worth more than this day!'* I want to ask you: *'Willst du mich heiraten?'*"

"Karl, are you asking me to marry you, again? Of course I will marry you over and over, *liebe*. Now I know why the girls are so secretive! When did you tell them?"

"That afternoon, right there at Tiffany's, I asked for Amie's help... We are renewing our vows today! I invited Pastor Meyer to officiate it."

"Pastor Meyer! Vows?"

"I am serious, Clara, we are doing it right this time, with our family, music and flowers! It's our wedding!"

I kissed him over and over, "Who said you are not romantic, *mein mann!*"

The girls were waiting for me, Katie and Louisa had bought me a long dress with just a hint of color, pink, so delicate, whimsical!

"Your favorite color, Mommy, baby pink, goes so well with your skin tone."

"I don't know what to say, I never really had a wedding celebration. Me, a sixty year old bride!"

When the girls and I went downstairs, I was surprised to see the children prepared for the occasion, the den's wide French doors opened, the room decorated with my most favorite flowers, pink roses.

Amie and Katie were standing as my bridesmaids. Erik was with Karl, and Gabriel was playing the Wedding March.

Karl held my hand and we walked slowly to Pastor Meyer, greeting us with a wide smile.

He officiated the ceremony, I was emotional like a young bride.

Karl told me words that he never said in the presence of others:

"Since the moment I met you, you taught me what love is. Now in the presence of our family and friends I publicly declare how much I love you!"

"Karl, with you I found happiness and fulfillment, you gave me the best life I could dream of, the best family! No man on this earth can be compared to you, you are my one and only true, lasting love of my life. Thank you for marrying me, again!"

Karl gave me a new wedding band, an exact match for my ring. Later Amie told me that he got it that day in New York while she distracted me.

We celebrated our marriage. Like in any other relationship there are joys and sorrows, challenges and victories, but where there is love anything is possible!

After our romantic ceremony Viktor told Katie, "Your parents are an example to follow, that is the kind of marriage that I want for us."

"Mommy, this was the first time Viktor talked about marriage."

Later in our suite Karl held me. "We will follow this day with a honeymoon. Where do you want to go, *meine liebe?*"

"Anywhere that's quiet and peaceful, anywhere that is just you and I, if you are there anywhere is the best place!"

I thanked life for this blessing. Once my dear friend Bertha told me, *'A happy marriage is like Heaven on earth!'*

"I am in Heaven!"

Our family and friends left the next day.

Hilda invited me to come and visit her in the Rhineland.

"One of the most romantic regions of Germany, very suitable for a couple like you."

"I'll see you, Hilda, and I will always remember how loving you were with my children, how much you helped me. You have friends here, you are always welcomed in our house."

Franz drove her to the train station.

He told me later that Hilda left on good terms, she apologized to him for the years of accusations and bitterness, and gave him the divorce papers.

Before Amie started her new job at the pediatric clinic, Fred took a couple of days to bring her to Wiesbaden to visit his family.

"Amie, feel free to invite your future in-laws to come here and stay with us."

"Are you sure, Mommy? I was thinking I should invite them for our engagement by the end of the year."

"That's great news, did you and Alfred discuss the wedding?"

"We did, we are together for almost three years, our relationship overcame the long distance."

She told me more about his family. His father Konrad is a landscaper; Hermine, his mother, is a medical office attendant; his sister Inge became a nurse.

"I would love to meet them, Amie."

"Mommy, I think they would be intimidated coming to our house, they live very modestly."

"We will make them feel welcomed. Tell them Daddy and I are looking forward to meet them."

Karl asked me, "Did you decide where you want to go for our honeymoon?"

"*There is no place like home, liebe!*"

"What do you mean, you want to stay home? Where did I hear that, Clara?"

"The Wizard of Oz! No matter how magical the world is, home is always the place we want to go back to. For me our home is the most romantic place to be, walking outside in the cool air of the fall in this peaceful garden, looking down the riverbank, sleeping in our own bed, loving one another.

This is the place where we built our family, this is where I want to be with you, Karl."

"I like the way you think, it is the most meaningful place for us, I agree."

At the beginning of November, Viktor's father called him, his mother was taking her last breaths, there was nothing the doctors could do. Katie accompanied him to Bonn. We asked her to call us, we wanted to pay our respects.

Two days later Katie called us. Viktor's mother had died. Karl and I went to Bonn to attend the funeral.

Viktor and his father were very touched to see us there. Herman embraced Karl. "So long, old friend, thank you for coming."

I hadn't met him before. Karl and Herman were collaborators and work friends, but he never had been to our house.

He told me, "I am glad to finally meet you, and I am very pleased with the relationship between my Viktor and your beautiful daughter. They make a perfect couple."

Karl, Katie and I returned to Dusseldorf, Viktor stayed a few more days, helping his father.

When he returned he brought Herman along, and told Katie:

"We decided to close the house in Bonn, I couldn't leave my father alone there. He is going to be here with me at least for a while."

Katie told me, "The house Viktor lives in was once his parents'. I won't spend time with him there for now, his father is mourning, I think he needs his time to reflect and consider how his life is going to be from now on. I hope this won't interfere with our plans. Viktor had talked to me about engagement and marriage, soon."

"Soon, Katie? Are you ready for it?"

"I think so, Mommy, I love Viktor, I want to live my life with him."

"Erik had told Daddy that he likes Viktor, and said he is one of the best directors the company has, and he is like one of us."

"That is how I feel, Mommy, he belongs in our family."

Amie was working at her new pediatric clinic and enjoying the new friendships that she has formed with the other doctors. Alfred was very absorbed with his duties. He shares a small apartment by the Hospital with two other doctors.

Karl told Amie that Alfred would be welcome to live in our house with her, after the wedding…

Katie assumed more responsibilities at work, Erik and Karl were impressed with her expertise and dedication to the job. Sometimes she stayed with Viktor in his house in the suburbs.

"It is a very nice house, but I would not want to live there permanently, I would rather live downtown, I am a city girl!"

I sat with Doris and Franz to discuss our plans for the holidays. "We are having a full house again this year."

"We will have all the help we need, and they love to come here for the extra holiday pay," Doris told me.

"What about you, Franz? Do you need any more help to decorate the grounds?"

"I have it all lined up already with the gardener's crew."

"What about time off? What are you planning?"

"I only need Christmas Day off, Frau Clara, I have to take my children to visit their grandparents," Doris spoke.

"The same," Franz told me. "I only need a day off to visit my friends."

The holidays are here! Gabriel, Elise and Marie-Claire are home with us. What a joy! As usual Erik, Louisa and the children came on Christmas Eve and stayed till the morning, they left after opening presents.

Viktor joined us on Christmas Day and he brought his father. Herman was doing better, he looked upbeat and told us he is going back to Bonn to make arrangements with the house and things that his wife left, and he will make the decision to come and stay with his son in Dusseldorf, permanently.

Viktor talked to Karl about him and Katie: "I love your daughter and I want to marry her. We have discussed it and Katie wants the same. Do I have your consent, Herr Weisenwert? I also want to tell you that I discussed a prenuptial agreement with Katie. I don't want anyone to have any concerns about my participation in the family business. I have no other interest but to be one of your employees."

"You are very welcomed in our family, Viktor, and you have my blessing to marry my daughter. Regarding a prenuptial, I think

Katie is the one to decide that."

Katie told me they won't celebrate an engagement this end of the year, first because Viktor recently lost his mother, and second she wants Amie to have her special day.

"But, Viktor and I have decided we are getting married next year!"

"So it is, we will have a double wedding at our house!"

The Bautzers arrived. What a jolly family! Konrad and Hermine are simple and warm people. Inge and Marten, Alfred's sister and brother-in-law, were also very kind. None of them disguised their astonishment seeing our house.

"This is a palace! And you are like a queen, Frau Clara!"

"Please call me Clara, thank you for the compliment but I am not a queen, I am a modest woman at heart. And I love this opportunity to share our home with your family, Hermine!"

The New Year's celebration was an engagement party, not only for a few of Alfred and Amie's friends. This time there were a lot of people, including some of Katie and Viktor's friends. It was a very beautiful night!

Karl and I stayed up later than usual, sharing the happy occasion with our family and friends. Our home was filled with cheers and joy!

As the year started, Doris asked to talk to me.

"I recognize that this is my personal issue, but I appreciate your opinion, Madame. I am very worried. My in-laws are threatening to take my children away from me, my son and daughter are terrified of them and they don't want to see them anymore."

"Doris, you have to tell me everything. Why would they threaten you?"

"Almost six years ago my husband abandoned us. I tried to keep my head above water, cleaning houses while the children were in school, but I ran out of resources. That's when my in-laws offered for the three of us to move in with them. They told me that I needed to pay for everything to keep the roof over our heads.

My father-in-law blamed me for my husband leaving us. That

was not true, I had put up with Egon's violent outbursts for years, and he was also lazy, quitting jobs frequently and not providing for us. When he left he said he was going to get rich and never told me where he was going. I am quite sure my in-laws know where he is. My mother-in-law has told me that Egon is coming back to take the children from me.

My in-laws were very upset when we moved out, and now they are saying that if I don't bring the children to visit every week, and also bring food for them, they are calling Social Services to remove Chris and Hanne from me."

"That's ludicrous, Doris, they can't take your children away. You are a good mother and you are providing for your son and daughter, I can testify to that. Did their father send any money since he has been gone?"

"Never, not a coin, not even a card. Hanne was five years old the last time she saw her father, she hardly remembers him, and Chris doesn't want to talk about him anymore."

"Have you made up your mind about continuing being married to Egon? Are you waiting for his return?"

"For Heaven's sake, no, I want him out of my life for good."

"I think you need help from Social Services, you need to file for full custody of your children. It can be a long process, they will guide you through everything. I'll find the office in our area and I'll set an appointment for you, Doris. They probably are going to investigate and corroborate with witnesses. They might provide you a counselor to deal with the legal matters."

"Thank you, Frau Clara. What should I do in the meantime? Egon's parents are demanding that I bring the children on Sunday again, but they don't want to go back there anymore."

"A social worker will tell you what you should do, Doris."

A few days later Doris went for her appointment with Social Services, she came back with paperwork to take care of. She asked me for time off to go back to the children's previous school to get testimonies. They recommended that she would not bring the children to the grandparents' home, but at her discretion they could see them in a neutral place.

"My in-laws were enraged, they said it is on their terms or nothing!"

"Just follow the legal procedures, Doris. Be patient, in the end things will work out. Social Services always looks after what is in the best interest of the children."

Katie was a little upset. Herman returned from Bonn and decided to set residence with his son. Viktor was happy to have his father around, he had told Katie that after getting married they could live all together. She disagreed.

"No way I am living in that house outside the city with my father-in-law. The house is pretty good, in a nice neighborhood, but it is not like ours where there is so much more space and privacy. I want to live in the city with Viktor, alone."

"I understand, Katie, and I support that. You need to have your independence as a new couple, even if you decide to live here, you could maintain that independence, but not in a smaller house."

"Exactly, Mommy, Viktor does not want to live here because it is much further away from the Industrial Park, and he doesn't want to commute a long distance."

"Katie, invite Viktor and his father to come on the weekend. Dad is friends with Herman, maybe he will find a way of talking to him and helping."

They showed up on Sunday for lunch. Herman told Karl that he had made his final decision to come back to Dusseldorf.

"Bonn was Marion's town, where her whole family lives. That's why I moved there, but here I have my only son, I would like to be close to him. Right now I am a little lost with nothing to do, I need to create new interests to keep myself busy."

"Well, do you want to do volunteer work, Herman?"

"Anything that I would feel useful."

"I can introduce you to Martha, our Foundation administrator, she might have something you could do to help in fundraising. I found that helping improve the lives of others is rewarding."

"Absolutely, Karl, I think I like that."

"Done! And we can also do something together in the spring and summer, just for fun. Do you like golf?"

"As a matter of fact, I do."

"After Otto retired, I meet him once a week at a golf course, and we play and move around, come along!"

And just like that, Karl gave a new perspective to Herman's life.

Gabriel called me to give me some totally unexpected news.

"Mama, I am on my way to Madrid to see Fabio. He called me with bad news, he is very distressed… Miguel has died. Fabio was flying and when he came home he found his father dead. It looks like it was a heart attack."

It felt like a punch to my chest, 'Miguel has died!'

"Mama, I am sorry to give you this news. Are you alright?"

"I am shocked, son. How are you feeling?"

"I feel like I lost one of my friends, and that my friend lost his father. I know how close they were, that's why I am going to visit him, I want to offer Fabio my support."

"That's noble of you, Gabe, I am sure Fabio appreciates your friendship. Are you sure you don't feel anything towards Miguel?"

"I feel grateful that I was able to get to know him, the image that I had in my head about him changed, I met a better man and I liked him."

"Gabe, I am sorry that he died alone, and I am glad that we found him, that also changed my memory of him for the best."

I had a sad feeling all day and I told Karl about it. He embraced me.

"I know, Clara, there was a time in your life when you loved that man, but you made peace with him."

"I feel sorry that not even his son was there at his side, Miguel was so lonely."

When Gabriel returned from Madrid he updated me on Fabio's state of mind.

"He is really sad, his father was his best friend, I feel empathy towards him. Fabio also told me that his father never got over the remorse he had for rejecting me. I think it is horrible to live with regrets."

"It is, son, but only people that have a conscience will feel regret. In essence he was a good man and I am glad I had the opportunity to wish him well, I meant it. May he rest in peace."

Amie and Alfred's wedding date was set for June. It will be at the local church with a reception at our mansion.

Katie and Viktor decided to get married by the end of the year, after they find a house in the city. Herman convinced his son that he will be alright living in their house alone, Viktor can always see him on his way to work.

The excitement was at a new level in our house, Amie was very calm about it, but I hardly could contain myself! We have discussed everything: dress, flowers, decorations, cake, dinner or buffet, guests.

"Where do you want to get your dress, Amie? In Frankfurt? Paris? New York?"

She laughed. "Oh, Mommy, maybe we can find one right here, after all Dusseldorf is Germany's fashion city! Anyway I like a Spanish designer, maybe we can order one online."

"A Spanish designer, online? No, Amie, you need to try it!"

"Mommy, I am half Spanish, aren't I? And I think they would sell it in a bridal boutique right here."

We went dress shopping, Katie, Amie and I. Amie found her perfect dress, and Katie took the occasion to try a few dresses, too. She had a pretty good idea of what she was going to get for her wedding.

"Two daughters marrying in the same year. That's fantastic!"

Luckily things at home were running perfectly. Doris was on top of the household management, and I could concentrate on the wedding.

Alfred had just one issue that he discussed with Karl and me. It was about living in our house.

"Amie doesn't want to move away from here, and I understand, I work pretty long hours at the Hospital and I like that she is not going to be alone, and who doesn't want to live in a palace! But I am not a free loader and I insist on contributing!"

"That's not necessary Alfred, but we understand your point, we will think about it. Anyway we like to have you around, two doctors are better than one!"

On a warm, sunny day in June, our younger daughter, the most beautiful bride, married her prince. Our granddaughters and some of their friends' children were escorts for the wedding party.

It was a beautiful, meaningful day for our family! Karl and I were delighted!

Amie was so happy, they looked like the perfect couple. But I couldn't shake off a nagging feeling... I didn't know why.

We accommodated Alfred's family in our house. They felt comfortable and so did we. Hermine, his mother, is one of the sweetest people I ever met!

The newlyweds didn't want to go anywhere crowded for their honeymoon. They chose to visit the wide, white, sandy beaches of Schleswig-Holstein. They rested for a few days on the sunny island of Sylt.

When Amie and our new son-in-law returned, they took the rooms that Amie had chosen on the third floor.

"It's like having our own apartment and still being in the house with you and Daddy!"

Karl told me, "I think our daughter feels responsible for her aging parents, it is her caring nature. Anyway, I love having her around, who would say that our youngster, the one that came as a gift into our lives, would be the one filling this house with joy and youth!"

"I feel happy to have her with us. But don't expect any babies anytime soon, she is not planning. She wants to invest time in her career first."

Gabriel and Elise went to his studio in Frankfurt, with two of her friends from the Opera House, for a recording.

"This is the first time that Elise agreed in coming for a recording," Gabriel told me.

As a bonus to me they left Marie-Claire for an entire week. I was thrilled! Hanne, Doris' daughter, helped me entertain her, we had a great time together.

Karl, the big Grandpa, had a brilliant idea:

"A mini golf course in our own backyard for the children and sometimes the adults to enjoy!"

He spent the rest of the summer teaching Liliane, Wilhelm, little Max and Marie-Claire how to handle the little golf clubs.

"I never thought it could be so much fun to spend the summer with the grandchildren in the backyard..."

He also told me that this was an opportunity for him to know Doris' children better. Her son Christof was very kind to the younger kids.

"This boy has leadership qualities, as soon as he learned to play he started teaching the younger ones and he was very patient. He is a nice boy and told me he has decided to follow a career in the military, as soon as he graduates from high school he will leave for training."

After Gabriel and Elise returned and took our little princess to Vienna, I started thinking about Katie's wedding.

She found the perfect place to live downtown. A duplex apartment in a new building, she was thrilled. Both fathers, Herman and Karl, offered to share the cost as a wedding gift! But, Viktor was not so sure he wanted to live in a modern complex.

Katie was frustrated. "I love the Dusseldorf architecture, why can't we have something new and perfectly located?"

I offered to help Katie with the décor as I started the preparations for her wedding. This time it's a different crowd, her friends, his friends, our family, some members of his mother's family will come too for a winter wedding.

It will be indoors in our house instead of our garden roses, it will be a winter wonderland of crystals and candles. But they need to decide where they are going to live first.

In the fall, Doris approached me.

"I'd like to give you an update, everything is being finalized. I have the divorce and custody papers, and they told me to deliver them to my in-laws, they should forward to their son. They still refuse to say where he is.

I'll be granted full custody of my children and the right to decide if and when they'll visit their grandparents. If Egon doesn't show up for court on the assigned date, the judge will grant it to me that same day."

"I am glad things are going in the right direction, Doris, and as far as I see, Chris and Hanne are happy too."

"Yes, they are, they love it here, this is the best place they ever lived. My children and I are happy. Thanks to you, Frau Clara."

Louisa came to help me with Katie's wedding preparations, and she commented that the last time they went to visit her parents Erik took the children and left abruptly. She was distressed.

"I don't know when we are going back there, they are my parents but they are wrong. I think Erik has put up with them quite a lot. This time was just too much for him to take."

"Is your father ever going to let go of the grudge he has against us? I really never understood why. And what about your mother, does she feel the same way?"

"My mother does not have a voice, she just follows what my father tells her. He is the one with strong opinions, he didn't like Karl first because he was more successful than my father is, second because of Karl's liberal ideas contrasting to my father's, you know!"

"I know, Louisa, and excuse me for saying your father is stubborn! He was here in our house only once at your wedding, and ever since he declined any invitations, that's why we stopped inviting him and your mother.

I'm sorry you are in the middle of this, you want to be at peace with your parents, your husband and your husband's family, that's a lot on you. But what did Adolf do this time?"

"He was talking to Will about the war times, and how proud he is of his name, and he was showing him some symbols...

Erik saw it, he grabbed Will and told my father to never try to project his views on the children. Erik yelled at my father, 'My children are learning the facts and they are growing up to be fair and just to everyone, everyone in this world!'"

"When Erik takes positions like that I see that he is so much like Karl. I applaud him. Louisa, your husband is right."

"He is, Clara, and I admire him for standing up. My parents are going to see much less of me and my children. I'm supporting

Erik."

"And thank you for supporting me, Louisa, I knew that your parents never liked me, they made no secrets in calling me 'that Spanish woman' with disdain."

"That's the result of their ignorance. Clara, you are the most classy and refined woman I know, and you raised a beautiful family. And talking about ladies, there is also something going on with the Countess Elsa. Erik's mother has come around, she wants to get closer to Erik and our children, she also said she wants to see Karl…"

"What is going on? Why didn't you tell me before? Does Karl know?"

"Erik told him, Karl does not want anything to do with her, neither do we. Sorry, we didn't want to upset you. No one is interested in getting closer to her, it is too late for that. You are my children's grandmother, they adore you. Erik grew up without her. Now that she is older and alone, she is just lonely."

"What happened to her Count?"

"They are no longer together, and she said she is tired of the social life of Munich."

Later I asked Karl: "Why didn't you tell me Elsa had come around?"

"Because she didn't come to see me, she came for Erik, and I had no intention to talk to her. Don't be jealous, *meine liebe*!"

I did feel a pinch of jealousy, but let it go.

Katie was very nervous as the wedding date was approaching:

"Mommy, I don't know what to do at this point, Viktor didn't agree in living in the city, and I will not move into his father's house to then decide where we are going. I am feeling rushed, I think I want to postpone the wedding for next spring!"

"Did you discuss it with him, Katie?"

"I did, but he is not taking me seriously, he says that his father's house is in an excellent location, which is true, but I don't want to live in the suburbs, I'd much rather be downtown."

"Is there anything else going on, Katie? This disagreement about the house might be just the tip of the iceberg…"

"I am very confused, Mommy."

"You need more time to think about it, sleep on it, you'll see things clearly in the morning!"

"Karl, Katie is postponing the wedding to the spring, she and Viktor haven't agreed on where they are going to live. She was very upset."
"I don't understand, they have options! Let's trust that Katie will make the right decision."

Gabriel and Elise had programmed to come for the wedding two weeks before Christmas, for that reason they accepted commitments to perform during the holidays in Vienna.
After Katie's change of plans they couldn't cancel their commitments any longer. In consequence we changed our traditional holiday celebration this year. We only had a Christmas Eve dinner with Erik, Louisa and their children, Amie and Alfred and Katie. Viktor joined us for the evening, but he was subdued.

The next morning, after the children opened their presents, Karl and I went to Vienna!
We had a wonderful holiday with Gabriel, Elise and our lovely and bright three year old granddaughter Marie-Claire. Elise told me that they are planning for another baby.
Our family will keep growing!

We stayed for a week and attended their New Year's Concert. This was something I always wanted to do. We enjoyed it very much, the colorful spectacle with music, ballet and singing.
It was delightful seeing our son and daughter-in-law performing together on that festive occasion.

This year was incredible, we are all healthy, our children are in love, living beautiful lives, one daughter is married, the other will be pretty soon!
There were some bumps on the road, but in the end we count our blessings!

At the year's beginning Karl did an inventory of the Foundation. "It keeps my concerns out of sight when I think about helping others."

His efforts have paid off, so many families have benefited from it, and some benefactors have found purpose, like Viktor's father who was so dedicated and creative, finding new ways of raising funds! With that, Herman was so much more optimistic and upbeat.

When we thought that everything was calm, Katie came to us with a very serious conversation.

"Mommy and Daddy, I didn't want to spoil the holidays, and I also wanted to give the best consideration to my feelings and expectations and Viktor's too. I need to tell you that our wedding plans are off!"

I was flabbergasted. "What do you mean? Why, Katie?"

Karl asked, "Is this about the house issue? How can I help?"

"No one can help, Daddy, I thought for a long time, I know myself, I am not cut out to live a provincial life. Viktor is a very good man, he is honest and has integrity, but we want different things in life. He wants the quiet life of the burbs, I want activity, energy, lights, the noise of a big town. I want to be challenged in my work and grow. I can't be tied up. I am sorry if I disappoint you both, I am just being true to myself."

Katie was sad. I embraced my daughter.

"Katie, is your heart broken? Do you love him?"

"Yes, Mommy, I feel heart-broken and I love Viktor, but honestly I don't know the difference between being in love and truly loving someone. I need to learn that."

"Did you talk to him about it? How is he dealing with it?"

"He was very sad, but in the end he understood me, I hope. I can't compromise! He can't either, he was very adamant about not living in our house or in the high rise in the city. That's all!"

Karl embraced her.

"Katie, you are right about not making a decision that goes against who you are to please anyone. I admire your courage in taking this step, many girls in your place would go with the flow... But I don't want you to be sad, my little one. What can I do to help? Do you want me to talk to Viktor?"

"No, Daddy, we had our last conversation, he understood. In reality he was always intimidated by the fact that I am your daughter. He will be alright, we'll be alright!

But Daddy, I have a new professional life plan, one that is all about our companies, and I was planning to call a meeting with you and Erik to present my idea."

"You look excited about it, tell me right now, Katie."

"Well, don't get me wrong, but I want to start a new life away from Dusseldorf, you have the satellite office in Frankfurt that deals with shipments to other countries. Erik has given me responsibilities and access to those foreign customers, and I absolutely love dealing with them!

Daddy, I want that office for myself, where I would be in charge of those customers' affairs at the same time that I would be expanding our commercial relationship and eventually going on trips to promote new business. I have so many ideas, you know that I am very serious about my job!"

"Yes, I know, you are bright, hardworking and also courageous. I understand that you want to start a new life in Frankfurt, a bigger city, I see the motivation."

"Please give me the chance, Daddy, I'll be working with you and for you, and I will always come home, we won't be far. It is all possible, isn't it?"

"Actually, Katie, it is a very good idea! Bring your proposal in writing and we'll discuss it with Erik, I promise I'll give it my best consideration, and if it benefits you and our company, we'll move forward."

And there ended the dream of a spring wedding...

I felt sad for Katie, at the same time very proud of her.

'Like father, like daughter!' She knows what she wants, she won't settle for less...

CHAPTER NINE

WOUNDED HEARTS

*G*abriel and Elise are coming in March.

Elise was invited by her friends from the Dusseldorf Opera House ensemble to perform with them in Barcelona.

She accepted the invitation and will fly out of Dusseldorf and will return with her friends.

That was very unusual, she hardly performs outside Vienna.

Gabriel told me:

"We will leave Marie-Claire with you while Elise is away, and I'll go for a recording in Frankfurt. Once I'm finished, I'll join her at your house, Mama."

"That's wonderful, Gabe, I'd enjoy some special time with Marie-Claire, and when you both come back we will commemorate Dad's birthday! He got a clean bill of health again, and we feel like celebrating!"

"Do you want us to bring Helene to help care for Marie-Claire?"

"No, give her some time off, I love to have Marie-Claire all to myself."

My Viennese family arrived, we spent a day together! The next morning Gabriel took off for Frankfurt, and Elise flew to Barcelona.

During three days Marie-Claire and I had the time of our lives, I spoiled her, like any grandmother would!

On the evening before her scheduled return, Elise called us to confirm her flight's arrival time.
"Franz will be waiting for you at the airport to bring you home, Elise. Your daughter can't wait, she is very anxious to talk to you, she is right here."
I gave the phone to Marie-Claire.

"Moma Clara, Mami said she is bringing me the most beautiful Spanish doll. Her name is Carmencita, she has black hair and a long red dress."

The next morning as Franz was getting ready to go to the airport, he called me very anxiously.
"Frau Clara, I just heard on the radio, a plane crashed in the southeastern mountains of France, it was a German airplane on a flight from Barcelona to Dusseldorf..."
I felt like my heart stopped and all my blood left my body.
"They might be mistaken, Franz! Can't be true!"

I ran to Karl, he was in the study at his desk.
"Karl, please put the TV on, a plane crashed in the French Alps, I don't want to say it, but I am afraid it could be Elise's flight."
Franz joined us, and in horror we watched the breaking news.
They confirmed the flight number.
We were shocked beyond belief!
"Oh, dear God, it is Elise's flight!"
"What should I do, Frau Clara?"

Karl immediately called the airline to obtain more details. They couldn't confirm anything yet.

I felt I couldn't breathe, he held me by my shoulders.

"Where is Marie-Claire?"

"She is playing with Hanne."

He told Franz, "Go to the playroom and tell Hanne to stay there, and no TV, no news at all!"

"Let's call Gabriel…" Before Karl finished, Gabriel was on the phone.

"Mama, did you hear the news? It is a hoax, can't be true, that's not Elise's flight!"

"I'm afraid it is, son. Dad is trying to obtain details with the airline. Let's not panic, there will be survivors! Elise will be well!"

"I'm coming home now, Mama! Please keep me informed."

"Come home safe, Gabe!"

I called Katie and Amie, they both left work to come home immediately. Karl heard on the news that the airline was having a press conference at the airport.

"Franz, let's go to the airport right now. I will call you, Clara. Please keep calm, don't think the worst!"

I sat alone in the study, for a minute the shock took over me. *'What is happening? Why is this tragedy happening to so many lives? This is unthinkable!'*

I felt like crying my eyes out, but I didn't, in my heart I wanted to hold on to the belief that they would come back to say that it was just a glitch in communication, everyone was fine! I hoped!

Gabe called from the road.

"Any confirmation yet? I am desperate!"

"Not yet, son, Dad is at the airport for the press conference. Who's driving?"

"Gunther, he left everything to come with me. Mama, please tell me this is a nightmare. This can't be real!"

"Please keep calm, son! I don't know what to say."

Amie arrived, she hugged me, "Mommy, the airplane crashed in the mountains, they are all presumed dead."

"Don't say that, Amie, they didn't confirm yet, there is hope!

Please take care of Marie-Claire, she is in the playroom with Hanne, don't let her watch TV."

Katie hugged me. "Mommy, I'm so sorry! I love Elise too, she is like my sister. I am in shock."

"I love Elise like my daughter. Poor Elise, is she frightened? Is she in pain? No, no, I can't imagine she won't come back to us..."

We watched the press conference on TV, and Karl called us as he heard:

"All one hundred forty-four passengers and six crew members are presumed dead. Air traffic control officials declared the plane to be in distress after contact with its crew was lost.

Recovery operations are expected to take several days, the area of the crash covers terrain that is too difficult to access."

Disbelief, devastation, horror took over our hearts. There were no words in any language that could describe what everyone was feeling.

Citizens and families of the passengers overwhelmed by the tragedy were waiting at the airport, hoping...

"All those young lives... Inconceivable!"

Gabriel called. Katie spoke to him.

"I am following the news, please keep Marie-Claire sheltered from this tragedy. I'll be home soon."

"She is, come home, my brother. We are all here for you."

The news kept coming...

Troubling facts emerged, incredulity took over, there indications that it was not a mechanical failure!

"What happened? Terrorism? A bomb? Did Elise and the other passengers see it coming? Were they scared?"

"Stop torturing yourself, Mommy. I pray that they didn't suffer..."

Gabriel arrived home accompanied by Gunther.

"I couldn't let him come home alone, under these circumstances."

"Thank you, Gunther, for bringing my son home."

I never saw Gabriel that way, he had no color, his lips were grayish. We could see the angst in his eyes. We embraced. He held on tight to me.

"Mama, tell me this is not true, it's a nightmare. Please tell me."

Karl hugged him.

"Son, I'll do anything to help, I am standing with you!"

"I want to go to the site, Dad, I need to find Elise."

"I have the information about the site, right now only the authorities are allowed there, but we will go as soon as they let us, I promise."

Doris stepped in. "Frau Clara, don't worry about anything, I have all the food prepared for everyone that is coming and all the guest bedrooms ready for the ones staying overnight. I don't know what to say, but I'll do anything to relieve your family's pain. I'm so sorry!"

"Thank you, Doris, I don't know what to say either."

Gabriel and I talked.

"Mama, I can't tell Marie-Claire... Please, you take care of that."

"We will tell her that Mami went far away and she can't come home. That's all I can say, Gabe. Amie is with her and she is the best to deal with children. You and Marie-Claire will be alright! I don't know what else to say right now, I have no words, my son..."

He asked me to call Gisele, Elise's sister.

"She might have no idea what is happening... I can't talk to her or anyone right now."

I called Gisele, she was surprised to hear from me. She heard something about an accident, but she had no idea that her sister was on that flight. She was horrified, like the rest of us.

"Gabriel and Marie-Claire are here with us, Gisele. Call later if you want to talk to him. And I am very sorry for the loss of your beloved sister, she was like a daughter to me. Like yours, my heart is shattered."

Everyone gathered together. Erik and Louisa joined us and stayed overnight, following up with the news and more details.

In those moments we were connected to all of the other families suffering the same pain in the same horrific circumstances. Massive disbelief and sorrow in an inexplicable manner took over all of us!

The people who perished in that horrendous tragedy were sons, daughters, mothers, fathers, brothers and sisters of all ages. They came from all walks of life, from our and other communities.

Our Elise was not alone, she was with her friends and enveloped by our love.

I brought Gabriel upstairs to the bedroom closer to mine, we sat on the bed, he was quiet, but all of a sudden he dropped to his knees, laid his head on my lap and cried, sobbed like a little boy.

"My son, my boy, I am so sorry."

I caressed his head, his long locks of dark hair, in that moment I saw him as my little boy suffering the most overwhelming pain of his life, and I cried with him. I could not offer him any other comfort but my own tears.

Exhausted, he crawled into bed and fell asleep.

"Thank Heaven! While he sleeps, he forgets what is happening..."

Karl was waiting for me in our room.

"Clara, you are emotionally and physically exhausted, I brought you some food, eat something and rest. Amie took Marie-Claire to her room, she is well up there, both Amie and Alfred know how to deal with children. She was upset that her Mami did not come home today, they will distract her."

Karl hugged me, "There is nothing I can say to ease this pain, but I am here, *meine liebe*, I am also heartbroken for our Elise, for all the other people in that plane. We need to be strong to survive this as a family and as a community."

I cried in his arms.

"Karl, I don't know how I am going to help Gabe and Marie-

Claire. I don't know what to do or what to say that could make a difference.

Oh, Elise, our daughter full of life and beauty, Gabriel's beloved wife and Marie-Claire's loving mother is gone! She is gone, she is not coming back to us!"

The next day Fabio called, looking for Gabriel. I told him he was with us.

"I'll do anything to help my friend, my brother. May I come to see him there in your house?"

"You are welcome here, Fabio, and you can help. There is something you can do for Marie-Claire. Elise called the night before and told her she was bringing her a Spanish doll with black hair and a long red dress. She might feel better if you tell her that her Mami sent her the doll."

"Absolutely, I know exactly what to bring her. I love Marie-Claire, and I loved Elise too, she was wonderful. I still can't believe this is happening."

When Fabio arrived, Karl was in the process of chartering a helicopter to fly over the crash area.

Gabriel was exasperated, "I'll find her, I'll find her!" He seemed irrational, not grasping reality, he believed there were survivors.

Fabio held him. "I'll go with you and your father, but it has to be tomorrow morning, and we will only be allowed to fly over. The rescuers are working down the mountains."

Early the next morning the three of them took a private airplane to a nearby town in the south, and from there they would fly over the site.

I was anxiously waiting at home. Karl called me:

"Gabriel and Fabio went alone, I gave my seat to a father of one of the children from our town. It is a clear day, but unfortunately there is not much to be seen, only fragments spread on the mountainside and valley."

"Karl, please bring Gabe home, we need to be together..."

The devastation was such that it changed the course of our lives, for most of us the losses were irreparable, nothing would ever be the same.

In those moments family was what mattered the most! The love and support that we drew from one another kept us going every day, facing life.

Solidarity and brotherhood were the words mostly used in the community during months, but there was also anger, mistrust, revolt!

There were memorials, celebrations of life in honor of the lives lost, but for many of the victims' families there would never be closure.

There was only one thing left to do: accept what happened, honor their lives, heal our wounded hearts, and get used to living without our loved ones, even when we couldn't forget them for a moment.

Our family attended many of those memorials and we shared the pain of many. Although we never met them before, that tragedy connected us, they were not strangers, we became one large grieving family.

As weeks went by, Gabriel went down into depression, wallowing in grief and filled with anger because he could not have his Elise back to give her a proper burial. He withdrew from everyone and everything. All of his commitments were cancelled.

Karl was the one following up with the authorities.

One summer day, I asked Gabriel to join me for a walk in our garden.

"Gabe, come, it is a nice day and I want to show you something."

I showed him a bed of lilacs, they were in bloom.

"It reminds me of the view of the gardens from your place in Vienna. I have been in touch with Helene, sent her money to keep up your house. Gabe, it is time to talk about what you are going to do. Are you going back? You need to start living again, son, you have a daughter, a life and a career. Elise would suffer if she could see that her demise destroyed you, she was your biggest supporter."

"I have been thinking, Mama, I do not want to go back to Vienna, the only reason I lived there was for Elise, for her career. I will get my strength back, I will be the father Marie-Claire deserves, but I need your help."

"You have me and our family supporting you. What do you need me to do, Gabe?"

"I want to sell the property in Vienna, for now I think it is better that I stay in Dusseldorf. Marie-Claire has all the love she needs right here. I want her to be in our hands, I know she will grow up whole and happy."

"I agree, son. Here with us, you can have your independence, and at the same time know that Marie-Claire is being cared for. But I think that first you need to go to Vienna to sort out your belongings and Elise's."

"Would you come with me, Mama? Are you in touch with Gisele?"

"I'll come, and yes, I have spoken to Gisele a few times. We could ask her to meet us there. I think you should give her some of Elise's things…"

I had a talk with Katie and Amie and apologized for those months that went by, when my time was consumed caring for Marie-Claire and Gabriel.

"It is not because I have been so absorbed with Gabe and Marie-Claire that you are not going to come to me. I am here for both of you too, in any circumstance. I'm sorry, girls, we hardly have talked about you and your lives lately."

"Mommy, we know how broken-hearted you are. Katie and I admire that you still can maintain everything in balance. It is hard for us to feel happy under these circumstances, but we are doing fine while our hearts hurt for Elise and our brother.

Life goes on…"

"Katie, how is your Frankfurt plan coming along?"

"Everything is going as agreed with Erik and Daddy. As a matter of fact I asked Daddy to get a bigger apartment for Gabe to stay with me when he comes to the studio."

"That's thoughtful, Katie, I like the idea."

"What about you, Amie? I haven't seen Alfred lately. Doesn't he come home every night? Is everything alright with both of you?"

"Yes, Mommy, he still has a room close to the Hospital, and on his long days or night shifts he stays there."

"I am sorry, Amie, I didn't mention it before, your first wedding anniversary is coming up. No matter what is happening in our family, life's memorable occasions are to be celebrated. Daddy had the idea to reserve a suite at the Dusseldorf Hotel for an overnight romantic dinner for both of you."

"Mommy, don't worry, Fred and I probably will go out for dinner if he is not working ..."

"Amie, you are newlyweds, you should be spending much more time together. What is going on? Is Alfred putting his work above your relationship?"

"Somehow! He is very determined about his career, he wants to be one of the best doctors in his specialty in Europe."

"Do you agree with this, Amie? It seems he didn't make the transition into being married."

"That is how I feel sometimes. Anyway it's giving me much more time to spend with Marie-Claire. I love her."

"You do! But don't forget about yourself and your marriage, *liebling*."

That evening I embraced my husband.

"Karl, I have missed you, I have been so absorbed with Gabe and I thank you for being supportive of him and me, but I miss my husband, our closeness. I want to feel happy in your arms again, *liebe*."

Gabriel and I went to Vienna, we brought Marie-Claire along.

"She should see her house one last time and say goodbye to Helene. She is there waiting for us, but she has another job lined up."

As Gabriel opened the door, Marie-Claire ran inside from room to room calling, "Mami, Mami, I am here!" That broke our hearts, again.

Helene came to greet us, she took Marie-Claire to see her room.

"Choose everything you want to bring to Moma Clara's house."

Gabriel was subdued. "It is very painful to be here without Elise."

"Gabe, she was happy with you here, she took that with her, the love and happiness of her short life were impressed on her soul forever...

Now choose everything that you want to take to our house. Gisele is coming tomorrow, I told her that we would pay for the transport to Linz for the things you are giving her."

I went to Marie-Claire's room, "Moma, I want everything! Everything!"

I helped Gabriel sort his belongings, his music room and a few pieces of furniture.

Gisele came alone the next day.

We hugged, we cried. She kissed Marie-Claire. "Don't forget, Tante Gisele loves and misses you."

On our second day Gabriel told me he wanted to go to the Opera House.

"They had the memorial and inauguration of Elise's picture on the Wall of Honor, I couldn't come, but now I would like to see it."

As we walked into the theater Gabriel went straight to a back wall in the atrium, and there it was, the most recent beautiful picture of Elise in honor of her tenure at the Opera House. There was an engraved plate underneath the picture, Elise Marie Melk - Soprano.

"She was only twenty years old when she came to this Opera House, here she lived her passion for almost fifteen years. She looked so beautiful in this picture. My Elise!"

We heard voices and music coming from the theater, the administrator approached us.

"Gabriel! I am glad to see you. I am so sorry, we are all heartbroken.

Come, they are at rehearsal and I bet the conductor and Elise's colleagues and friends would love to see you."

We walked into the empty, dark theater. There was a group of singers on stage and the orchestra in the pit. The conductor immediately came to greet him.

Agnes, Elise's friend, ran off the stage and hugged him, she couldn't say anything, she was already crying, "Gabriel, oh, Gabriel!"

Then she turned to me, "Do you remember me from their wedding?"

"Yes, of course, you were Elise's best friend." We hugged.

Gabriel asked the conductor to borrow a violin. A young player came and gave him his instrument.

Everyone took a seat, Agnes sat beside me. Gabriel went on stage alone, with no special illumination, no special attire, just his presence, he tuned and adjusted the instrument, brought it up to his chest, and said: "Für Elise."

I saw my son playing the violin in the most delicate and heartfelt way, the melancholic sound touched us. We were all teary.

That was the first time he played in public since that tragic day in March.

When we were leaving, Gabriel told me, "My Elise's spirit lives here, I feel like her angelic voice echoes through these halls..."

Gisele left. "Gabriel, I wholeheartedly thank you for loving my sister and for everything you are giving to us. It means so much to me and my mother to have all of these remembrances of our Elise."

Before leaving Vienna, we went for a walk at the Belvedere Gardens. Marie-Claire, skipping ahead of us, Gabriel held my hand.

"I moved to Vienna because of Elise, I am moving out because of her. I am saying goodbye to Vienna, to the beautiful life we lived here, to the love we've shared... But I'll never say goodbye to my love!"

When we arrived home in Dusseldorf, I thanked Karl for being understanding and taking care of all the legal issues for Gabriel and asked him if he had any news from the rescue team and authorities.

"Nothing, they found nothing, and there is no hope of finding any remains. But, I had another meeting with members of the victims' families and the airline representatives, we will follow up with legal charges. They have to take responsibility for this tragedy!"

"Karl, these months have been horrible for our family and for us. I feel guilty I have been neglecting you. I'm sorry, *liebe*."

"I understand, *meine liebe*, you are trying to divide your attention between the ones that need you the most. This shall pass, and we will find some kind of normalcy again."

"We will, Karl. For now Gabriel is staying with us. I have enrolled Marie-Claire in the same school our daughters went to. Someday, somehow our lives will be normal again."

The next morning Gabriel told me that Fabio was coming to visit.

"He is always welcomed here, Gabe, and if he is willing to help, you should install your things in your new room. Take the east suite, this room will be for Marie-Claire, I want her close, the baby room adjacent to mine is small and I want to rearrange her furniture once the truck arrives from Vienna."

That afternoon I talked to Doris.

"I couldn't manage anything around the house, and you have been exceptionally helpful and efficient. I recognize you went above your duties, thank you, Doris!"

"You don't have to thank me, Frau Clara. You gave me a new life, and I am committed to helping you and your family for the long run."

Amie and I went for a stroll in the garden, and we heard the sound of the violin. Marie-Claire wanted to run back into the house. "Papi is playing, Papi is playing!"

"He is, let's just listen, it is so beautiful and melancholic."

"Gabe is playing with his heart, Mommy, I am glad that he can express his feelings through music again…"

The same day Fabio arrived, the Vienna delivery also came. All the music apparatus were taken to Gabriel's suite. Fabio helped him enormously.

Marie-Claire asked for her entire room, and with Doris and Hanne's help, we did it!

My little granddaughter was so happy placing her dolls and picture frames, lots of them with her Mami holding her.

"My Mami is an angel in Heaven! When is she coming back, Moma?"

During his visit I had a conversation with Fabio. He is the kind of person who the more I know, the more I like him. I do see some similarities between him and Gabriel. I asked him how his life is in Madrid, now that he is living alone. He told me:

"I think of my father every day, his early demise still hurts me but sometimes I smile at memories of things we did together. He was funny, witty, above all he was my best friend."

"That is so nice to hear, Fabio, it is right to nurture the good memories, the love, and move on."

"When I was fifteen my parents separated and he told me that he was going to live the life he was supposed to. He was very happy when he got the job at the airline in Madrid, he told me that was the place he should never have left. He taught me everything about airplanes, and I developed a passion for flying.

Later, against my mother's will, I went to live with my father.

After he met you and Gabriel, he told me the past story. My father spoke of his remorse for what he caused you. He had strong feelings of self condemnation, never forgave himself.

My father taught me to not go by others' prejudices. And that is how I learned to live an authentic life, my father was my best example."

"Fabio, I am glad Gabriel was able to know him and be his friend. But, what about you? Do you have someone special?"

"Yes, I am going to marry the woman I love. I didn't tell Gabriel yet because he just lost his beloved wife, but he knows of Alicia. I am happy professionally, I was also just promoted to first officer and down the road someday I want to have my own private jet company."

"Your father was proud of you! I wish you much success and

happiness. I like you, Fabio, I see in you the best of Miguel, I am so glad you are my son's friend and brother, and thank you for supporting Gabriel during this most painful time."

We celebrated Marie-Claire's fourth birthday. Gabriel did not want to celebrate his, but Gunther came from Frankfurt to see him anyway.

"It has been more than six months and I need you back in the studio, come with me, Gabriel."

During the days he was away I spent much more time with my daughters. One day Amie took me out for lunch, then we went together to the Children's Home, we met some of the parents and the little patients. I haven't been there for so long, it felt good to extend my heart to them.

I also spent time in the city with Katie. She was happy with the prospects of her new life.

"So proud of you, my independent, business girl!"

"Things are coming along in Frankfurt, and I am excited about it. I am going to help Gabriel, motivating him to be more active with his studio in Frankfurt. He needs to get busy."

"I'm glad Gabriel is going to spend more time with you, you can cheer him up. But I'll miss you, *liebling*."

"I'll only be a little over two hours away. Frankfurt will be my place of work and social life, but this is where I belong. I'll come home every week. I want to see you happy again, Mommy. What about if we start planning for the holidays? I think we need to do something different this year. I know it is not going to be festive, but we can't let it be sad either..."

"You are right, Katie, when I went to Vienna I bought a beautiful angel doll for Marie-Claire, and that gave me the idea of having 'an angelic Christmas.' Dad has the addresses for the victims' families in our area, I thought of sending each one of them an angel, with a message from a family that lost an angel to another... What do you think, Katie?"

"I think it is a heartfelt gesture, this season is so devastating for so many, maybe that could bring them a little comfort. I'd like to help you with this project. Do you want me to order the angels,

Mommy?"

"Yes, Katie. I really like that Austrian angel."

Karl spoke to Gabriel about the lawsuit the families are filing against the airline.

"Dad, I don't want to proceed with this, sometimes I feel angry, I want to blame someone for what happened, and sometimes I want to forget."

"I understand, it is part of the grieving process, but making sure that people take responsibility is pivotal so that it will never happen again. And I also want you to remember that I am standing with you and I'll do anything that is just and fair. If I could, I would heal you, son."

"Thank you, Dad, you are right. Let's fight for our loved ones, nothing could bring them back to us, but fighting for them makes us feel stronger."

I wouldn't tell anyone, but my heart was not as resilient as before, all of those emotions did affect me. I was trying my best to heal, I had a hole in my chest. I hurt for Elise, for Gabriel, for Marie-Claire, only the love I have for my family kept me moving forward, but I was craving tranquility and peace.

Day after day I observed Amie bestowing her love and attention on Marie-Claire.

"Amie, you are loving, dedicated and a natural mother to Marie-Claire. Don't you want to have a baby of your own? Is Alfred committed to having a family?"

"I give all my maternal love to my little patients and to my niece. One day I'll have children, but I don't think it will be with Fred."

"It is time for you to tell me what is going on, *liebling*. Clearly, something is wrong, he hardly spends time with you."

"I didn't want to worry you, Mommy, but I am getting to the end of my rope. Fred is excessively ambitious, his excuse for not coming home is that the twenty minute drive is too much for him, he would rather walk two blocks to the apartment he shares with others for a few hours of sleep.

When we got married he offered to rent an apartment for us

right there by the Hospital. I declined because I knew I would be alone most of the time.

He likes to come here only on his days off. He says that our home is like a luxurious hotel, a resort."

"That offends me, Amie. This is a home where children grow up, where a family lives and loves. If he comes here just for the amenities he doesn't have to come at all! We invited him to live here as your husband, not as a weekend guest."

"Mommy, I have told him those same words. I am tired of this, I don't feel like I have a husband."

I discussed it with Karl, he has been upset over this whole situation, and many times he wanted to talk to Alfred about it. I asked him not to.

"It is hard for us to keep out, but Amie is mature and very logical, she will decide what is best for her, we can only support our daughter."

Days later, Amie came to us with some unexpected news.

"Because of his cutting edge cancer treatments Fred got an offer to go to a specialized clinic in Zurich. It is a great opportunity for him, he wants me to quit my job to come with him."

For a moment I got a chill thinking our daughter would move to Switzerland for the chance of building her marriage.

"What did you decide, Amie?"

"For all that I know of Fred, since our time in New York, his unlimited dedication to his career has proven that he does not have time for me or our marriage. I would be starting over in another country, alone. I told him I won't leave my pediatric clinic or my family to follow his ambitions. This is not an emotional or rushed decision. I am done!"

"Oh, Amie, I'm sorry things didn't come out as they should. He has proven to you and to us he can't be the husband you deserve. I am proud of you for your rational decision. But how are you really feeling, are you sad, *liebling*?"

"A little sad, I feel empty, but I am being realistic. I am letting him go. The next step is a divorce."

Karl hugged her, "Come here, my *little doctor*, I'll take care of you. Do you want me to talk to Alfred?"

"No, Daddy, I think he is the one that should come and give you the satisfaction of an explanation."

I went upstairs with Amie to her room, and there she hugged me and cried.

"*Liebling*, I am here for you. Your heart will heal and you'll find the one that really deserves you, I am sure!"

Before leaving for Zurich Alfred came by our house to pick up his things and had a conversation with Karl.

"I do love Amie, she is the best I could ever have in my life, I thought she understood my professional ambitions. I am sorry, I didn't want our marriage to end."

"She does understand, she knows that you are a very good doctor, also overly ambitious. Me, personally, I think that you are an intelligent man, but lack emotional intelligence. You don't know what love and commitment are. I am sure you will reach your goals, you'll be rich, famous and lonely!

I am letting you know that to protect my daughter's interests, I have hired a lawyer, you won't take anything else from her but her time and a piece of her life that you already took."

On that note, Alfred left our home and our daughter's life with his head down.

Karl and I hurt for our loving and sweet daughter.

After another restless night of sleep, I just couldn't get out of bed.

"What is going on, *meine liebe*? Are you ill? You don't look right, Clara!"

"Karl, I think I need to rest all day, I feel very tired."

He left our room and went to get Amie. She immediately decided to bring me to the Hospital.

As soon as we arrived there she called my physician and a cardiologist. They started running tests.

Katie and Gabe came soon.

Amie stayed at my bedside.

"Doris and Hanne are with Marie-Claire, I need to be here with you, Mommy."

I felt horrible making my family worry, but I welcomed the medical attention, for months I have been feeling chest pains. I thought it was the heartache...

A little later the cardiologist explained to us that I was having symptoms of heart failure, and they kept me overnight.

Karl was devastated. Amie sent everyone home and she stayed with me.

My daughter explained everything I needed to know about the heart condition and how to manage it. She made me feel very calm.

She is my biggest emotional supporter, the fact that she lives with us is a balm to my soul.

After two days in the Hospital I went back home.

I never saw Karl so worried about me. "You need to be healthy again, *meine liebe*, you are the heart and soul of this family."

"I am sorry, I didn't know I had a condition, I thought it was the pain of heartbreak and stress. I will be alright, Karl, and you too. Relax!"

I asked my family not to fawn over me. I didn't need the unnecessary attention, I reassured them I was committed to taking care of my health. All I wanted was a normal life again.

My *little doctor* took good care of me at home. I was doing well.

Gabriel spent more time with me. "Mama, I am not going to give you any more distress, we need you well and healthy! I am your older son, I should be the one taking care of you! You are the soul of our family, the harmonic, melodic rhythm that connects us all, with your sweetness and strength you keep our music going, in *allemande* style!"

"Oh, my talented son. You make me feel better! Gabe, you didn't bring me stress or pain, life did. And that word you just said brings memories of Bertha, she used to call me *Alemana*, that reminds me of her saying, 'Instead *of crying, rejoice for the beautiful life you've shared with your loved one. Remember to live!'* I want to see you smiling again, son."

"Someday, somehow, Mama, our broken hearts will be mended..."

Louisa came to see me and told me that this year Erik decided not to go away for the holidays, they will spend the entire week with us. That made me happy!

"Erik is busy at work, he feels that he hasn't been here enough for Gabriel, he wanted to be more proactive and bring him some fun times. He is planning to take Gabriel on a country ski walk, maybe make a bonfire, things that they did when they were younger. And from my side I'd also like to spend more time around you, Clara."

"That's so thoughtful! Thank you, Louisa!"

"There is another reason. Elsa has been insisting on coming for the holidays. As a matter of fact when you were in Vienna with Gabriel she came to the downtown office and spoke to Erik and Karl. Did he tell you?"

"No, Karl didn't tell me!"

"Elsa asked him to talk Erik into welcoming her. I personally think it's too late for her to establish a relationship with her son."

"I think so too. Elsa hardly saw him growing up."

"Karl told her that Erik is a mature man, he would not tell him what to do."

"I agree, Louisa, but I feel sorry for her. Sometimes we take too long to recognize our mistakes, it might be too late for Elsa."

I invited Gabriel to come with me and Amie to the Children's Infirmary and the Home to share our holiday party.

"Let's bring a smile to the young patients. You have been a contributor to our Foundation, and it makes us feel better when we expand our hearts to others and we try to soothe their suffering, that makes us forget our own."

Gabriel came along, and for a few hours he forgot about his sorrow! Our sorrow!

"Thank you, Mama, for this opportunity, there is so much suffering in this world, and when we share, it gets lighter.

My first concert this coming year is going to be in benefit of the children."

"So, you decided to go back onstage, Gabe? That is good news!"

"I decided right now. I am going to talk to Martha to organize it.

I need to bring my life back on track. Bringing joy, entertainment to others is a form of healing!"

My son was showing signs of strength, not that he forgot Elise, his heart was full of love and pain for her, but his spirit was strong! I prayed that the day would come that when thinking of her he wouldn't hurt anymore.

Amie, too, was smiley. She was healing from her heartbreak and disappointment.

It has been difficult to create a balance between the immensurable loss and at the same time hoping for better days. But that is how life is for so many, isn't it?
Grieving is a long process, has its ups and downs, and we can't allow it to take over our lives. We need to learn to live without our loved ones while honoring their lives.
Secretly, I wished the same for myself, my heart can't take any more sorrow.

Karl had a new idea:
"We did it before, when the children were younger. As we are going to be all together for a week, I decided to hire a company to set up an ice skating rink on the tennis court for all of our children, grown and small, to enjoy."

We had a full house, all of our children and grandchildren enjoyed the ice rink, including Doris' children. Chris and Hanne joined Erik, Louisa, Katie, Amie, Lili, Will, Little Max and Gabriel, holding Marie-Claire's little hand, trying to teach her to dance on the ice.
They laughed, they smiled! And in our granddaughter's smile we saw Elise's! She will always be part of us!

The devastating events of life can make us withdrawn from living or have a new appreciation for the little things, little pleasures.
In those fleeting moments of joy the pain subsided...

We had one theme: Angels! "Angels were among us!"

We all agreed in not talking of sadness, but we remembered the wonderful beings that are in Heaven now! They were not forgotten, thinking of them brought us a tear and a smile, feeling gratitude for the time we shared.

Karl and I sat on a bench, wrapped up in blankets. He said:
"Here we are, the old, solid couple. We hope that our three children will heal and won't be alone... And soon they will find their life partners, like we found each other!"
"It is comforting to see our family united through the best and the most difficult times, supporting and loving one another!
They are the biggest achievement of our lives, we created this beautiful, strong family."

CHAPTER TEN

TIME TO HOPE

*A*fter the holidays Katie finally moved to Frankfurt.

"Mommy, I couldn't go last year with everything that was going on, but I am not moving out, this is my home, and I'll be back often, we'll talk every day. You keep well. I love you!"

"I love you too, *liebling*, and I'm proud of you."

She thanked her father.

"Daddy, thank you for the opportunity, you'll be proud of me, expect big results and more business."

"You are a winner, my girl, I am already proud of you. I'll surprise you one of these days in your new office."

She took Gabriel along, he will spend a few days at the studio. He has been trying, step by step, to get more involved with recording and responding to invitations to play. He has asked Gunther to select some cities where he might consider booking events.

In March, a year after the tragedy, it felt like it had just happened. We clearly felt the emotions of that unthinkable day, when we all gathered around Gabriel and Marie-Claire in support of him and each other.

To honor the lives of our never forgotten loved ones, Dusseldorf came together in a celebration of music and lights.

The concert at the Opera House was heart-wrenching. Gabriel was one of the performers and touched us all with the sound of music. We saw a difference in his playing, it was more profound, there was more soul to it, every note came from his heart.

Karl and I were touched by the kindness of many that had received an angel and approached us to give thanks for the remembrance. There were many tears, we felt connected to one another, feeling each other's pain and loss vividly.

"We are in this together, your pain is our pain, and we will mutually support each other in healing."

In the end we collectively felt that our loved ones were and forever will be alive in our hearts!

Gabriel has been going to Frankfurt once a week to work with Gunther. Before leaving this time, he told me:

"Mama, your home is my home base, this is where Marie-Claire will grow up. I'll never take her away from here, and I will spend all the time I can with my family and my daughter.

You and Amie are the source of love and support in her life. Did you see? She doesn't call her '*Tanti Amie*' anymore, now she is '*Mamie.*' I am grateful that my little sister loves my daughter and she is filling the void."

"I agree, son, that is something to be grateful for."

Marie-Claire loved her pre-school, I brought her every day, she made new friends and mostly loved her dance classes. "I am going to be a ballerina!" She fills our lives with light and pink tutus.

Gabriel got a call from Fabio.

Later he told me, "He is getting married next month and invited me to the wedding. Mama, I don't feel like participating in any parties, but he is my friend and has been here for me through this time, I think I need to go."

"You should, you need to get out, socialize and mostly be with friends, and Fabio is a very special one."

While Gabriel went to Madrid I prepared a surprise for Karl. I asked Doris to bring our dinner to our suite. I set a romantic table with flowers and crystal candlesticks.

As soon as Amie came home I asked her to take Marie-Claire to her suite for a sleepover, which they both loved.

I went to the study and told Karl: "Come with me, *liebe*, we are having dinner upstairs tonight. I am sorry I forgot last year, I promised you when we renewed our vows that we would always celebrate our day. But as things were happening, it went by... I want to reaffirm to you that no matter what happens you are my priority. Tonight we will only speak of love."

We hugged, kissed, and for moments our world felt right again!

Amie is doing very well, she has told me she is over her break-up with Alfred.

"I am starting to feel that he never happened!"

She accompanied me to all my medical appointments, I can't keep anything hidden from her. She knows exactly how I feel and knows that I am responsible and attentive to my own health.

I want to become an old lady, I want to be with my beloved family for a long time, I want to see my children happy, my grandchildren grown. That's my purpose!

In the meantime, I see Katie often. She comes home always radiant, happy about her work achievements. She is also meeting new people, but no one special, so far.

"I am taking my time, I have learned from my mistake jumping from one relationship to another too soon. For now I am just focused on my work."

"Good thinking, Katie. I see that you are thriving in your work and also being a very supportive sister to Gabriel, which I truly appreciate. I am sure that everything else will come in time, *liebling*!"

Gabriel came back from Madrid. The wedding was simple, just a few friends and Alicia's family.

"Did you meet Fabio's mother?"

"She did not come, she did not approve of him marrying a flight attendant. What a stuck up woman! But their friends were very pleasant and I made an effort to have a good time."

"I am glad you did, Gabe. Did you meet anyone special?"

"Alicia made an obvious effort in putting me and her maid of honor together. She is a very nice and pretty girl, but my heart is still taken, I don't think I will ever love again, Mama."

"You will, Gabe, with time you'll heal the wounds, and believe, one day you'll find happiness again."

Gabriel went for a concert in Prague, he hasn't performed in another country for the longest time. He returned feeling accomplished.

"The effort paid off, I was feeling like a bird with a broken wing, but I can do this again, one concert at a time…"

He tried to conceal it, but I know he still experiences bouts of emotional pain alternating with days when his heart lightens with hope. My brave son is resilient and realistic, he accepts what comes his way, even the most difficult events. I prayed for better days for him, for all!

Erik came to see us, but before leaving he talked to me alone.

"We have shared many one to one conversations since I was a boy. For me you were the example of the perfect mother, Clara. I didn't share this with Dad, but let me tell you, I saw my mother recently, she came around again and I agreed in talking to her, and I am glad I did.

My mother can hardly see, she has a degenerative cornea disease and pretty soon she will be totally blind. She wanted to see me one more time, she said she wanted to remember my face.

She was very sad and apologized for her past absence. She is living with an *au pair* in an apartment downtown, not far from my house to make it easier for me to come and visit her once in a while. Mother said I am the only one that she wants in her life.

Clara, I felt so sorry for her, I got emotional, I hugged her and cried."

"Oh, Erik, I know, you are just like your Dad, strong, tough, but you have the kindest heart. Are you planning to visit her?"

"Do you think I should? Why do we love our mothers, no matter what? Why do we feel like a child in their presence?"

"Because, a mother and child's bond is unbreakable. When she left you, she didn't know that she could not break away from you. She gave you the gift of life, you won't regret giving her a little of your time once in a while."

He hugged me.

"Thank you, Clara, you always have the right thing to say."

"Feel good, Erik, and bring the family on the weekend, Marie-Claire loves to play with Max, her *bestest* friend, and I love to see Lili and Will, too."

I didn't drive anymore, but I took Marie-Claire to school every day with Franz. On one of those mornings we talked about him.

"Franz, you are much more than a driver, you are a friend to us, and I regret the time that we hardly talked. How is everything with you?"

"Frau Clara, you are very caring and I know how much you have been enduring. It doesn't feel fair to say, but I'd like to share that I am actually happy with my life. Doris and I have connected, we love each other and we are planning to be together."

"Franz, you have all the right to be happy. How did I miss that? I see you and Doris being friends, talking, laughing, but I had no idea!"

"Doris is shy, she didn't want anyone to know, but I don't feel that way, we have no reason to keep our relationship a secret.

Christof is leaving for the Army, and after that, I am planning on moving into the apartment with her and Hanne. I do get along with the children, we are like a family."

"Are you planning to get married?"

"I want to. What do you think, Frau Clara?"

"Both of you deserve a happy life, and I would love to give you a wedding celebration. Tell Doris to talk to me about this, no reason to be shy, I support both of you."

"Thank you, Frau Clara, thank you!"

"Franz, I have been in touch with Hilda, she seems happy there, she adores being a grandmother to her niece's children. Have you heard from her? Does she know about you and Doris?"

"I got a Christmas card, she wished me well. I didn't tell her anything. If she talks to you, please tell her. I don't think she would mind at all that I am going on with my life..."

I talked to Karl that same day.

"I do support their relationship and I am happy for both of them. Did you notice anything, Karl?"

"I did, I thought Franz had a crush on her. She gets giggly around him. Something happened on those rides to the supermarket..."

Katie talked to Karl about going on a business trip to New York. He agreed with it. Erik said he couldn't go at this time and he had total confidence in his sister.

She came home to select a few business items for her trip.

"I wish you could come with me, Mommy, you certainly need a vacation."

"Maybe next time, *liebling*, I would love to go back to New York with you."

She invited Gabriel to come along. He couldn't, he was preparing for a concert. But later this year he might go to New York, he has plans in the works there.

Katie went alone, she took off from Frankfurt. She came back a week later, all smiles! Success!

"Business went very well and I had time for some shopping. Most of all I had a wonderful flight, I met someone successful, smart, single, handsome... And he lives in Frankfurt!"

"Oh, boy! There we go, it has been a long time since I see that sparkle in your eyes! Who is he?"

"Stefan Beuren-Breis!"

"I have heard that name before, Katie."

"Of course you have, he is a champion, the famous tennis player. His name is also a sports clothes brand."

"Oh, that one! Where did you meet him?"

"At the airport, in the VIP lounge, there were some people around him, I thought he looked familiar, maybe he was a movie star, and I didn't pay much attention, but when we boarded he was just there in the seat across from mine.

He smiled at me like he knew me. I said, 'Hi, I am Katherine.' He responded, 'Hi, I am Stefan.'

Just then I recognized him, I had seen him on TV many times. We started talking, he said he didn't sleep on flights and asked me to have dinner with him. I agreed, he moved to the empty seat next to mine, we had champagne and a delightful dinner. Business class was great!

We talked all the way across Europe and the ocean. It was a fabulous flight! When we landed in New York we felt we had known each other for a long time..."

"Katie, you are so excited, maybe a little too much! Please, protect your heart, *liebling*."

"Don't worry, Mommy, I saw him twice in New York and we are going to meet again when he is back. He is still there on business, he is not only a talented tennis player, he is a savvy businessman, and I appreciate that. He is also open minded, laid back and a real people's person."

I shared the news with Amie: "Your sister met someone special, now it is your turn. You have to give yourself opportunities, don't spend all your free time being Marie-Claire's *Mamie*, you need to go out and make new friends. And I love taking care of her."

"All of my friends at the clinic say the same, '*Go out, meet someone.*' I am open to it, but I believe it will happen when I expect it the least."

Over time I saw Gabriel making an effort trying to overcome his heartache.

But he still had some down days when he forced himself to go on. He had expanded his work at the studio and also booked a couple of concerts.

"I am not going on tours anymore, that would take me away from my daughter for long periods of time, but I'll come and go to other cities, maybe for three, no more than four concerts, a year."

"That is very wise, Gabe. When is your next?"

"I am invited to go back to Madrid, it has been a long time, the last time I played there you were with me, remember, Mama? I was also invited to Barcelona."

"Barcelona? Do you feel like going there? That might bring you many emotions."

"I am sure, that was the last place Elise performed, and it will be at the same theater. I do admit that I have mixed feelings about it, but I need to face it.

Fabio would join me there for moral support, and he would return with me to Madrid."

"Fabio is supportive of you, he is a very good friend. I am grateful to him."

"He is a real brother, Mama. After Madrid he wants me to go with him and Alicia to Costa del Sol, they rented a house there for the summer to relax. She is not flying anymore, she is pregnant!

I might go with them only for a few days, then I want to spend the summer here with my Marie-Claire."

"Or you might take Marie-Claire to a beach too, she would love it!"

Amie is progressing with her partnership in her practice and making a good name for herself. She does rounds at the Hospital to support her patients and visits the other children. She has a good circle of friends, but she always finds time for our family.

This is our younger daughter's thirtieth birthday, and we are celebrating it in style.

"Amie, invite all of your friends and choose what you like better, a formal dinner or a pool party!"

"I think Saturday afternoon fun at the pool, with good food, a little wine will do. I'll invite my friends and co-workers, all of them."

I talked to Doris, "We will cater for about twenty people, I want Amie to have the best day she has had lately. The sad times are over!"

That day Katie showed up to celebrate her sister's birthday.

"I thought of inviting Stefan, but I didn't want to take the attention from Amie today, it's her day!"

"Good thinking, Katie, I am sure people would fuss over him. How are things with both of you?"

"Wonderful, he invited me to Wimbledon, I couldn't go because of my business commitments, he respected that, but he wants me to come along for the next tournament.

I am having a great time with him, we have so much in common, maybe I'll bring him home soon to meet our family."

Karl and I talked about vacations.

"Do you remember, *meine liebe*, when was the last time we had vacations, just the two of us?"

"It has been too long, Karl. Where do you want to go?"

"Somewhere peaceful, surrounded by beautiful nature."

"For me Germany is entirely like that. But Hilda had invited us to go the Rhineland, as she says, it's one of the most romantic regions. The other option would be Salzburg, Austria, once you said you wanted to go there."

"Yes, I want to, but this time we might go to the Rhineland, I would not stay in Koblenz for more than two days, I don't want to depend on Hilda's hospitality for too long."

Gabriel came back. He called right after the concert in Barcelona to say that he was very nervous, but did alright.

"I felt vulnerable. The feeling of being on the same stage as Elise was for the last time made me very emotional, but I played for her, like she was there listening." He sighed. "Fabio was with me all the time, and he and Alicia came to the Madrid concert, also. Then we travelled to Marbella, Costa del Sol. I was surprised, never thought it was so stylish. I enjoyed it, but I was in a hurry to return home. Fabio and Alicia were trying to match me with one of their friends."

"They are trying to play matchmaker? Did you like the girl?"

"She is Alicia's best friend, she is very nice, I had met her at their wedding, to be honest I told her that I am not ready for a relationship. I still feel married to Elise."

"I can understand that, but someday you will move on, Gabe. You'll keep the love for Elise in your heart and make room for new experiences, a new life. I want to see you happy again, son."

"Maybe, someday..."

"Tell me more about this girl. Who is she?"

"Micaela is a typical Spanish girl, beautiful dark eyes, black hair, she has your colors, Mama. She is an artist, she paints portraits in her spare time, and she works at a museum in Madrid. She is intelligent, mature, and a nice friend!

Anyway she asked me for a picture of Marie-Claire to paint a portrait. I gave her the one I had in my wallet."

"Open your heart, Gabe! Let light and love in! *Remember to live*, son!"

Karl and I went to Koblenz.
I called Hilda in advance. She was thrilled!

The city located where the Mosel and Rhine Rivers merge is a modern metropolis and the center of cultural life in the Rhineland region.

We went outside the city where Hilda's place was situated, an adorable house with magnificent views, more impressive than I expected.

It was heartwarming to see Hilda, she looked happy. She offered us the best room, which she prepared carefully, I could see her personal touch!

"I missed you, Hilda, but I can see that you are happy in this beautiful place."

"I am, Frau Clara, I have a full life with my family and the children. My niece's children are very attached to me, I love them, they are the light of my life."

"I agree, children bring light. I have my little granddaughter living with us, she is delightful."

"How is Gabriel doing? I feel so heartbroken for what happened in your family. And how are my girls? I miss them so."

"Gabriel is playing again and trying hard to continue living, working. He is a wonderful father, he's at home with Marie-Claire now.

The girls miss you too, Katie is happy, expanding her work and with a new boyfriend. Amie is successful in her practice and doing well after the divorce. She is a loving mother figure to my granddaughter."

"Please, send my love to Gabriel and the girls, and I am sure that one day all of them will find happiness again."

"I hope so, Hilda. What about you, besides the children do you have any other love?"

"No, I am very fulfilled being a grandmother now. How is Franz doing?"

"Franz is happy and in love, with Doris!"

"Franz and Doris! Doesn't surprise me, I wish them both well. Franz is a good and loyal man, sometimes I regret being so hard on him, but it's all in the past now, I moved on, he moved on."

Hilda gave us directions to places to visit. Karl and I went around. We sat on a bench, contemplating the water. "It is really beautiful here, and as romantic as they say, *liebe.*"

After a couple of days we went to Mainz, visiting many beautiful places on the way. We had a great time, Karl and I, just like old times…

When we arrived at home, before going to Frankfurt, Gabriel told me that after observing more closely how Amie is a mother to Marie-Claire, he made a decision.

"They are bonded like mother and child, I am happy that my girl doesn't have a void in her life and I am making it official, I am writing a will, leaving full custody of Marie-Claire to Amanda in case something happens to me. I am out in the world, travelling, you never know. I want my daughter to always be happy with you and her *Mamie*, no matter what."

My heart hurt, thinking that something could happen to my son, he already suffered so much. But I was grateful that he saw the love that Amie bestowed on our Marie-Claire and how well our little princess was doing.

In September Erik asked Katie to come to Dusseldorf to take his place, he decided to take his family to the U.S. Louisa was excited about the prospect of going to New York, mostly for Liliane, she has been acting up. She and Erik had been frustrated about it.

"Lili is all about trouble now. Who said that sixteen is sweet! The clothes she wears, the make-up, her interest in boys… Everything is out of control."

"Keep calm, Louisa, it is hard to deal with a rebellious teenager, but it will all come into place, she will grow out of it."

"Are you sure, Clara?"

"No, but keep hoping and keep her under your wing, it is not time for her to fly solo yet."

It was good to have Katie back at home for an entire week.

She told me that she was inviting Stefan to come, he just returned from the U.S. Open tournament, but he has other commitments to attend in Sweden and France. He will be travelling again soon.

Stefan came and made a good impression. He is one of those men that people are drawn to. He is amiable, a little loud, natural, what I would call authentic. He felt at ease in our home with us.

Karl appreciated his businessman approach. Stefan told him he knows the reality that his career as a tennis player is short lived, and decided to invest the prize money he gets in tournaments into businesses.

He has an athletic clothes line distributed in Europe and several tennis training centers for adults and children all over Germany, and recently he started investing in real estate.

His first acquisition was the modern building where he lives in downtown Frankfurt. He is well off! And he also praised Katie's entrepreneurial skills.

I could clearly see a good match between him and Katie, around him she was relaxed and cheerful.

I told her of all the men that she previously dated I liked Stefan the best. I have been wrong before, but I cautiously believed he was the right one for our Katie. I had a good feeling about their relationship.

He enjoyed our tennis court and gallantly didn't beat Katie or Gabriel. They played well, he said, and he showed them some new skills.

Every three months Amie takes me to my cardiologist appointments. Sometimes I wish she would forget about it.

At Dr. Vogt's office I noticed another doctor that I hadn't seen before at the nurses' station, he had his eyes glued on Amie. I called her attention.

"Do you know that doctor? He was staring at you!"

"That one looking at the charts, Mommy?"

"Yes, he is looking at you again. Go, talk to him."

"Mommy, are you playing cupid? No, I am not going, but he looks familiar... Maybe if I see his name tag I'll remember."

He went back in.

After we saw Dr. Vogt, as we were leaving, the other doctor was coming in the hallway. He addressed Amie.

"Amanda Weisenwert, I thought I recognized you!"

"Lukas VonGartner, I remember you now!"

He asked her to wait a minute outside, he was going to ask Dr. Vogt a question.

"Mommy, Lukas was an assistant professor at the medical school about ten years ago..."

He came out into the waiting room and they had a brief conversation, I was just observing them. She told him where she works and gave her clinic's phone number.

"I'll be glad to talk to you again, Lukas."

As she was driving back home, I told my daughter, "You lit up, Amie. Was that because of the encounter? Or because Dr. Vogt said I am doing fine."

"Both, Mommy," she laughed. "Lukas taught us a class during my second year in medical school. He was a new doctor getting a specialty in cardiology, as I remember he said he wanted to be a surgeon, a heart surgeon. I never saw him again. What a coincidence he was at Dr. Vogt's today!"

"He looks charming, Amie, if he calls you, the first thing you need to know is if he is single. And then..."

"Oh, Mommy, you are seeing things. Do you know who he reminds me of? Now that he is a little older Lukas resembles a doctor on a TV show that I watched in New York, they called him Dr. McDreamy."

"Really? Dreamy!"

Days later Amie told me that Lukas had called her, they had a long conversation about their work, and personal.

"He is a thoracic surgeon, still practicing, takes many years to perfect. Like me he is divorced, no children, and he invited me out for dinner!"

"That's great, Amie! How old do you think he is? The white hair on his temples doesn't mean anything, but he could be too old for you."

"Not old at all, he is thirty-eight. Daddy is much older than you, and you never complained, Mommy."

In November Katie announced that she was going to Paris with Stefan for the Paris Masters Tournament. I told Karl:

"It looks like our daughters found love, Katie is going steady with Stefan, and Amie has seen her *dreamy doctor* a few times. She likes him a lot!"

"We need to meet him sooner rather than later, I don't want my *little doctor* to be hurt again! What about Gabriel? How is his broken heart?"

"He is fighting back, more involved with his music, and he has a new friend, a certain Spanish girl, I have a glimmer of hope that he might open his heart…"

"I would tell him if he likes a Spanish girl, don't let her slip through his fingers, he might become the happiest man. I can tell!"

"And the Spanish girl would be the happiest she could ever be with her German man. Oh, Karl, I had to live this long to learn that love never ages."

But not all was right, nor bright!

Karl had a persistent cough and went for a check up. The doctors found a nodule on his lung.

Initially he didn't tell me, I found out accidently, I overheard a conversation he was having with his doctor on the phone.

A biopsy was scheduled and I was terrified, very afraid that the disease was haunting my husband again. What an anguish!

I didn't know if my heart could take it.

"Please, Karl, you can't hide it from me."

"I don't want to worry you, *meine liebe*. I am sure it will be nothing. They recommended that instead of a biopsy I should have minor surgery to remove it, and I opted for that. The question is, when? Dr. Jung said we can wait a few weeks, I think it is better to do it after the holidays."

"I would say do it now! We won't have peace of mind during the holidays at all, one way or another. Do it now, please."

Karl was annoyed with me because I asked Amie to obtain more information about the risks.

"I don't want our family to worry about me, Clara."

"We need to know, Karl, and if it is the disease again we have to attack it head on."

Louisa told me that again this year they are spending the holidays with us. "Last year we were together to give our support to Gabriel, and that time was very special for all of us. We want to do it again, the children, Erik and I are looking forward to it!"

In the beginning of December, Karl went for surgery, Amie accompanied us and sat with me in the waiting room. I was shaking.

"Mommy, at this point I am more worried about you than Daddy, please relax."

"How can I relax? Karl keeps getting one blow after another. What do we do?"

Gabriel came too.

"Keep calm, Mama. Dad has been a rock for me through the worst of times, I am stronger now and I am here for both of you."

After two hours they came out with an update.

"The nodule is completely out, it was a little more delicate procedure than it seemed initially, but the preliminary tests confirmed it is benign!"

I broke into tears convulsively, looked like the anguish of years was coming out of me all at once.

"My Karl is alright!"

Gabriel held me.

"You are releasing all the anguish and pain that you have bottled up always for the sake of others, of us. Cry, Mama, cry, let it all out."

After that my heart felt lighter.

Karl was free of cancer. My son was coming back from the dark times.

Life was full of hope!

Returning home, Karl was having a slow recovery, spending much more time alone in our suite. He lacked energy and looked depressed, that was not like him, I was concerned, all I wanted was to cheer him up.

I had an idea:

"I don't know why I didn't think of this before! We are going to have an elevator, all the way to the third floor. That's my new home improvement project for the beginning of the year."

"Why, Clara? You really think I am getting too old to handle the stairs, don't you?"

"That's not it, Karl, but on occasions like this it gets very challenging, and you are spending much time away from our family. It will be good for all of us."

"You are the lady of the house, you make the decisions, and I think I might enjoy it, *meine liebe*!"

A week before the holidays Gabriel got a delivery, a large square package, he opened it carefully.

"Marie-Claire's portrait! Absolutely gorgeous!"

"Gabe, it is wonderful! How could your friend do this kind of work copying from a small picture? It is absolutely perfect, Micaela is very talented!"

Marie-Claire, jumping around, was shouting: "It's me, I am so beautiful! Bring it to my room."

Gabriel told her, "No, *liebling*, if we put it in your room nobody else is going to see it, let's ask Grandma where she wants to hang it."

I decided to put it in our family room, next to Elise's portrait.

Marie-Claire was happy. "Look, that's me and my Mami!"

"I want my little princess's picture to be right here, for all to see, and you, Gabe, should call the artist and give her our compliments for her beautiful work."

Gabriel spent a long time on his phone.

Later he told me:

"I told Micaela that I was very impressed by her work and I'm looking forward to seeing her next month when I come to Madrid for Fabio's baby christening. After all, Daniel is my godson!"

"I am glad, Gabe, and I wish Fabio would bring your little nephew for us to meet."

Gabriel smiled a big smile.

"Thank you, Mama, for saying that. Yes, Baby Daniel is my nephew."

All of a sudden he got a little teary and hugged me.

He whispered, "Life goes on, life goes on... But *she* will always be in my heart."

"Oh, our beloved Elise, I miss her dearly!"

We are expecting a full house again this year, I would say fuller. Stefan is coming with Katie and staying for the weekend, and Amie has invited Lukas for our end of the year celebrations.

Karl had an ice skating rink set up again for the winter. It was cold, very cold, and Karl and I stayed in.

From our balcony window we observed our little ones and our big ones having fun, dancing, stumbling, falling and getting up, laughing and smiling.

Our hearts were full of love for our family, and we were grateful for this time together, seeing our children and grandchildren going on with their lives, with challenges and victories, sorrows and joys. Living!

Karl softly recited his favorite Goethe quote, reminding us to live in the present. *"Nothing is worth more than this day."*

We both hoped that moments like those, with our loved ones, would last forever, but we knew forever will only last until...

ABOUT THE AUTHOR

M. Carolina Bento, a passionate world traveller, adapts her memories, giving wings to her imagination, adding relevant views and beliefs of love for family, country and people in all of her writings, as well as in her third novel, *Alemana*.

In her heartwarming storytelling style, her characters keep moving forward, achieving, or not, their objectives and goals, but always finding meaning and purpose in what life will bring them. Like it should be...

The writer lives in a suburb of Washington, DC.

www.ingramcontent.com/pod-product-compliance
Lightning Source LLC
Chambersburg PA
CBHW032118170626
46808CB00006B/1991